GUNNING FOR TROUBLE

A JO GUNNING THRILLER

RENÉE PAWLISH

Gunning for Trouble: A Jo Gunning Thriller
First Digital Edition published by Creative Cat Press
copyright 2022 by Renée Pawlish

AUTHOR'S NOTE

I have exercised some creative license in bending geography and settings, and law-enforcement agencies to the whims of the story.

CHAPTER ONE

She wasn't like all the other teenagers who lounged nearby. The others had the look of runaways with time on the streets—disheveled and worn clothes, uncombed hair, dirt on their faces and under their fingernails. They tried to look cool, with forced laughs and nonchalant nods at each other as they smoked. But their eyes betrayed them, hollow and haunting, speaking to their lives on the run.

The girl who hung on the periphery was different, though. Her shoulder-length, wavy brown hair was neatly styled, her heart-print V-neck blouse unwrinkled, her white shorts clean. This girl hadn't been a runaway for long, and her innocent gaze spoke volumes. It wouldn't be long before someone took advantage of her.

A teen boy with tattooed arms held out a cigarette to the girl, who shook her head. He pressed her to take it, and she finally did. Once he lit it for her, she took a drag, then coughed. He laughed, showing a toothless grin. She shrugged and tried to act cool as she took another drag. This time, she didn't choke on the smoke as much.

The other kids mostly ignored her as she looked off into the distance.

Jo Gunning watched it all, at first mildly disinterested, but her gaze kept going back to the girl. There was something of herself in this one. Not the girl's naïveté; Jo had always been able to read people, and she had street smarts. However, she knew what it was like to be a fish out of water, to not fit in.

It was a pleasant Monday, and people walked about Rawlins Park. A few mothers pushed babies in strollers. The gaggle of teenagers loitered by the fountain, too high to do much. The afternoon sun beat down, and Jo wiped sweat off her brow. A skinny girl with stringy black hair approached the girl in the V-neck blouse, and they began talking.

Jo edged her way nearer. Trouble was brewing. None of them seemed to notice her, even as she got close enough that she could hear them talking.

"I'm Sammy," the skinny girl smiled. "You gotta trust me, okay?" She was obviously trying to convince the other girl of something.

The brown-haired girl shrugged and shook her head. Sammy pointed toward the far end of the park. Jo's gaze followed her finger to a man in jeans and a blue T-shirt. He lounged on a park bench, one leg crossed over the other, smoking a cigarette. But he was eyeing the group of teenagers. The brown-haired girl looked toward the man.

"I don't know," she said.

Sammy smiled and offered a joint. The girl shook her head, and the others laughed. Sammy motioned with her head, and the man on the bench stood up. He smoothed his blond hair as he sauntered toward the teenagers. Sammy began talking faster.

"Leroy will be able to help you." Her jeans hung a bit too loose, and she fiddled with an earring as she talked. "And you're gonna need it, you know? You don't got a place to stay tonight."

The brown-haired girl shook her head. "No, but I'll be all right."

"Yeah, I said the same thing. But Leroy's okay. He can help you, you know? Get you something to eat, that kind of thing."

"I guess I could talk to him," the brown-haired girl replied.

Leroy closed in, but before he could talk to the brown-haired girl, Jo stepped up and blocked his way. The man's eyes were so cold and dark, she felt a chill run down her spine.

"Why don't you move along," he said with a hint of a Southern accent.

Jo glanced over her shoulder at the girl, who was watching them cautiously.

"I could say the same thing to you," Jo said as she turned back to the man.

Leroy stiffened, and his brow furrowed. She smelled cigarette smoke on his clothes, saw the danger in his eyes. He gestured toward the teen girls.

"I'm just going to talk to them." His tone was smarmy.

Jo slowly shook her head. "I don't think so."

"Hey lady," Sammy said. "Leroy's okay."

Leroy smiled. "See? Sammy thinks I'm okay." He licked his lips as he stared at the brown-haired girl.

"Leroy's just gonna talk to her." Sammy nodded at the other girl. "Tell him your name."

Before the brown-haired girl could say anything, Jo held up a hand. "Don't tell them."

The brown-haired girl looked at her. "Why?"

"Because knowledge is power," Jo said. She glared at Leroy. "And he doesn't need it."

Leroy swore softly. "You trying to interfere in my business?"

"Nope."

"You know her?" he asked the brown-haired girl as he jerked a thumb at Jo.

The girl shook her head. "No," she said softly.

"Then there's no problem with you and me." Leroy grabbed the girl by the arm. "Come on."

Jo shook her head as she took a step toward him. She was five-nine and in shape. Leroy wasn't much taller, and he hesitated, clearly feeling the threat of her presence. He had a threat of his own, though. With his other hand, he inched his shirt up to reveal a small pistol tucked into his waistband. The brown-haired girl gulped, and the teens stepped back.

"Don't mess with Leroy," Sammy said.

Jo met Leroy's gaze carefully. Then she leaned toward him and whispered in his ear. "Let her go."

Leroy shook his head. Jo never underestimated an opponent, but Leroy had made two critical mistakes. His right hand was occupied with the girl's arm, and his left was holding up his shirt. He could do nothing as Jo struck out with a fist and punched him in the gut. Leroy sputtered as he let go of the girl and doubled over. A heavy blow to the solar plexus caused instant pain and a desperate struggle to breath. The other teens stepped back and murmured in astonishment as Leroy gasped for air. He tried to swear, but no words came out.

Jo stepped back and looked at the brown-haired girl. "May I have a moment of your time? I think I can help you."

The brown-haired girl hesitated, then looked at the other teenagers around her. Finally her gaze rested on Leroy. He glanced up with a leer, and that made her decision for her.

"Sure," the girl said.

Jo backpedaled a few steps and gestured for the teen to follow her. They walked away from Leroy and the others, who muttered among themselves.

CHAPTER TWO

"Hey," the girl called out. "What's going on?"

Jo kept her stride long as she headed to the far end of the park, where an unoccupied bench sat under towering maple trees. She took a seat and gestured for the girl to join her. Rush hour traffic was growing, and the buzz of cars disturbed the peacefulness of the park. The girl eased herself down. Glancing over, she drew in a breath and waited.

Jo looked across the park. The teenagers still loitered around the fountain, and Sammy was talking to Leroy, who had managed to get to his feet. He held one arm over his stomach, waving his other hand angrily. Sammy gazed toward Jo and shrugged, but she wasn't moving. Jo felt sorry for the girl. She would probably have a long night ahead, and who knew what Leroy would do to her? Something to address, but not now. She shifted and rested an arm on the back of the bench, then contemplated the girl beside her.

"What's your name?" Jo asked.

The girl smiled slyly. "I thought you said I shouldn't tell. You know, the knowledge that you would gain."

Jo nodded. Not a bad reply. "Yeah, okay. You got me there." She tipped her head toward the kids at the fountain. "But I did save you from a bad situation. Isn't that worth something, like your name?"

The girl shrugged. "I'm not sure you saved me from anything. I could handle them."

Jo looked down her nose at the girl. "Please."

Her cheeks reddened. "I could have," she said in a small voice. She managed to meet Jo's gaze, then quickly glanced away and sighed. "It's Brooke."

Jo stared at her for a moment. "That's a nice name. Better than mine." Time to use the intelligence-gathering skills that she'd acquired over many years in Civil Affairs. She could make people comfortable, and she used that to her advantage. Jo had been a highly trained Army soldier with CA, and she was fluent in several languages, was an expert markswoman, and had worked with several secretive Special Operations units. She'd gathered human intelligence in dangerous places, where those who were caught were generally tortured or killed.

The girl looked at her. "What *is* your name?"

"It's Jo. Short for Josephine." She frowned. "I never liked Josephine. It's too long, sounds too fancy."

Brooke laughed. "Yeah, my name is like a river. But I kinda like it."

Jo waited while two men in shorts and T-shirts walked by. Seeing Brooke up close, studying her, Jo was even more certain that the girl had gotten in over her head. Her haircut was stylish, her makeup artfully applied, nail polish on manicured fingernails. She didn't belong with that group of teenagers, not at all.

"You live around here?" Jo asked.

Brooke shook her head. "North Springfield."

Jo nodded. "Nice area. Want to tell me how you ended up in the park today?"

Brooke shifted, stretching her feet out in front of her and crossing her arms across her chest. She stared down at the ground. "I ran away from home."

"I gathered that. Why?"

"Because it sucks at home. My parents argue a lot, and they completely ignore me. It's like they've been in their own little world, and they don't seem to understand what I'm going through."

"What are you going through?"

Brooke gnawed her lip. Then she wiggled her foot. Jo waited. Finally, the girl went on. "There's a couple of girls at school. They give me a hard time, tell me that I'm stupid to focus on my grades, that I'm a teacher's pet. Just because I don't want to hang out and party with them all the time." She snorted. "I've done things, you know? I've been drunk, and I've been high."

Jo tended to doubt the last, based on the girl's defensive tone, but she wasn't going to point that out. She stared across the park again. The group of teenagers had moved on, and so had Leroy. But they'd be back.

She looked at Brooke. "You think you fit in with that group of kids by the fountain?"

"Sure," Brooke said, a bit too fast.

Now Jo laughed. "I don't think so. You couldn't even smoke that cigarette without gagging."

Brooke's cheeks turned red again. "So what?"

Jo softened her approach. "You said your parents were arguing a lot, but was anything else going on?" The girl shrugged, and Jo went on. "Did your parents do anything to you?" It was a not-so-subtle way of asking if she'd been abused. A lot of teenage runaways faced some kind of trauma at home.

Brooke shifted once more. "No, nothing like that."

Jo believed her. "I have to be honest, it doesn't sound like there's too much going on." Just a lot of teenage angst, she thought but didn't say.

Brooke wiggled her foot for a moment. "What do you know?"

Jo considered that. Her own childhood had been okay. Her parents had been strict with both Jo and her younger sister, Avery, but Jo wasn't sure how unfair the treatment had been. She'd always felt as if she needed to overachieve, and she had. Just not in the arena that her parents had hoped for. They certainly hadn't wanted her to join the military, which eventually led to working with Civil Affairs.

Growing up, Jo had never once thought about running away—although her choice of career, which had taken her all over the world, could've been seen that way.

She pointed across the park. "You don't want to end up with those kids, and certainly not with Leroy."

"Why?"

"You can't be that naïve. Most of those kids were strung out, and you know Leroy's a pimp. He saw you as his next mark, and before you know it, you'd be doing the same thing Sammy is. She'll be working for Leroy to get her next fix." She knew she sounded harsh, but she wanted to make a point.

Brooke stared at the ground, her body tense. Then she nodded. "I suppose you're right."

"I know I'm right."

Brooke turned to look at Jo, surveying her. "How do you know so much? You a cop or something? You hit Leroy, and it looked like you knew what you were doing. You weren't scared of him."

"I can handle myself." Jo arched an eyebrow. "Which is more than I can say for you."

"I can take care of myself," Brooke mimicked her, a little too harshly.

Jo let out a sharp laugh. "Leroy would eat you for lunch. You don't know how to handle someone like that."

"Oh, and you do?" Brooke didn't hide the sarcasm.

"I've done a lot worse," Jo said, her tone cautioning.

The girl stared at her for a moment. "Like what?"

"I've . . . taken care of the bad guys."

"Who?"

"No one you need to know about."

Brooke sat straighter. Her curiosity made her seem innocent. Her guard was coming down a bit. "What do you do?"

Jo hesitated before answering. She didn't like to share about herself, but she wanted to keep the girl engaged in the conversation. "I used to be in the Army."

"When did you get out?"

"About a year ago."

"Why'd you leave?"

Jo's reply caught in her throat. How could she explain that it was because she'd made a mistake? Officially, that hadn't been the case, but she knew. Things had happened, terrible things, all because she'd missed the signs.

"It was just time."

"And Virginia's your home? You work with the government now?"

Jo smiled. "You ask a lot of questions."

"Hey, I told you about me."

That brought out a laugh. "You remind me of my little sister. She would ask a lot of questions, too."

"Yeah?" Brooke said. "I don't have any siblings. Is it nice having a sister?"

Jo stared past her toward the street, where cars zoomed by, streaks of color against the gray canvas of buildings behind them. "She's ten years younger than me. I haven't seen her in a long time."

"Why?"

"I was busy with my job."

"Were you deployed?"

"Something like that."

The look Brooke gave her carried understanding, a shrewdness Jo hadn't expected. "My parents work for the government. I hear things. You weren't just a grunt, were you? Not the way you act. Were you part of some special forces? Something like that?"

Jo shook her head. There was a lot of classified information that she supposed she could talk about, but she wouldn't. She still had too much loyalty to the military. "It's nothing you need to worry about."

They both stayed silent for a minute, listening to the symphony of Rawlins Park, people talking, kids laughing. Stretching, Jo tapped Brooke on the arm.

"Are you going to go home?"

Brooke shrugged. "I guess."

"Trust me, it's way better than being on the streets."

The girl nodded slowly. She seemed lost, but Jo knew what she was talking about. Brooke would never survive out here.

"I don't know." Brooke pursed her lips. "My parents might be mad."

"Do you have any money?"

She shook her head. "A few dollars."

"No credit card?"

"No."

Jo sighed. "I can get you an Uber or Lyft," she offered.

Brooke shook her head. "You don't need to do that."

"I don't mind."

She shook her head again. "No."

"Why don't you call your parents to come get you? If they don't know you ran away, you can make up something so you don't get in trouble."

Brooke drew in a breath. "I don't have my cell phone."

"Were you worried about being tracked?"

"What? No. I didn't even think of that. I left it at home because I didn't want them calling me."

Jo rubbed her forehead. "And you didn't get a new one? A phone is a lifeline, especially on the streets."

"I guess I made a mistake." A petulant tone.

"I'll call your parents." Jo pulled out her own phone.

"No way."

She let out a heavy sigh. "I'm just trying to help."

Brooke crossed her arms, closing herself off again. "I'll call them when I'm ready. And don't try calling the police." She gestured around. "I'll just leave here, and the cops won't find me."

Jo nodded. She couldn't force the girl into going home. But if she was going to stay on the streets, she at least needed a phone. Tapping on her screen, Jo found a Target five blocks away. She pocketed her phone, stood up, and gestured at Brooke.

"Come on."

Brooke stared up at her. "Where're we going?"

"To get you a phone. You can use it to call your parents, when you're ready."

"You don't have to."

Jo put her hands on her hips. "Listen, kid, at least let me do this."

Brooke let out a huff of air, thinking for a moment. "You sure are pushy."

Jo smiled and walked away from the park bench, trusting that the girl would follow.

CHAPTER THREE

"Where're we going?" Brooke asked, running a few yards behind.

"There's a Target a few blocks from here," Jo called over her shoulder.

The girl caught up as they reached the street. "Don't you have a car?"

Jo shook her head. "I don't have one. Too much hassle."

A horn honked as they walked along the sidewalk, and Jo glanced around, always wary. They stopped at the corner, and as they waited to cross the street, Brooke looked pointedly at some parked cars, then back at Jo.

"What?" Jo asked.

Brooke shrugged and stared at a Subaru parked nearby. Jo hid a smile. The teen couldn't fathom that she didn't have a car. But it was too much hassle, too much expense.

The light changed, and Jo struck out across the street with Brooke hurrying to keep up with her on shorter legs.

"I can't believe you don't have a car," the girl said.

"I can't believe you don't have your phone," Jo shot back.

Brooke clamped her mouth shut as they walked down the block. "Do you live around here?" she asked after a minute. "Do you have an apartment somewhere?"

Jo wiped sweat off her brow. "I've got a place nearby."

"Is it nice?"

"It works."

She didn't want to tell Brooke that she'd been staying in a cheap motel for months. The previous fall, Jo had left Civil Affairs. She'd thought she would head back to a small cabin nestled in the mountains near Salida, Colorado that she'd bought nearly a decade ago. It had been years since she'd been to the cabin, but something about going there with winter coming, and seeing her father and sister, had depressed her, so she never left the DC area. Even though she'd quit the only job she'd ever known, the only job she'd ever been good at—even after her mistake, she enjoyed the familiarity of DC, being near people she had worked with, near the military bases.

"You don't talk much," Brooke observed.

"No," Jo replied, and left it at that.

They walked a few more blocks to the Target. It was after five, and cars packed in like gridlocked traffic. They went inside, found the electronics section, and perused the selection of pre-paid phones. Brooke gravitated toward the colorful ones.

"I don't have any money," she said.

Jo picked out a simple black phone. "This is on me. I want you to get home safely."

"Why do you care so much?" the girl asked as they headed toward a counter where a salesperson waited.

Jo stopped and looked at her. In some ways, she was so like Avery. Avery had just turned eighteen the last time Jo had seen her. She was pretty, like Brooke, and had the same gullibility. Jo had often told her sister to be careful, to not assume it was always safe everywhere. Avery would laugh and say that Jo's job left her too jaded. Maybe that was the case, but she hadn't wanted her sister to get into trouble. And Avery could have.

Jo sighed. She didn't want Brooke to find herself in a predicament, either.

"Come on," she said.

They approached the counter, and a young woman with long hair helped Jo with purchasing the phone, then with purchasing a card and getting minutes and data. She paid with cash.

"It's easy to use," the young woman said.

She wore an eager expression as she spent a couple of minutes showing them how everything worked. When they finished, Jo and Brooke walked to the food section and picked up some Lunchables.

Once they'd paid and gone outside, Jo handed Brooke the bag with the phone, charger, and food. "I'll bet you're hungry."

"Yeah," Brooke said, but she didn't open the bag.

They moved away from the doors to sit on a concrete retaining wall by a flower bed. Brooke set the bag next to her and pulled out the phone, then carefully studied the flowers, avoiding Jo's penetrating look. Jo shielded her eyes against the sun, staring at Brooke.

"Are you going to use it?" She pointed at the phone in the girl's hand. "Call your parents?"

Brooke hesitated. "I don't know. I guess I'm kind of scared to call them. Neither one will be home from work yet, anyway."

"What would your parents think you did all day?" Jo asked. It was July, so she wouldn't have been in school.

Brooke ran a hand through her brown hair. "I usually go out with my friends, or sometimes they come over and we hang out at the pool."

"You have a pool?"

She nodded. "It's okay, I guess. It's nice when it gets hot."

"A lot of people don't have a pool," Jo observed, unable to keep a degree of wryness from her voice.

"Yeah, I know. It's cool."

"Do you think you can talk to your parents about how you're feeling?"

Brooke's face twisted for a moment. "I don't know. If I tell them I took off today, they're going to be pissed."

They sat and watched people going in and out of the store. Plenty of nice cars zipped by—North Springfield was a fairly high-income area.

"How'd you end up so far from home?" Jo asked.

"I took the Metro." Brooke sighed. "I rode it around for a while, got off near here. The park seemed nice."

Jo waited, hoping that she would use the phone right then to call her parents. But the girl didn't. Finally, Jo suggested something else.

"If you don't want to call them, how about a friend? Someone could pick you up and take you home. You could tell your parents you're hanging out with your friend and you lost track of the time."

Brooke stared at the phone in her hand. "I don't know any of my friends' phone numbers. I put their names in my phone, and that's it. I never pay attention to the numbers."

Like most people, Jo thought. She rested a hand on Brooke's arm. "Don't go back to Rawlins Park. You don't want to run into Leroy again. He's bad news—for you, and for those other kids. Tell me you'll stay away from all of them."

Brooke nodded. "I won't go back there." Then she grinned. "Tell me you won't, either."

"I'm pretty sure Leroy wouldn't want me to."

The girl snickered. "After that punch you gave him, probably not." She fiddled with the phone for a moment. "What's your number?"

Jo hesitated. "Why do you want my number?" The words came out a little too quickly.

Brooke sat back, stung. "I guess I thought . . . that you might want to know that I made it home safely. But if you don't . . ."

She nodded. "Oh, I gotcha." It was a good sign, Brooke saying she would go home. Jo didn't want to give out her number, but if the girl trusted her, that was okay. "You can have my number, as long as you promise to tell me you got home."

"I promise," Brooke said.

Jo rattled off the number, and the girl entered it into the phone. Then she typed for a moment.

"I just sent you a text."

Jo's phone rang, and she pulled it from her pocket. Brooke had sent a simple "Hi" with a smiley face.

"The phone works," Brooke said.

"Yes, it does."

She bit her lip. "Do you think—maybe I could be alone now?"

Jo took the prompt and stood up. "Are you going to call your parents?" she asked yet again.

"Maybe." Brooke held up the phone. "But they wouldn't recognize this number. If I get home pretty soon, they wouldn't even know I'd been gone. Then I guess we'll have dinner."

"Who're you going to get to pick you up?" Jo wasn't going to let her off the hook.

"I don't know. I could take the Metro."

"Sounds like a good plan." Jo looked down at Brooke and held out her hand. "Good luck. And do me a favor. Work things out with your parents. I can tell you have a lot of potential, and you don't want to throw that away."

Brooke shook her hand. "Thanks." She locked eyes with Jo. "And you be careful, too."

"I always am."

"Are you going home?"

"I have something else to do, but don't worry about me."

Brooke nodded. Jo waited for a car to pass, then started across the parking lot. When she got to the street, she looked back. The girl was staring at her phone. Hopefully she'd make a wise choice and call her parents to come get her.

After a moment, Brooke took the Lunchables from the bag and began eating. Jo smiled grimly. Maybe a crisis had been averted.

She headed back down the street toward the park. She had something else to do.

CHAPTER FOUR

When Jo got back to Rawlins Park, none of the teenagers were by the fountain. Several people milled about, some families with their kids, some joggers, and others just out for a stroll. Jo looked all around but didn't see Leroy. It was still hot, and she found a bench under a tree with a view of the fountain. Some birds chirped pleasantly, and the traffic sounds died down. A man with a little girl came up to the fountain, and the girl put her hand in the water and laughed in delight. Other people took pictures in front of the fountain.

Jo's gaze roved around the park. Her stomach growled, but she ignored it. There'd been plenty of times where she'd gone long hours without a meal. She was used to it.

After a while, she glanced at her phone. Nothing from Brooke. Jo frowned. Hopefully she was on her way home and hadn't changed her mind.

The shadows grew longer, and the park remained full of people. The sky had turned a deeper blue tinted with orange in the west, the air cooler now, not so sticky. A couple of the teens Jo had seen earlier milled around the fountain, mostly ignored by other people. But she didn't see Sammy or Leroy. The sky morphed into a deep blue as the sun set. Then she saw him.

Leroy approached the fountain from the other side of the park, pausing to talk to a young teenager in loose-fitting jeans and a sleeveless shirt. The teen gave Leroy some money, and the man pressed something small into his hands. Drugs, Jo assumed. Leroy was pimping out both boys and girls. Sadly, there was a market for both.

The teen said something to Leroy, then sauntered off in the other direction. Leroy glanced around, but he didn't notice Jo. He pulled a pack of cigarettes from his pocket, lit one, and smoked for a moment. Then he took off in the other direction.

Jo got up and followed.

Leroy exited the park and strolled down the street, pausing a couple of times to talk to some teenagers before moving on. Jo paused at the corner, letting him cross the street. Down the next block, she saw Sammy loitering in a doorway. Leroy stopped, and the two of them began talking. Jo waited for a car to pass, then darted across. She kept her head low as she moved toward Leroy and Sammy, who were facing the other way. Jo crept to the corner of a building and listened.

"You gotta keep busy tonight," Leroy was saying.

"I'm doing it," Sammy said. "It's been kind of slow."

"Maybe I should replace you. What about that sweet thing that was in the park earlier?"

"If I see her around, I can talk to her." Sammy didn't sound enthusiastic.

"You should've kept her around earlier."

"Hey, I was trying," Sammy protested. "What about

that woman? If she hadn't come around, maybe I coulda talked to the girl longer." Accusation filled her voice.

"What're you saying?" Leroy's voice took on a dark tone. "It was my fault you didn't make a connection with the girl?"

"Well . . ." Sammy hedged.

"I shoulda hit that bitch, but I didn't."

"Yeah, like you could."

A crack racked the air, then the sound of Sammy whimpering.

"Hey! Why'd you do that?"

Jo peeked around the corner. The skinny girl stood in the deepening darkness, a hand to her cheek.

Leroy glared at her. "Don't get smart with me, you hear?" he said.

"All right," Sammy said. She began to rub her arms and fidget.

Leroy shoved her. "Get going. You got plenty of time."

"Fine," Sammy said, shoving her hands in her pockets. "I'll see you around."

"Count on it."

Leroy watched Sammy shuffle down the street, then turned in Jo's direction. She ducked into the gloom of the alley and pressed herself against the building. Once he'd passed by, she followed him.

He spent the next few hours in the same area, touching base with various teenagers, exchanging drugs and money, asking some of the kids if they'd seen Brooke around. None of them had. Finally, close to midnight, Leroy walked to a Metro station and got on a train. Jo thought she might lose him when she had to pay for her fare, but he was walking slow, like he didn't have a care in the world. He waited for the blue line, and she stayed on the far end of the platform, out of the way.

When the train came, Leroy got into a car, and Jo stepped on as well, at the back of the same car. She sat down by the door and shielded her face with her hand, but kept an eye on him. He stood near the far door and leaned casually against a rail, his hand on a grab bar.

They went several stops, and Leroy transferred, then finally hopped off at the U Street station. She got out as well, careful so he wouldn't see her. Leroy rode up the escalator alone, his head bobbing to imaginary music. Jo reached the bottom just as he stepped off. A horn honked, but he still didn't look around. She raced up the escalator, light on her feet, making no sound. When she got outside, he was sauntering down the block. Initially, she walked in the other direction, giving him time to put some more distance between them. Then she whirled around and followed him once more.

Even though it was late, a few people still hustled about, but they gave Leroy space, seeming wary of the man. He walked a few blocks to a cheap apartment building with outside stairs and walkway. He still hadn't noticed Jo as he went up to the second floor and disappeared inside an apartment. She waited until a light came on in a window, then quietly ascended the stairs and tiptoed down the walkway. Pausing by his door, she listened. Just the sound of a TV. The rest of the building was quiet.

She knocked. The door opened a moment later.

"Who the hell—"

Jo shoved the door inward, and Leroy stumbled back. He swore as he put a hand on a cheap table to right himself.

She shut the door and stared at him. The man's jaw

dropped as he recognized her. "What the hell are you doing here?"

Jo held her hands at her sides. A greasy smell, worse than a dive bar, filled the air along with cigarette smoke, but neither was enough to mask Leroy's rank body odor. She quickly surveyed the apartment. A living room with a threadbare couch and a flat-screen TV sitting on a cheap stand. A matching coffee table with a few beer bottles and a bong on it. A table and two chairs near Leroy, and behind him, the kitchen. Down a short hallway, she saw two open doors, a bed through one, a toilet through the other.

"You live alone?" Jo asked.

Leroy didn't say anything. No one emerged from the bedroom or bathroom, and she didn't hear anyone moving around.

"Nice digs," she said sarcastically.

He looked around and shrugged.

"What's your full name?" she asked.

"I don't have to tell you."

"The girl you saw in the park today."

"What about her?" Leroy asked.

"If you ever see her again, you steer clear of her."

"Or what?" he sneered. "You don't own her."

Jo took a step forward. "And neither do you."

"I can do whatever I want." Leroy shoved his hands in his pockets. Not a good move. He wouldn't be able to act as fast if necessary. "If that sweet thing wants to come with me, she can."

His Southern drawl grated on her.

"If you so much as talk to her," Jo said in a low voice, "I'll know it. You don't want that."

Leroy stood straighter, glaring at her as he squared his shoulders. He was going for tough, but he looked small and timid, like a scared squirrel. "You got a lot of nerve, coming in here." His left hand subconsciously covered his stomach. "And for hitting me earlier. You're going to pay for that."

He pulled his right hand out of his pocket, stared at her for a second, then took a quick step forward and threw a right hook at her. But the man was slow and out of shape. Jo easily deflected the punch and lashed out with one of her own. This time, she didn't hit him in the stomach but square on his nose. His head rocked back, and blood ran down his lips.

"You bitch!" he snarled.

Leroy tried for another punch, to no avail. Jo hit him in the face again, splitting open his cheek. Finally, she struck him in the stomach. He crumpled to the floor and gasped for breath, groaning, one hand covering his bloodied nose.

Jo took a step back, bent down, and grabbed his shirt. "Leroy, look at me."

His face didn't budge, but his eyes, full of pain, met her gaze. She raised a fist. "What's your last name?"

"Doherty," he wheezed.

"Don't mess with that girl, and don't mess with me."

"Yeah, okay," Leroy said nasally. "Just leave me alone."

She let go of his shirt, and he looked away like another second of eye contact would be too much humiliation to bear. She stood straight, backed up to the door, and left.

CHAPTER FIVE

After Jo left, Brooke hung out near the Target for a while, then took the phone charger from the bag and stuffed it in her pocket. She stood up and started back toward Rawlins Park.

Brooke didn't call her parents, because she'd decided against going home. She'd heard what Jo had said, how life on the streets would be harder than living there, but she didn't think the woman understood. Brooke had been practically invisible at home, her mom almost always out of town, her dad busy with his job. Would they even notice she was gone?

The girl looked around. She was resourceful; she could make do. Then she frowned. She didn't want to run into Sammy or Leroy. Jo was right about them, at least.

Turning, she walked in a different direction. The traffic eased as she wandered the streets. At a Starbucks, she ducked inside and used the Wi-Fi to download a couple of games onto the phone. She sat and played them for a while, then left.

A little before dusk, as she was standing near a street corner, she saw Sammy get out of a Mercedes. Before the girl could spot her, Brooke hurried the other way. She didn't want to talk to her.

She wandered around until she made her way to a smaller park several blocks away from the Target store. There was no fountain, just a sandy area with a jungle gym at one end, although no kids were playing on it. Now it was dark, and she was tired. She sat on a bench for a while, the muggy heat enveloping her, and played the games until she grew bored. A few people walked by with their dogs, then it grew quiet. It was still hot, so she lay down on the ground near a tree. The grass seeped coolness into her, but as the minutes ticked by, she grew cold.

Getting up, she walked back to the bench and sat there for a long time. She couldn't see far into the darkness, and her imagination took over. Brooke remembered some of the horror movies she'd watched, how the teen girls always seemed to get murdered in the most savage ways. Those movies seemed amusing at the time, so unrealistic. But now, out here alone, she was rethinking them. Every noise scared her. She finally lay down on the bench but didn't really sleep. A few times, she heard voices, but she didn't see anyone, and hopefully no one saw her. She didn't want the police called, and she didn't want to be taken back home.

Somewhere in the early hours of the morning, she dozed off.

———

Brooke opened her eyes and bolted up. She was still on the bench. A kaleidoscope of sunlight burst out over trees at the far end of the park. She yawned, stretched, and rubbed her eyes. It wasn't the worst sleep in her life, but it certainly hadn't been much. She'd been scared to death of every noise, frightened of the homeless people wandering the park during the night. Even though it was July, it had been surprisingly chilly, and her shorts, short-sleeve shirt, and sandals had done nothing to ward off the cold.

Brooke sighed. She had to go to the bathroom, but she didn't see any facilities nearby. Her stomach growled. She hadn't eaten much since yesterday morning, and she was starving. As a couple joggers ran past, her mind wandered to Sammy and the other teens. They must've dealt with this a lot. Brooke contemplated her situation—she was a runaway now. It had seemed like a good idea when she'd left the house yesterday, even after talking to Jo, but after a night on the streets, she wasn't so sure. She raked a hand through her hair to try and get it to some semblance of normal, and smoothed her blouse.

"I must look terrible," she muttered to herself.

Brooke studied the backs of her hands, then turned them over and looked at her palms. Plenty of dirt. She rubbed them together to try to get them clean, but it didn't really do much. She thought about Sammy, how skinny the girl was, how dirty she'd been. And what had Sammy been doing in that car last night? Brooke shuddered at the thought. She was glad she'd avoided her—and Leroy.

Reaching into her pocket she took out the prepaid phone and some money. As she'd told Jo, she only had a few dollars, but the hunger was too much. She stared at the phone for a moment. She was tempted to call the woman, but she didn't think Jo would want to hear from her, especially after Brooke had ignored her advice. She put the phone back in her pocket and felt her house key.

She held it for a second, then let go and pulled her hand out.

With a sigh, Brooke looked across the park. A few people were jogging along the path, and a woman with gray hair walked by with a smile. Brooke nodded back. She again realized she needed to go to the bathroom, so she got up and hurried out of the park. She didn't know the area, but she remembered where the Target was, so she headed in that direction.

In the same general shopping area was a McDonald's. Brooke used the restroom and washed her hands, then tried to touch up her makeup with her fingers. Finally giving up, she washed her face. What she'd give for a shower.

Her stomach growled again, so she went out to the lobby and ordered an Egg McMuffin and a Diet Coke. It felt as if people were staring at her, as if they knew she was a runaway. She sat at a table and wolfed down the breakfast. It tasted really good. When she finished, she sipped the soda, played on the phone for a while, and then set it aside. What to do next?

If she were at home, she might go out to the pool or call some of her friends. But those choices weren't available at the moment. She had nowhere to go, so she just sat and people-watched. When she finally went outside, the heat was oppressive.

Brooke decided to go back to Rawlins Park. The skinny boy with the tattoos on his arms was still there by the fountain, but she didn't see Sammy or Leroy. Some other teens joined the boy, but Brooke kept to herself. As the minutes ticked by, she kept thinking about what Jo had said, about how things couldn't be so bad at home that she'd want to stay on the streets. Maybe the woman was right after all. She could be sitting at home by the pool, drinking a Diet

Coke, with food in the refrigerator. Now she was getting hungry, and thinking about that didn't help, so she tried to think of something else.

Brooke had wanted to go to college, wanted to get a degree in business. If she stayed on the streets, she could kiss that goodbye.

Glancing at her phone, she saw it was close to eleven o'clock. Her stomach growled. She put her hand in her pocket and fiddled with the loose change left over from the McDonald's breakfast. That was all the money she had. Then she sighed. What the hell was she doing? It was hot, even in the shade. She finally made a decision, got up, and marched to the nearest Metro station.

When she got there, Brooke was faced with another dilemma. She didn't have enough money for the fare, and she didn't see a way of getting past the kiosks. People hustled about, ignoring her. She was a ghost, invisible, worthless.

Feeling the change in her pocket again, she realized she didn't have any other choice. When a woman with a small girl headed toward the station, Brooke approached her.

"Ma'am, I was wondering if you could help me out?"

The woman shook her head, tugged the girl's arm, and hurried on. Brooke sighed and tried a man with a briefcase, getting the same cold reaction. She kept asking people, feeling humiliated the whole time. She'd turned into a beggar. Finally, she approached an older man with thinning hair and asked him for some spare change. He was about to say no, but when tears welled in her eyes, he took pity on her and gave her a few dollars. She thanked him profusely, then went into the station, bought a ticket, and got on a train.

After what seemed an eternity, she finally made it to

Blacklick Station. From there, she transferred to a bus, and then it was a long walk home. But she'd made it.

The front door was locked, but Brooke still had her key to let herself inside. She'd thought the house would be empty, that her dad might be at work, but she heard noises in the kitchen. As she headed that way, she ran into him as he was coming toward the foyer.

"Brooke!" Connor said, then breathed a sigh of relief. He rushed to her and wrapped her in his arms. "Where the hell have you been? Are you okay?"

She nodded and smelled his cologne, a woodsy scent that reminded her of a warm winter night by the fire. It was comforting. He stepped back, his hands on her shoulders as he surveyed her, staring into her eyes.

"You're okay? No one hurt you?"

Brooke shook her head slowly. "I . . . um . . ."

Connor stepped past her to the front door and peeked out the peephole. A few moments later, he finally opened it and looked out, glancing quickly back and forth before locking up.

"Come into the kitchen."

As she followed him, she grabbed bottled water from the refrigerator and drank it. He gestured for her to take a seat on a stool at the kitchen island, then walked past a square wood table in a dining area with a view of the lawn and pool. Parting the blinds, he looked out.

"Did anybody follow you home? Nobody's after you?"

Her brow furrowed. "Why would anybody follow me?"

"I . . . never mind."

After a second, he seemed satisfied she was telling the truth, and he came back into the kitchen. He leaned against the counter and crossed his arms, towering over her with a penetrating glare. He wore khakis and an Oxford shirt, not his usual suit and tie.

"Why aren't you at work?" she asked.

Connor ran both hands over his dark hair. "Are you kidding me? You've been gone all night. I didn't know what to do, and I've been worried sick. I wasn't going to work when I didn't know what happened to you." Anger crept into his voice. "I called your friends and their parents. Nobody knew where you were. I was scared half to death."

Brooke hadn't given much thought to what he'd been doing while she'd been gone. She couldn't meet his gaze.

"I'm sorry I ran away," she said quietly.

"What were you thinking?"

She shrugged. "I don't know. I just . . . it's been weird, lately." As his expression grew angrier, she wondered how much trouble she was going to be in. "You and Mom are so preoccupied. It's like I'm not even here."

He put a hand to his mouth, stifled a reply, then drew in a breath. "Where were you last night?"

"I took the Metro down to Springfield. I ended up in some park."

He stared at her, incredulous. "Nothing happened?"

She shook her head. "No, Dad, I keep telling you that. I'm fine. Just hungry."

"Oh, of course."

Connor expelled a long breath, and with it some of his ire, then went to the refrigerator and rummaged around. "You want a sandwich? There's some chicken salad from Costco."

"That sounds good."

Normally he wouldn't wait on her like this, but she was tired, and if he was offering, she wasn't going to argue. He got bread and fixed a sandwich, then put it on a plate and pushed it across the island before getting her a Diet Coke as well. She gobbled up the sandwich while he watched her. When she finished, she drank half the soda. Connor ran a hand over his forehead, then covered his eyes. Finally, his fingers dragged slowly down his face and dropped to his side.

"I can't believe you'd do that," he said. "And what with your mother—" He stopped mid-sentence.

"What's going on with her?" Brooke asked as she gulped more soda. "She's still out of town, right?"

Her dad glanced away and nodded. "Yes, she is."

Brooke studied him. He seemed weird, unsure of himself. It was that same odd behavior, more of that tension that had been around the house the last couple of weeks.

"Could I take a shower?" she asked.

He nodded. "Sure, and then we need to talk."

The dreaded talk, she thought. But she couldn't blame him. She wasn't stupid enough to think that running away wouldn't mean a talk about it all. That was fine. She could placate her dad, let him know that she felt sorry about what she'd done—which was true—and then maybe she could go out to the pool for a while. She'd probably be grounded and wouldn't be able to see her friends for a while, but that wasn't the worst thing. Sliding off the stool, Brooke headed toward the doorway. Then she turned around.

"Thanks for the sandwich," she said.

Connor had moved back to the windows and was looking out again. "Go take a shower."

Brooke walked upstairs, went into her bedroom, and shut the door. Her gaze rested on the bed. Boy, one night was all it took to miss that. She shook her head ruefully as she peeled off her clothes and dropped them on the floor. Heading into her own bathroom, she started the shower.

When the water was pleasantly cool, she stepped in. It felt wonderful. She soaked it in for a minute, then finally scrubbed herself clean, washed her hair, and got out.

Toweling off, she blew her hair dry and went back into the bedroom. She donned clean shorts and a T-shirt with the Washington Nationals logo on it. Then she picked up the old shorts and took out the prepaid phone and charger. Brooke stared at it and remembered her promise to Jo, that she would let the woman know that she'd made it home safe.

"Brooke?" her father called out. "Are you about finished?" He sounded impatient.

"Yes," she replied. "I'll be down in a second."

Brooke looked around the room. Where was her phone? She'd left it on the desk in the corner, but it wasn't there now. Her dad must've taken it. She hid the new charger in a desk drawer, stuffed the prepaid phone in her pocket, and padded downstairs on bare feet, completely forgetting that she was going to text Jo.

Her dad was in the kitchen.

"Dad, where's my phone?" she asked as she entered.

He was peeking through the blinds into the backyard again. She stared past him but didn't see anything.

"Is everything all right?" she asked.

Connor turned around and nodded. "It's fine."

The words came out a little too quickly. She craned her neck to see, but there was still nothing.

He gestured at her. "Could you help me downstairs? I got new food for the safe room."

Brooke wasn't sure how many people had a safe room in their house, but her family did. Both her parents worked in government, her dad for Senator Macintosh, in a position that she didn't know much about. It was high enough up that they had a security system and the safe room. It seemed like too much, but whatever. If it made her parents feel happy, she didn't care.

"Sure," she replied. "And then can I get my phone?"

"We'll talk about that," he said.

Oh. Was she was going to lose phone privileges for a while? Brooke frowned, but she followed him downstairs. They crossed the game room, making their way around the pool table, the TV, and the couch. The bar area dominated one wall, but her dad went to the dark-paneled wall adjacent to it and pushed on a section. The paneling slid back to reveal a short hallway.

Connor took a key out of his pocket and unlocked three bolts on a heavy door at the other end of the hall. Stepping into the room, he flicked on a light, then held the door open for Brooke. She entered the rectangular room that she'd only been in a couple of times—in one corner, a bar stood next to a refrigerator, sink, and microwave. The cupboards above were stocked with food. The walls were heavily fortified, and there were no windows. A couch was positioned across from a flatscreen TV hanging on a wall opposite the door, and a small twin bed sat in the corner. It was all designed so that if, for whatever reason, they needed to stay safe, they could—for a long time. Brooke had always thought it was overkill, something out of the movies, but her parents seemed to think it was necessary.

Her dad pointed to boxes of cereal on the bar counter.

"It's some of the healthy granola that you like," he said. "And there's almond milk in the refrigerator."

Brooke glanced at him. "Okay."

"Why don't you put it in the cupboard," he suggested, "and then we need to clear out some of the old food."

She shrugged and headed toward the counter.

"Let me get some boxes for the old stuff," he added.

Brooke picked up one of the cereal boxes and looked at it, then glanced toward the door. It was swinging closed, her dad on the other side, avoiding her gaze. The door shut, and she heard sounds of the locks clicking into place.

CHAPTER SIX

Jo awoke with a start. The room was dark, with just a sliver of light seeping in through a crack in the heavy curtains. She took a few deep, calming breaths to chase away the dreams that haunted her. Then she thought for a moment.

Last night, after she'd left Leroy's apartment, she'd taken the Metro to Crystal City, where she'd been living in a motel kitchenette since she'd left the CA the previous summer. The small room was functional, and she didn't have any possessions beyond some clothes and toiletries. In her career, she'd always been on the go, rarely having a place to call home, so Jo had never collected any possessions. The motel also had no cleaning service, which she liked. No one to bother her.

She swung her legs over the side of the bed, sat up, and stretched. Her phone showed the time as eight o'clock. Longer than she'd meant to sleep. When she'd returned to the motel, Jo hadn't been tired, so she'd watched mindless TV for a while before her eyelids had drooped and she'd crawled into bed.

Now she got up, used the bathroom, splashed cold water on her face, and returned to the main room, where she performed the series of exercises that she had done most days of her life. Jo had a firm core and little fat. She was proficient in many forms of martial arts that would help in close-quarter combat. She especially liked Krav Maga, a fighting system developed in Israel where size wasn't as important as leverage. It emphasized tactical thinking, focusing on the most efficient ways to subdue an aggressor. She'd had to use those skills, usually against men who had the advantage in size and strength, to survive in some very dangerous situations. But she also used her wits. Anything so that she won.

When she finished exercising, Jo was dripping in sweat. She toweled off, slipped on shorts and a sleeveless shirt, and went for a long run. She never knew when she might have to escape on foot. Upon returning, she took a cold shower to soothe her sore muscles, dressed in jeans and a short-sleeved shirt, and finally opened the curtains. The sun shone from a cloudless blue sky. It was hot out there, but inside, the air-conditioner hummed, keeping the room cool.

Jo looked onto an empty parking lot, then fixed a small pot of coffee and prepared a quick breakfast of eggs and toast. She sipped coffee and ate with the TV on. The news was all the same—a war here, political disruption there, and so on. The world never changed. She was glad she wasn't part of all that now, but she still felt aimless.

Glancing at her phone again, Jo wondered what had happened to Brooke. Hopefully the girl had gone home and just forgotten to call, but there was nothing she could do now. Brooke had to make her own choices, just as she did.

Jo finished her breakfast and the last of the coffee, put

the dishes in the sink and rinsed them, and turned off the TV. Enough of the news. She sat in a chair at a small table by the window and looked out. A few cars crossed the parking lot, but otherwise it was quiet. So many times, she was alone with her thoughts. It was part of why she often left the motel room, wandered the city, sometimes even volunteered at a shelter or some other place in need. Anything to keep her mind preoccupied, to keep from thinking about what had happened before she left her position in Civil Affairs.

The video call on her phone rang, the special ringtone for Dack Pendleton. He always seemed to call her when she was at her lowest.

Jo glanced at the phone, tempted not to answer. But she'd never ignored Dack when they were in the field, and she wouldn't now. She swiped to answer the call, and smiled as his face came on the screen.

"Hey, Dack. How're you?" she asked.

Jo enabled the live-caption feature and waited. A moment later, a typed message came through that was then transferred into an altered electronic voice.

"Hey, Jo. You doing okay?"

She imagined hearing Dack's tenor voice, even though he hadn't actually been able to speak in a couple of years. He was a good-looking man with a tanned face, an angular jaw, blue eyes, and a wide smile that melted hearts. He still kept his brown hair closely cropped, military style.

"I'm doing fine," was all she said.

Dack stared at her with those intense eyes, then cocked an eyebrow as he read her reply, probably knowing that she had just lied to him. She hadn't been fine in a long time. He typed for a moment, and soon his reply came through.

"You know who you're talking to. How is everything really going?"

Jo sighed. He knew her too well.

"It's okay. The usual stuff. I'm not sure what I'm going to do today."

He twisted up his lips and typed. She waited and listened.

"It's been almost a year. The weather is beautiful now. Don't you think you should go now?"

Jo thought about that. She was running out of excuses, and she knew it.

"What am I going to do when I get back to Colorado?"

He shrugged. "Why don't you cross that bridge when you get to it? You've done a lot of good over the years, and I'm sure you can do a lot of good there."

Jo stared at him, thinking about what he'd said. She didn't feel as if she had done a lot of good. At one point, she'd felt that way, but now she wasn't so sure. She'd gotten rid of some very bad people over the years, but had it been worth it?

It was a question she'd never asked until that last mission with Dack. As if he knew what she was thinking, he started typing.

"You've got to stop blaming yourself for what happened to me. I know I keep repeating myself, but it wasn't your fault. Things happen. We all knew the risks, and I'm living with that now. But I'm doing fine. You know that." He nodded at her.

Jo smiled. She couldn't argue with Dack about that. After everything that had happened overseas, he'd come home, convalesced, and never blamed her. He now owned a private security company and was doing very well. It wasn't surprising, given his skill set and how smart he was.

"If you don't go home, you can always work for me," he added.

It wasn't the first time Dack had offered her a job, but Jo hadn't wanted to do anything when she'd left her position. She *had* said she would go home, but that hadn't happened, either.

"What? I'd be like one of Dack's Angels?" She grinned at him. "Can I be Kristen Stewart?"

He smiled back. "You can be whatever you want."

Jo's grin vanished, and he gave her a wan look. She glanced away.

"You're out of excuses, Jo. You know I'm here to help any way I can, but you wandering around DC isn't doing you any good."

He'd said that plenty of times, and as she stared out the window, she knew he was right. Something about seeing Brooke had emphasized that as well. Jo couldn't become homeless, aimless, like those kids.

"You're better than you think you are," Dack said.

"You're right," she said, though the words struggled to get out. "I've got to quit fooling myself, don't I?"

He nodded slowly. "Yes, you do."

Jo, not usually impulsive, made a sudden decision. "I'll get my things packed this morning, and I'll head out."

"I think that's best. Keep me posted." With that, Dack was gone.

Jo stared out the window for a few more minutes, trying to find reasons to stay put. There weren't any. She finally got up, went into the kitchenette and cleaned out the refrigerator, then packed everything she owned into her duffel bag, in neat military rows.

Zipping up the bag, Jo looked around. She wouldn't miss this room. She was about to head out the door when her phone rang. The number wasn't familiar at first. Then realization dawned on her.

"Hey, Brooke," Jo answered. "Are you doing okay?"

"I need your help!"

CHAPTER SEVEN

"What's going on?" Jo asked, taking a seat on the edge of the bed. "Where are you?"

"I'm at home. My dad has me locked in the safe room," Brooke spoke quietly, but she was frantic.

Jo's mind raced. Brooke was home—that should've been a good thing. But what was going on?

"Are you hurt?"

"No, but I can't get out of this room. You've got to help me!"

"Back up," Jo said. "You have a safe room, and your dad locked you in there? Where's your mom?"

"She's out of town."

"Where's your dad right now?"

Brooke sighed. "I have no idea. This room is sound-proof, so I can't hear anything outside the door. If he comes back in, I'll have to hang up."

Her voice was getting calmer, and she seemed rational. But the thought still crossed Jo's mind—was the girl making all this up to get attention?

"Why don't you call the police?"

"No way," Brooke said. "I had a friend who ran away, and her parents called the police, then social services got involved. I'm not going through that."

"Did you use your other phone and talk to your friends?" Jo asked. "You could get them to come over."

"I can't. Dad has my other phone."

"How did he get it?" she asked. "Here, just tell me what happened since you left the Target store yesterday."

Brooke quickly gave Jo a rundown of her activities, ending with how her father had tricked her into the room.

"Why do you have a safe room?" Jo asked. "Who are your parents?" She realized she didn't even know Brooke's last name.

"My mom's named Fran, Fran Whigby. She works for the Department of Defense. My dad's Connor. He works for Senator Macintosh."

Jo had seen Elaine Macintosh on the news but didn't know much about her.

"What's going on with your dad?" she asked. "How did he react when he found out that you'd run away?"

"He was upset, but he was acting weird, too. He kept looking out the windows."

"He wasn't at work because you'd run away?" Jo deduced.

"Yes. He'd been trying to find me. I don't know if him locking me in here is some weird way of punishing me or what. I have no idea when he'll be back or what's going on. I thought I'd call him, but then he'd know I have this phone."

"No," Jo affirmed, "call the police."

"No way."

Jo frowned. "Do you have food and water?"

"The room is fully stocked, and there's even a bathroom and a bed in here." The girl muttered something under her breath. "I could be here for a long time and never need anything. I can even watch TV, but the phone that's usually in here is gone."

"Has your dad ever done something like this before?"

"No," Brooke said. "Like I told you yesterday, most of the time my parents hardly notice I'm around. I was surprised he got as mad as he did about me running away."

She sounded a bit peevish. Jo wondered again if she might be making the whole thing up. It seemed rather drastic on the dad's part—unless there was some kind of abuse or other things going on that Brooke hadn't mentioned. Jo grimaced.

Brooke's voice changed. "He's coming in! You've got to come over here and help me." The line went dead as she said the final word.

She stared at the phone for a moment as she thought what to do. If she called back, would she be alerting Brooke's dad to the phone? Jo decided not to call, instead getting on the internet and looking up Connor Whigby. He was forty-four years old, born in upstate New York, had gone to Yale. The only picture she could find of him was from a few years earlier. He looked tall in relation to the people around him, with broad shoulders and dark, wavy hair. He'd been working in DC since his early twenties, and he'd been on Senator Macintosh's staff for several years. Jo didn't find a lot of other information on him, not even his official position. How closely did he work with the senator?

Macintosh was the next search. The senator was in her fifties, divorced, with two grown daughters. She was considered a moderate Democrat and served on a couple of committees, including the Senate Select Committee on Intelligence. But as far as Jo could find, Macintosh hadn't done much of anything distinguishable until a few weeks back. Her name was in the news because she was one of a handful of politicians who had voted against sending money to yet another foreign nation to aid a war the United States maybe shouldn't have been involved in.

Jo looked up Brooke's mother, Fran. Her LinkedIn page didn't have a picture, and the Department of Defense job description was boilerplate. The woman had grown up in California but graduated from Yale as well, presumably where she and Connor had met. Jo found nothing else remarkable on either parent, certainly nothing that might indicate that Connor would be capable of locking his daughter in a safe room.

Jo looked out the window for a moment. She was sorely tempted to call the police, report what Brooke had said, and leave it at that. After years of being in dangerous situations, she wanted to lead a quiet life, not get involved in anything. Brooke was probably exaggerating things with her father, and this would all blow over. Jo tried to convince herself, but she wasn't succeeding. The girl had reached out to her for help, and even if the call, the claim of being locked in a safe room, was made up, she still needed help.

With a sigh, Jo stood up. She looked up the Whigbys' address and studied the location. Their house was at the end of a cul-de-sac, the back yard butting up to a wooded area. Satisfied that she knew the exterior layout, Jo used an app to request an Uber. She pocketed her phone and eyed her duffel bag. So much for leaving. Frowning, she put the bag in the closet.

As she closed the motel room door on her way out, she tucked a tiny piece of paper in the upper corner, between the door and jamb.

Jo avoided passing the front office—the day manager always wanted to chat with her. That didn't go well with keeping a low profile. Instead, she walked to the back of the building and waited. A white SUV soon pulled up. Jo verified the ride, then got in.

The driver tried to make conversation with her, but he soon lapsed into silence. They headed southwest, arriving about twenty minutes later in North Springfield. Jo had the driver drop her off at the end of Brooke's street. He sped off, and she stood at the corner for a moment. The neighborhood was mostly two-story brick homes on big lots, with tall maple and oak trees providing ample shade. The sky was cloudless, the heat oppressive. A few birds chirped from the trees, and a squirrel darted by. After a moment, she started walking down the street.

The cul-de-sac was short, and soon she was near the Whigby house. Jo kept her head down as she stood on the sidewalk for a moment, studying the property. The home was two stories, with a small balcony centered over a white front door. No one was around outside, but she spotted security cameras on some eaves. Probably a doorbell camera as well. Everything seemed ordinary, nothing going on, no movement behind the front windows. She checked the side windows, wondering if one was Brooke's bedroom. Still no activity, so she walked up to the front door and rang the bell.

CHAPTER EIGHT

Connor Whigby was even bigger than Jo had originally thought, probably standing about six-two or so, with broad shoulders and hands that could palm a basketball. He looked older than the picture that she'd seen too, his hairline receding slightly, gray around the temples. He was fit—though not in the way that Jo or other people she knew in the military were—with the beginnings of a paunch and a little fullness creeping into cheeks beneath some stubble. Crow's feet flared from the corners of his eyes; he seemed to be a man with heavy concerns. And he looked worried now, his eyes narrow as he stared at Jo.

"Yes?" he said in a baritone voice, a hint of annoyance carrying through.

"You're Connor Whigby?" she asked. She shifted her position, keeping her head low so the security cameras wouldn't get a good look at her. She couldn't do much about the doorbell camera, but hopefully the man was blocking it to some degree.

Connor nodded, his lips pressed into a firm line. Jo cleared her throat. On the Uber ride over, she'd thought about what she was going to say. Now that she was standing before him, she hesitated.

"I'm a—I guess you would call me a friend of Brooke's," Jo said. "I ran into her last evening."

"You saw Brooke last night? Why didn't you get her home?" His words tumbled out.

Jo nodded. "I talked to her, offered to get her an Uber, but she refused. I tried to get her to come home, but she apparently didn't listen. I did get her some food." She didn't mention the pre-paid phone. "I thought she was going to go home last night."

He put his hands on his hips. "She didn't show up until today."

Jo dodged the fight he seemed to be looking for. Glancing past him, she saw a large foyer with a dark wood staircase. She couldn't see or hear anything beyond that. Looking back at Connor, she smiled.

"Is Brooke around? I'd love to talk to her."

The man shook his head. "She's . . . at a friend's house now."

"Oh, I would've thought maybe she'd be in trouble, that she wouldn't be allowed out."

He stared at her. "That's between Brooke and me."

"I'd sure like to talk to her," Jo said. "What friend is she with? Sarah?" She threw out a name.

He shook his head. "She's at Val Lindbergh's, the next block over."

"Okay." Jo acted as if she knew who that was. "You said she didn't get back until today. Was she okay?"

He nodded. "She's just fine. I'm sorry, but I need to go. I'm working." He glanced over her shoulder, maybe looking for a car, then eyed her. "Thanks for helping my daughter."

The door slammed closed. Jo stood on the steps for a

moment, staring at it. She wasn't sure what to think. The man's answers had been plausible, but she didn't like his attitude. He'd slipped when he named one of Brooke's friends, and now Jo was going to check into that.

She spun on her heel and walked down the sidewalk, then looked back. Would Connor confront Brooke about her visit, and if so, would he find the phone? Jo wanted to call Brooke, but if the prepaid phone was working and for some reason Brooke wasn't answering, she'd inadvertently alert Whigby to the phone.

If Brooke was in the house and her father talked to her now, the conversation would likely only last a few minutes, so while she waited, Jo looked up Val Lindbergh. She lucked out—the girl was on the high school swim team. A profile listed some of her accomplishments and noted her parents' names as well. Jo googled them and found a website that gave an address. As Connor had noted, the Lindberghs lived on the next block over, which dead-ended at the edge of the nearby woods.

Jo jogged around the block to an older ranch-style brick house. On the front porch, Jo paused, straightening her posture. She knew she could carry herself with a bearing that commanded people's attention, and she did so now. After ringing the bell, she waited.

A moment later, a teenager with long blond hair opened the door. She wore slacks and a shirt with a Subway logo.

"Yeah?" she asked.

Jo went with a direct question. "You're Val Lindbergh, Brooke Whigby's friend?"

"Uh-huh." The girl gave her a wary stare.

"Is she here?"

Val shook her head and snapped her gum. "I haven't

seen her in a couple of days. Um, is she in some kind of trouble?"

"When was the last time you talked to her?" Jo asked in a rush.

"It's been a few days. I called her last night, but she didn't answer. Is everything all right?"

"Yes," Jo replied. "Have you talked to her parents recently?"

"No." She sounded more suspicious now. "Um, I gotta go. I'll call Brooke later."

Val shut the door, and Jo walked back down the street. Connor Whigby had lied to her. Not a surprise, but it was also not a good sign. As she walked to the corner, she looked up the Springfield Police Department's phone number and called. When a sergeant answered, Jo spoke quickly.

"I have reason to believe that a girl named Brooke Whigby might be in trouble," she said. She rattled off the address. "I'm not sure what's going on, but she ran away yesterday, and today I haven't seen her around. I don't know if her father might have harmed her when she returned home."

"What makes you think that might be the case?" asked the sergeant, a woman with a high-pitched voice.

"Can you do a welfare check?"

"I'd like to get a little more information, if I may. What makes you think Brooke might be in trouble?"

Jo hesitated. "Brooke called and told me that."

"What is your name?"

"If you could send someone for a welfare check, I'd appreciate it."

With that, Jo repeated the address and ended the call. With luck, that would be enough to get someone to stop by the Whigby house. She hurried back around the corner,

then continued down the block to where she could still see
Cawthorne Drive.

Finally, after walking back and forth, keeping the street
in sight, she saw a squad car approach from the opposite
direction. It turned onto Cawthorne, and Jo picked up her
pace. As she neared the corner, she looked down the cul-de-
sac. The vehicle parked in front of Brooke's house, and two
officers got out and walked to the door. Jo watched from
behind a tree. One of the officers knocked on the door, and
it soon opened again. Connor Whigby said something, but
she couldn't make out his expression. He talked to the officers, gesturing calmly. Both officers periodically nodded
their heads. After a few minutes, they turned and left.

Jo whirled around and jogged down the street. Darting
onto the next block, she peeked back. The squad car soon
reached the corner and drove off in the other direction. She
wiped sweat off her face, frowning in frustration. She
would've loved to have heard the conversation between the
officers and Whigby, but the conclusion was obvious: he
had convinced them nothing was wrong, or they wouldn't
have left so quickly. She also knew that in a welfare check,
the police didn't always push to find out if the person in
question was really in trouble, and without cause to enter
the house, there wasn't a lot more the officers could do. If
Brooke was indeed locked in a safe room, what would her
father do next?

She was debating what she should do when she saw a
silver Lexus stop at the corner of Cawthorne. Connor was
behind the wheel. As the car turned in her direction, Jo
dashed behind some bushes at the side of the nearest house
and ducked down. The Lexus continued down the street—
she was sure Whigby hadn't seen her.

Once the car disappeared from view, she jogged back to

Cawthorne Drive and stopped a few houses down from the Whigbys'. She watched it for a few minutes, and when nothing happened and no one came outside, she ran to the next street and stopped at the house at the end. She rang the bell, and when no one answered, she hurried around the side of the house. Peeking through slats in a cedar-wood fence, Jo saw nothing, so she opened the gate and tiptoed in.

Jo crossed the yard, climbed the back fence, and dropped down on the other side. The woods were filled with oak and maple trees, and as she walked in, the shadows enveloped her, the cooler air a relief. She picked her way along until she was directly behind Brooke's house. The neighborhood remained quiet as Jo climbed a tree where she could see into the Whigbys' back yard. It was large, with a big lawn and a pool surrounded by deck chairs. Jo waited and watched. If Brooke was making up a story about being locked in, would she see the girl come out, now that her father had gone? But no one appeared.

Jo called Brooke, but she didn't answer. Then she realized that if Brooke hadn't had a chance to charge the prepaid phone, it might've died. Or maybe her father had discovered it and taken it from her. In either case, that meant no way to contact her, nor any idea whether she was okay.

The minutes ticked by, the muggy afternoon air thickening around Jo. She shifted her position, ignoring the occasional bug. She'd been well-trained to stay still and quiet in the most uncomfortable places. After a while, the neighbors to the right of the Whigbys came home, and soon a man was out mowing his lawn. The neighbors on the other side returned as well, and Jo heard their voices through an open screen door in the back.

At dusk, lights finally came on in the Whigby house.

Connor appeared in the kitchen, but she couldn't tell what he was doing. He occasionally came to the back door and peered into the yard. Jo never saw anyone else, certainly not Brooke. She continued to watch as dusk deepened into night. Kids played in the neighborhood, their squeals carrying into the woods. It cooled off slightly, and Jo found herself longing for some water. She hadn't planned on being out here all day.

A half-moon rose, silver rays slipping past the tree branches. Finally, the neighborhood sounds died off. Connor appeared at various windows, shutting the blinds one by one. Then the lights went off, and in the surrounding houses as well. Jo was about to climb out of the tree when she heard a noise nearby.

She was not alone.

CHAPTER NINE

Jo froze and strained her ears to hear. She heard the sound again, below her and to the right. Peering into the darkness, she saw the slightest movement in the woods. Her eyes were well adjusted by now, and she made out a man, crouched low. He was dressed all in black, barely visible. She didn't move a muscle, continuing to watch.

The man crept through the foliage, pausing near some trees close to the Whigbys' back fence. After a few minutes, he stole up to the fence and peered through the boards into the yard. Jo momentarily lost sight of him as he worked his way along. Then she heard a faint noise. The man appeared again, finally standing straight. He watched through the fence boards for a long time before he skulked back into the woods. When he was a safe distance away, Jo quietly dropped out of the tree and followed.

The man was good, hardly making a sound as he traversed away from the houses at the edge of the woods. But Jo was better. She sneaked behind him, careful with her footfalls, barely breathing. When the man paused to listen, she halted behind a large maple. The moonlight filtered into the trees, but it remained dim. It was too early for crickets, the night utterly still. The man glanced around. Seeming satisfied, he continued on.

He crossed the woods, and at the other side, houses sat across a road. Pausing, he listened for a moment, then approached a dark sedan. He glanced around one final time, unlocked the car, and got in. The engine started, and Jo risked a little more noise as she dashed toward the edge of the woods. The car pulled into the road, headlights off, and even though Jo got as close as she dared, she couldn't make out the license plate. She swore to herself as the sedan disappeared from view.

The night was still again, just the occasional sound of a car in the distance. Finally satisfied she was alone, Jo trekked back toward the Whigby house. As she approached, she made sure she was quiet. She watched the fence and woods near the back of the house for a long time, and when she didn't see anybody, she approached another tree near the Whigbys' back fence. Climbing up and out onto a branch gave her a view into the back yard. The house was quiet, so she dropped to the ground and examined the fence. Near the center, she discovered a tiny camera inserted into a crevice between the boards, focused on the house.

Jo glanced around as she processed the discovery. Who wanted to spy on the Whigbys, and why? Did it have something to do with Connor and his association with Senator Macintosh, or with Fran and her job at the DoD? Jo didn't give an answer much thought at the moment, instead pulling out her phone and taking a picture of the device. Then, for good measure, she searched the fence again, with painstaking focus, but she didn't find any other surveillance devices.

She wiped sweat off her face and waited to see if anybody else would show up. When no one did, she stole out of the woods the way she had come in that afternoon. At this point, she was more worried than ever about Brooke, but she was also concerned about who was watching the house.

Whatever was going on, Jo was going to make sure nobody knew she had been around, so instead of calling an Uber, she made the long trek to a Metro station. As she walked, her previous training kicked in. Even though she was certain no one had any idea she'd been around the Whigby house, she was keenly aware of her surroundings and made sure no one was following her.

When she arrived at the station, she bought a ticket and walked to the platform. One other person was waiting for a train going in the opposite direction, and only a few people populated the one she took back to Crystal City. When she got off, she looked around again for a tail, but all seemed clear. Then it was another long trek back to her motel.

As she approached, she stopped in the doorway of a store across the street and studied the building. The parking lot was dark and quiet, no one around, no lights on in any rooms. Jo sneaked up to her door. The piece of paper she'd put in the upper corner of the door was still there. She listened for a moment, then quietly let herself in. After locking the door without a sound, she finally turned on a light. For good measure, she searched the space before going into the kitchenette.

Jo wrapped a hand towel around the door stopper so the door couldn't be opened, then put a chair under the handle.

She hadn't eaten in hours, and only now realized how famished she was. She ate some granola and a banana, then stripped off her clothes and took a cold shower. The water felt good as she scrubbed the dried sweat from her body. After she toweled off, she tumbled into bed.

CHAPTER TEN

After Brooke ended the call with Jo, she pushed the phone in between the couch cushions and stared at the door. She was sure she'd heard a key in the lock, but nothing happened. Her dad didn't come in. Listening hard, she still couldn't hear anything. As she waited, fear arose in her. The girl wanted to believe Jo would help her, that she would come by and see what was going on. But Brooke knew she was being stupid to not call the police.

Screw whatever happened, she finally thought.

She grabbed the phone and swiped the screen, and then her heart sank. The battery icon was red. She dialed 911 and waited. When nothing happened, she looked at the screen. The call wouldn't connect, and then the screen went blank. Brooke tossed the phone onto the coffee table and cursed. Too many stupid games. She hadn't thought about charging the phone, hadn't known that she might need it. She shook her head. So much for that.

Twisting her lips, she slumped on the couch and propped her legs on the coffee table. The time crept by, and she kept glancing toward the door, wishing that Jo would come in. Or anybody to rescue her. But again, nothing happened.

Finally, Brooke grabbed the remote and turned on the TV. At least she had that to while away the time. She flipped through channels, found a *Catfish* episode on MTV, and began watching. A young woman in New York City had been lured into a relationship by a man in London, but his online persona was fake. He actually lived in New York City as well, but he wasn't an entrepreneur as he claimed. Brooke shook her head. How could people fall for those kinds of scams?

Another episode came on, but she was hardly watching. What was Jo doing? Had she even tried to come by the house? After a few more episodes, Brooke got tired of the show and flipped channels again. She glanced at the door. Had her dad gone to work? He sometimes worked odd hours, available for the senator whenever she needed him. Brooke snorted. What would the Senator Macintosh think if she knew that one of her key men had his daughter locked in the basement?

Brooke turned off the TV and flopped back on the couch, where she stared at the ceiling and waited. Her eyelids drooped, and she dozed off.

When she awoke, she had no idea what time it was—the artificial light in the room revealed nothing. She turned on the TV again, went to the guide, and noticed that it was six o'clock. Her stomach growled, and she went to the kitchen area. Her dad had put bread and sliced turkey in the refrigerator, along with cheese and condiments. She made a sandwich and ate it with some chips she found in the cupboard. The fridge was stocked with bottled water as well, and there were plenty more in a cupboard. She rummaged around and found other snacks. One thing was for certain, she wouldn't starve for quite some time. The thought made her uneasy, though. How long did he plan on her being here? The last bite of her sandwich went down hard as she thought over her circumstances.

Moving into the middle of the room, she looked around. Was there a way out?

Brooke turned and studied each wall closely. There were no windows, and the ceiling was concrete, as were the walls and floor. The room was virtually impenetrable. She grimaced. Surely there was a way out, some secret passage. She walked to a corner and worked her way around the entire space, looking for cracks in the concrete, any kind of odd seam, but when she reached her starting point, she hadn't found anything. She should've known it would be that way, but she needed some sliver of hope.

Back in the bar area, she checked the cabinets, cleared out the contents, and tapped on the back sides. Nothing sounded hollow. The refrigerator was on rollers, and she pulled it out and looked behind it. No other opening.

Brooke got up, went into the bathroom, and scrutinized the walls, floor, and ceiling. All was as airtight as the main room. She noticed a small fan in the ceiling, though—that would mean air ducts. Maybe she could pull the fan out and call for help. She had no idea where the ducts led, but if she was lucky, someone passing by might hear her. Or she could make enough noise that her dad would see the futility of keeping her locked in the safe room. She could be annoying when she wanted to be.

With that in mind, she carried a stool and a plastic knife back into the bathroom. On her tiptoes, she was able to reach the fan. She unscrewed the fan and lowered it, but frowned at what she saw. The fan was connected to wires and had some kind of contraption with a filter on it. She studied the small opening in the ceiling before reaching up and feeling around. There was a cavity, but no duct work. She swore softly. The fan wasn't connected to any kind of ventilation system. There wasn't even anything to bang on, anything to make noise, let alone a way to call out.

Brooke stood on the stool for a minute, defeated. As far as she could tell, there was no way out of the safe room. She should have known that, but she'd gotten her hopes up.

She didn't want Connor to know what she'd been up to, so she put the fan back in place, returned the stool to the bar area, and sat on the couch. She didn't feel like watching any more TV, so she waited. A while later, her stomach growled, so she went to the bar and grabbed some potato chips. She ate a handful, drank some water, and went back to the couch.

Brooke didn't know how much time had passed before she heard the locks on the door rattling. Standing up, she started toward the door. Her dad came into the room and quickly shut it, blocking the way. He crossed his arms.

"Are you doing okay?" he asked.

She stood before him, hands on her hips. "What the hell's going on, Dad?"

Connor glared at her. "You watch yourself, young lady."

Even though she'd run away, she wasn't a bad kid, and she'd been taught to be respectful. Just hearing her dad's tone made her back off. She mumbled an apology. He gestured for her to sit down, so she moved back to the couch and perched on the edge of it.

"Are you okay?" he repeated.

She nodded, staring at him. He looked haggard, with dark circles under his eyes, and his mouth was pinched with worry.

"Are you in some kind of trouble?" she asked.

He shook his head. "It's nothing for you to worry about. There's just some . . . stuff that I need to take care of. And I can't have you running away again."

"Where's Mom?"

"I told you, she had to go out of town."

"When will she be back?"

He didn't answer, just stared past her. "There's enough food for you."

Brooke glared at him. "How long will I be in here?"

"I'm trying to get things taken care of. You need to trust me. This is all for your own good."

She huffed. "Come on, Dad. Don't you think this is excessive punishment for me running away?"

It was as if she hadn't said a word. "You talked to a woman at the park yesterday?"

He'd spoken to Jo. "Yeah. She was trying to help me," she said. "Why? Did she come by here?"

"What's her name?"

"Jo. I never got a last name."

Connor narrowed his eyes. "You told her where we live?"

"Not yesterday. I mean—" She wasn't sure how to answer.

He drew in a deep breath. "This will all blow over, then maybe we can take a vacation. We could go to, I don't know, Mexico? Sit on the beach, get a tan."

"I can get a tan in our back yard." Brooke made sure to put plenty of snark in her tone.

He didn't say anything for a moment. "I'll be back to check on you again."

She leaped to her feet. "You gotta let me out of here. This is ridiculous."

"I promise it won't be for too long."

"Where's Mom?" she asked again. "Let me have my phone so I can talk to her."

He shook his head. "She can't take your call right now."

"What's going on?" She fired off questions before he could answer. "Does she know that you have me locked in here? She's going to be pissed at you, you know? And maybe Jo will call the police. What will they say about me being down here? You're going to get in big trouble. You can't do this to me."

He took a step forward, staring at her with hard eyes. Brooke sometimes forgot what a big man her father was. Then his gaze fell to the coffee table.

"What's that?"

She looked where he pointed. The prepaid phone was next to the TV remote.

"It's a phone Jo got me," she said. She snatched it up.

"Did you call the police?" The words came out in a menacing whisper.

"I called whoever I wanted."

His face turned white as he held out his hand. "Give it to me."

"Fine!" She threw the phone at him. "It's dead anyway."

The phone hit him on the chest and bounced, but he caught it in midair. "You need to listen to me, okay?" His voice remained low and forceful. "I was worried to death about that stunt you pulled, and it can't happen again. You don't know as much as you think you do."

Brooke took a couple of steps forward, and Connor did, too. His face contorted like an ugly Halloween mask. She'd never seen him like this, and she was suddenly scared.

"Sit down," he said.

Brooke backed up and slowly sank onto the couch. Her dad pointed a finger at her.

"I've got enough going on without you . . ." He didn't finish. "I have to go. You'll be fine in here."

With that, he backpedaled toward the door. Brooke should have done something, but she was scared of him. He quickly let himself out, and she heard the locks again. Only now did she run to the door, grabbing the knob and twisting it. It wouldn't open. She hollered, but she knew he couldn't hear her. Stepping back, she stared at the blank surface before her.

Brooke felt totally helpless.

CHAPTER ELEVEN

Connor Whigby sat at the kitchen island with a glass of Crown Royal. He hadn't even bothered with ice, just drank it straight. The house was still, no TV on, no music.

How had things gotten this far, this fast? He took another big gulp of the whiskey, then put the glass down. He desperately wanted to get drunk, so drunk that he couldn't even think, but he had too much to do. And the senator might need him.

Connor swore silently. The job had been great for a long time. But the responsibility tied him down. He contemplated the glass on the counter. Macintosh should be okay tonight, but he never knew. The senator had a habit of calling at the oddest times, always wanting something. And with her recent work on the credibility of individual terrorist cells operating in Eastern Europe, his job had become even more difficult, with even more demands.

He thought about Brooke, too. He and Fran had done everything for her. She didn't believe it, of course—the whole running away thing proved that. Connor shook his head. He'd lain awake last night, frantic about what might've happened to her. To then find out that she'd just run away . . .

He shook his head at her reasoning. They hadn't been paying attention to her.

Connor snorted as he took a small sip of whiskey, regulating his intake this time. His hand shook as he thought about how much he and Fran had done for Brooke over the years. They'd been at all her school functions, all her swimming activities. They'd even moved to a house with a pool so she could swim at home. All the sacrifices. But Brooke was right. They hadn't been paying much attention to her lately. Things beyond his control had dictated that. She'd never understand, and he couldn't tell her. Hell, he couldn't tell *anybody*.

Another small sip. When did things get to be such a cluster? You start out, you think you're trying to do good, but there are always temptations. Connor stared at the glass. Would there be any way that they could try to make things right?

Glancing at the prepaid phone he'd taken from Brooke, he felt his heart race. Who had she really called? Just Jo, or the police, or someone else as well? He had no idea what Brooke had told that woman, but it had been enough for her to stop by.

And the police. Jo might've called them, not Brooke. When they'd first come to the door, they didn't seem to have much information, other than that they'd been asked to do a welfare check. Connor had told them she was fine. They'd wanted to see Brooke, but he'd been able to convince them she was sleeping upstairs. He hadn't told them she ran away, just that she'd been out late the previous evening with a friend. He was a smooth talker, and they believed him and left. But did he need to worry about Jo? Hopefully she would move on, not worry any more about his daughter.

Picking up the phone, he swiped at the screen. It was dead, just as Brooke had said. He slid off the bar stool and rooted around in drawers until he found a charger. A battery icon appeared on the screen when he plugged it in, but he still couldn't get to the main screen. He swore, set the phone down, and checked the back windows.

The light was fading. Connor could hear the faint sound of kids playing in the neighbor's yard. Blackness blanketed the woods behind the house, and he couldn't shake an eerie feeling. He went back to the counter and checked the phone again. Now he could log in, but it asked for him to enter a pin number. Damn. He'd hoped that Brooke wouldn't have thought to put a pin on it. But she was his daughter, and he'd trained her well. Never let someone steal your information.

He tried several number combinations Brooke might use, but none worked. Then he set the phone down, still connected to the charger. There was no way his daughter would tell him. Not now, anyway. He was sure she hadn't been able to call her friends, or he would've heard something from them or their parents. But what had she told Jo?

A slow anger continued to build as he fumed at his daughter. She'd screwed things up, whether she realized it or not. At the moment, she hated him, and he couldn't blame her. But Connor had told her the truth. He could *not* afford to have her running away again, and he couldn't trust her to stay while he was gone. Hell, he didn't know what would happen even if he was there. What if they came to the house? He shook his head. No, Brooke had to stay where she was, as horrible as it was to think about that. She was safer downstairs. He pictured the look on her face after she'd thrown the phone at him—fear. She was scared of him, and that broke his heart. He'd never intentionally hurt her.

Yanking the phone from the charger, Connor pushed both away. He swore into the silence, his voice echoing against the high ceilings of the house. That made him feel slightly better, if only for a moment. He got up, walked around the house, made sure the windows and doors were locked, and closed the blinds. Then he returned to the kitchen island.

The glass of whiskey sat there, just a finger left. He'd been good, hadn't drank that much. Screw it. Connor tipped his head back and gulped down the rest of it, feeling the burn in his throat. Then he pulled his own phone from his pocket and checked it. No missed calls or texts. He tapped the screen, willing it to ring. Fran should have been calling. The silence around him was deafening. He stared at the phone.

Ring. Please, ring.

CHAPTER TWELVE

Light through the crack in the curtains woke Jo at seven. She'd only gotten a few hours of sleep, but she felt completely alert. She rolled out of bed and checked her phone. Nothing from Brooke. Jo was again tempted to try her, but she didn't know where Connor was, or if he'd discovered the phone. Now Jo had no idea what might be going on with the teen. But given all that she'd seen yesterday, she wasn't going to leave DC until she knew what had happened.

Jo turned on the TV, switching to the news in case Brooke had been reported missing, but the anchor never mentioned the teenager. She kept it on as she stretched all her muscles, but she skipped a workout. After dressing, she fixed up some eggs and sausage patties for makeshift Egg McMuffins. She ate one sandwich as she again googled Connor Whigby, this time being more thorough in her research. She finally found him referenced in a few articles, and his associations with Senator Macintosh seemed innocuous at best. He didn't have any social media accounts that she could find.

She tried Fran Whigby again as well, thinking that a mother might have a Facebook page or other account to share updates with family and friends. But try as she might, she couldn't find anything.

The news droned in the background as Jo ate the other breakfast sandwich and thought through what to do next. Something was going on at the Whigby house, something potentially more serious than Brooke being locked in a safe room. Jo didn't know if anyone had seen her watching the house. If so, she herself would potentially be in danger, and that meant she had to be more cautious now. She couldn't rely on public transportation and walking anymore, which presented a dilemma that she needed to address.

She wiped her hands on a napkin, then used a knife from the kitchen to undo the screws from a heating vent near the floor. After retrieving a small key from the heating duct, she replaced the vent, then called for an Uber, and went outside. Again, she tucked a piece of paper in the upper corner of the door.

When her car arrived, Jo asked the driver to take her downtown. She kept an eye out on the way but never saw a tail. The man dropped her off on K Street, north of the White House, and once the car had driven away, she walked down the street to the corner and looked around. A few groups of tourists meandered by, easy to spot with their maps in hand. Today's heat would be intense if they were sightseeing. Jo strode down Seventeenth Street NW, past Farragut Square, then around another block and back to K Street. No one was following her, so she headed east to a bank on the ground floor of a ten-story high-rise and walked inside.

The lobby was a refreshing change, cool and quiet. Soon, a clerk escorted her to a safety deposit room. They used their keys to unlock a deposit box, and then he showed her into a private room and shut the door.

Jo opened the box and pulled out a few driver's licenses and credit cards, all with fake names. She knew how to get fake documents on the street, but that might take some time, which she didn't have. She pocketed all of them, taking some cash from the box as well.

As she was leaving the building, she paused in the lobby, acting casual as she looked around. No one appeared to be watching her, but she remained vigilant as she went outside.

The sun hit hard as she walked to a nearby Metro station, hopped on, and rode to a stop near an Enterprise car rental. She paid for an older-model SUV, gray and nondescript. The attendant inspected the car and noted some scratches on it. He seemed embarrassed about the condition, but she didn't care. An older car attracted less attention. He gave her the keys, and when she got in, she put her original ID and credit cards, and the extras, in the glove box.

Googling pawnshops, she found one close by, and headed straight there. Jo hadn't driven a car in months, and at stoplights she adjusted the seats and mirrors, trying to get comfortable. Still no tail.

When she arrived at the shop, she purchased high-powered binoculars and a solid folding knife from an older man with a heavy beard.

"I could use your help," she said quietly as he rang them up.

"What can I do?" he asked with a smile.

"I need a tracking device."

"We don't carry anything like that."

"It's my husband." She put emotion in her voice. "I think he's cheating on me. I can't go to the police because he's . . . well, he's threatening me. But if I can find out what he's up to, I might be able to get his family to believe me and help me."

It was the kind of lie she knew would work. Domestic violence pulled at people's heartstrings. The man nodded and touched her elbow.

"Has he hit you?"

She nodded, her chin quivering. "Sometimes."

"Come with me."

He got someone else to cover the register, then led her to a back room. Heading behind another counter, he pulled a box from a nearby shelf.

"This device works with a burner phone," he said as he opened it. "In case he takes the one you have, you can still find out where he's going."

"Good," she said.

"The tracker has a solid range, and it comes with a magnetic case, so you can put this on his car. I'll set up the phone, and you'll be good to go."

"What about listening devices? You know, bugs. So I can find out what he's doing when I'm out of the house."

He smirked. "You're really worried about him."

"Yes."

"Well, I've got something for you." Another box came down off the shelves. "You can stick these to almost any surface." The man held up a tiny bug transmitter, no bigger than the tip of his finger. "I'll set up the monitoring software on the burner phone as well."

"Thank you."

Jo purchased a monthly subscription plan for the tracking systems, and the proprietor set up the device and the bugs, then showed her how it all worked.

She drove into North Springfield, stopped at a conve-

nience store for snacks and water, and finally headed to the
Whigby neighborhood, parking down the block from
Cawthorne Drive. The house was quiet—no cars in the
driveway, no activity. She trained the binoculars on each car
on Cawthorne and typed the license plate numbers into a
notepad app on her phone. Studying each house in the
neighborhood, she saw no unusual activity, no sign that
somebody might be spying on the Whigbys.

After watching for a while longer, she left and drove
through the neighborhood until she found the road where
she'd seen the dark sedan the previous night. Traffic was
heavier today, and she pulled over to let a few cars pass.
There were no cars parked on the street directly across the
woods from the Whigby house, so she drove on. When she
passed the spot where the sedan had been, no one was
around.

Farther down the street, a blue Chrysler minivan with
tinted windows and a rooftop cargo box was parked across
from a two-story house. Bumper stickers were plastered on
the back of the car. To most people who passed by, the
minivan would seem like nothing more than the perfect
vehicle for an on-the-go soccer parent.

But Jo suspected different.

CHAPTER THIRTEEN

After driving past the blue minivan, Jo stopped when she was almost out of view. Even though there were two other cars parked between her and the vehicle, she still had an angle on it. The minivan was the perfect vehicle to spy on the Whigbys. It didn't appear out of place, and if listening devices had been placed at the house, it would be in range.

However, it was hot outside, and that presented a problem. If someone was spying from the van, they would need some way to keep their vehicle cool inside without the engine running, probably an air-conditioning unit within the rooftop cargo box. Jo didn't have that luxury. She had to risk rolling down windows, otherwise she might suffocate.

Grabbing the binoculars, she crawled into the back of the SUV and trained them on the van. The cars partially blocked it, but she still had a decent view of the back.

The minivan had no markings on it, nothing that said it might be a business vehicle. The bumper stickers all appeared to be from a local high school. She couldn't see in through the back windows. The car could've belonged to someone who lived in the neighborhood, but she remained suspicious.

Jo looked up the license plate. It took some time as she had to keep an eye on the minivan, but she finally found the vehicle registered to someone named Kelly Smith. Could be a male or female. She googled the address, and her suspicions were confirmed—it didn't exist.

Again, she peered through the rear window at the minivan. It had to belong to the government. She wasn't sure which agency, probably the FBI, but she had to find out.

Jo munched on mixed nuts, sipped some water, and waited. At some point, the agents inside the minivan would either need to use the facilities, or they would be relieved by another team. She smiled at the pun.

Several cars drove by, and some kids came outside to ride their bikes up and down the street. Another minivan parked on the road, and a woman and her daughter got out, crossed the street, and went into a house. At noon, another older-model white minivan parked some distance behind the blue one Jo was watching. No one got out of the second vehicle. Then the original one pulled into the street, heading in her direction.

Jo ducked down and waited until the minivan passed, then scrambled into the front seat. She started the SUV and blasted the air-conditioner, thankful for the sudden cool rush. The minivan was far ahead already, almost out of view, and she followed.

When it reached a stop sign, it turned left. Jo sped up. The new street was busier, and for a second, she was afraid she'd lost the minivan. She turned left as well and spotted it at a stoplight. A few cars had gotten between them—good. The light turned green, and the minivan drove east for a bit before pulling into a gas station convenience store. That made sense. There was only so much you could do cooped up in a surveillance vehicle before you needed a bathroom. *Especially if you've been drinking coffee,* she thought with a wry smile.

The van pulled into a space at the far end of the store, and two men in trousers and white shirts got out. They casually walked into the store as Jo turned into the parking lot. She circled the building, parked on the side, and hopped out, peeking around the corner. No one was in front of the store. She approached the rear of the minivan. A woman was pumping gas, facing the other way, the only customer outside.

Jo bent down as if she'd dropped something, then carefully put the magnetized tracker in the minivan's wheel well. It took her only a second. As she stood, the woman at the gas pump was still looking the other direction. Jo hurried into the store. The bathrooms were down a hall at the back. She kept her head down and walked along an aisle. Soon, one of the men in the white shirt emerged from the hall and joined the other man. Both had bulges at the ankle, where their trousers covered guns.

Each of them grabbed a soda and a bag of peanuts, then paid and went outside.

Jo stood near the door. Neither man bothered to look around the minivan as they got in. At some point, the tracking device would be found, but likely not until after they'd reached their destination. Jo glanced the other way as the vehicle backed up, then turned onto the street. She didn't have to worry about tailing the minivan too closely— the tracker had a long range. She took the opportunity to use the facilities herself and buy a premade sandwich before returning to the SUV. She grabbed the burner phone and turned on the tracking device. A blue dot blinked on the screen, showing the minivan still traveling east.

Pulling into traffic, Jo followed the same route. After the heat of the morning, the car was wonderfully cool. She munched on the sandwich as she drove. It wasn't very good, but it would do. The minivan took Interstate 395, and so did Jo. She sped up a bit, weaving around cars so she wouldn't be too far behind it when it reached its destination. Traffic was heavy, but moving, and she and the minivan made steady progress. Then the target crossed the Potomac River into DC, and the dot on the phone stopped moving. She followed the map until she reached a large cinderblock building that spanned an entire block.

She'd tracked the vehicle to an FBI field office. Jo didn't see the minivan—it must've pulled into an underground parking garage. How long would it be before somebody swept the vehicle and her tracking device was discovered? But she had the information she needed. The feds were watching the Whigby house.

The question remained, though: Why?

CHAPTER FOURTEEN

Jo knew surveillance cameras would be surveying the
street, so she drove onto the next block, found a
parking place, and pulled in. She didn't know what
was going on, but whatever it was couldn't be good for the
Whigbys. The feds didn't put your house under
surveillance for no reason.

She thought back through the last twenty-four hours.
She'd been careful when she'd talked to Connor Whigby,
but now she wondered if the feds had any surveillance on
the front of his house, someone who'd spotted her when she
came to his door. And did they know about his daughter?

Traffic passed by, but no one paid attention to the SUV.
Jo glanced back toward the FBI building. She had no idea
what she'd gotten herself into, or how much danger Brooke
might be in. Gripping the steering wheel, she swore. Since
the moment she'd gotten out of Civil Affairs, she hadn't
wanted to be involved in anything like this. She was
through with secret operations, dangerous situations, and
innocent people getting hurt or killed. She'd known she
should just walk away, and she thought she had.

And then this. Jo didn't know Brooke, didn't know her family. She wasn't obligated to do anything. But she thought about her own sister. If Avery got into any trouble, Jo would want somebody to help her.

She sighed. She couldn't walk away. But that meant finding out what the feds were doing at the Whigby house, and she needed some help for that.

Jo stared at the phone for a moment. She could call Dack. He'd have the resources to get more information on the Whigbys, and he just might be able to find out why the FBI was interested in them. But since she had no idea who she was dealing with, or how dangerous things might be, she wasn't going to risk involving him. She already blamed herself for the incident in Syria; she wasn't going to risk putting him in danger now, even though she knew he'd help her.

She had a contact at the Department of Defense, a man named Arnie Evans. Jo had gotten to know Arnie while she was with a female engagement team in Iraq. Over the years, he'd risen through the ranks, and he was now with the Defense Counterintelligence and Security Agency. He could get information for her, but she and Arnie had clashed at times. Coming up against her, a woman as good as he was, hadn't set well with him. He'd never made it a secret that he distrusted Jo, that he felt she would be better suited to a desk job somewhere rather than in the field. Even when she'd earned the respect of others, Arnie had still been cool to her. He was also a cagey guy, and she didn't know what he would do if she called after all these years. But she had something on him that might prompt him to help her now.

She stared at the FBI building, then finally got on the internet and looked up the number for DCSA. She called, and although it was a pain and she was transferred multiple times, she was finally connected to Arnie's office.

"I'm afraid he's unavailable at the moment," a woman with a perky voice said. "If you'd like to give me your name and number, I can have him call you at his earliest convenience."

Jo had expected as much. The best she could hope for was that when Arnie saw her name, he'd be willing to return her call. He'd probably be curious enough to know why she was reaching out to him, so she gave the woman her information, thanked her, and ended the call.

At a Starbucks nearby, she ordered a latte, positioned herself near a window, and sipped it. People entered and left, but she never spotted anyone who might be tailing her. Just after she finished her coffee, her phone rang, a number she didn't recognize. She faced the window as she answered in a low voice.

"Hello?"

"Jo Gunning."

She instantly recognized Arnie's voice. It hadn't changed, still deep and resonant, still that same trace of disdain. That was Arnie, a man who thought he knew everything about everything. With those two words, it was clear his attitude toward her hadn't changed, either. But curiosity as to why she was calling after all this time meant he wouldn't blow her off.

"Arnie. How're you doing?" she asked politely.

"Things are going well. I'm busy, but nothing I can't handle. What have you been up to since I last saw you?"

Jo knew there was a dig in that. Arnie kept up with people that he'd worked with, and he had to have known that she wasn't with Civil Affairs anymore. He would also likely know that she wasn't doing anything new. Many people had expected her to work with Dack.

"I'm keeping myself busy," she said.

"That's great to hear." The tone said he couldn't have cared less. "So why are you calling me?"

"I need a favor."

"From me?"

"I wouldn't be calling otherwise."

He hesitated. "You're doing nothing, but you need my help. What's going on?"

Jo stared out the window at the cars racing by. "A man named Connor Whigby is involved with the feds. I need to know why."

An audible sigh came through the phone. "What aren't you telling me?"

Jo couldn't get anything past Arnie. Oh well. It wouldn't hurt to tell him some of what was going on.

"I know his daughter, and there are some issues with her dad." That was vague enough.

"So how are the feds involved?"

She chuckled at that. "That's what I want you to find out."

Jo heard a clicking sound—she could picture him tapping a pen on his desk. She remembered that habit of his well and knew not to interrupt him while he was thinking. His mind would be racing, wondering if she had another angle. She'd be doing the same thing if the situation was reversed.

Finally, he made a decision.

"What's the guy's name?"

"Connor Whigby." She spelled it out. "His wife's named Fran, and his daughter is Brooke. They live in North Springfield."

"And I suppose you need this info fast?"

She smiled grimly, though he couldn't see. "Yes."

"And I should do this why?"

Of course he knew the answer, but he asked it anyway, almost a dare. Her lips formed a thin line before she answered.

"Because of what happened at the FOB."

When she'd been deployed with Arnie at the forward operating base, the females had lived in metal containers similar to shipping containers—small apartments for two people with cots, a little shelving system, and a tiny desk. One time, when Jo left to shower in a shared bathroom area, Arnie had snuck in and tried to have his way with her. She'd left him with a black eye and swollen balls, but she'd never told anyone for fear of what reporting the incident might do to her career. Arnie had given her a wide berth after that, and then she'd been assigned to a different task force.

"You'll never let me live that down, will you?" he snapped. "I could deny it, you know?"

"You sure could. But things have changed. People might believe my story now. It's not like back then."

There had been news stories recently about sexual assault in the military, how the problems had persisted for years. Some women were coming forward with their stories, and Jo could, too. And even if Arnie denied it, the stain would be there. They both knew it. He sighed again.

"Give me a bit and I'll call you back."

The call went dead. Jo set her phone on the table and sat back. Arnie wasn't happy to help, angry that she was pulling strings and getting him involved. She didn't see another way to get the information she needed, though. Fiddling with her coffee cup, she remained wary for anything suspicious. The coffee shop was busy and noisy, full of the bitter but somewhat sweet coffee aroma she loved. She didn't know how long it would be before Arnie called back, or if he'd change his mind.

Twenty minutes later, her phone rang again, and she snatched it off the table. This time she recognized the number.

"What'd you find out?" she asked.

Arnie's voice was forceful. "Where are you?"

She frowned, puzzled. "I'm near the Mall." No way would she give him her exact location.

"Meet me at the mall at Pentagon City in half an hour. Sit outside the Shake Shack."

Again, he ended the call abruptly. Jo hurried out of the Starbucks. She'd expected some resistance from Arnie, but this was different.

Something was up.

CHAPTER FIFTEEN

Arnold "Arnie" Evans looked the same as she remembered him. He was a small man, narrow in the shoulders, but wiry and muscled. He wore slacks and a white shirt, his brown hair cut short, his face tanned. His angled jaw tightened when Jo approached. The table umbrella offered a modicum of shade, a small respite from the heat. He pulled out a chair across from her and sat down. She gestured toward the restaurant behind her.

"Would you like . . ." she started.

"Cut the crap," he interrupted. "Tell me what's going on."

Jo proceeded cautiously. "I'm not sure what you mean."

He glanced around, and his chair scraped as he pulled it closer and rested his elbows on the table, giving her an intense stare. "Why did you ask me to look into Connor Whigby? You're not part of an agency, are you? One that wants to keep its activities under wraps?"

She sipped her coffee and stared at him. "What happened?"

He contemplated her for a long moment, then sat back.

Arnie was a smart man, and she knew he was thinking through everything.

"Okay, that was a dumb question." He studied her. "If you were part of another agency, you wouldn't need me."

She took a second to answer. "That's true. Want to tell me what's got you so spooked?" Jo thought she knew the answer, but she waited.

He let out a slow sigh. "I hardly did any checking on Connor Whigby before I had someone in my office asking me what was going on, and why was I looking into the Whigbys." It was later in the day, and people were starting to leave work, hustling by them. But no one paid any attention to their conversation. "I might've expected somebody to find out I was looking into them, to ask me some questions at some point *later*, but not so soon."

"Who was asking?"

His head drifted back and forth, and he tapped the table with his index finger. "Someone showed up fast. Whigby's glowing, and I want to know why."

Jo sat up straighter. Multiple agencies were looking for him?

"That's what I'm trying to find out," she said. "Back up and tell me everything you did find out."

He searched her eyes. "You're not deep undercover? I can't afford to have things go bad for me, you understand?"

She nodded. That was typical Arnie. He was climbing the ranks, and he wouldn't let anything—or anyone—stand in his way.

"You got out last summer, right?" he asked. She nodded again. "What have you been doing since then?" His finger tapped the table emphatically. "Details."

"I haven't been doing anything, Arnie." She rested her hands in front of her. "You know I wasn't happy at the end, after everything with Dack, so I got out. I was going to head out west, but I just haven't made it there yet. I've been . . . hanging around."

"Hanging around?"

She shrugged. "After years of crazy schedules, waking up in places all over the world, looking over my shoulder all the time, the anonymity is nice. I haven't wanted to be a part of anything."

He crossed his arms. "You've gotten into a situation now."

She couldn't tell him much. If somebody had been asking him questions when he first looked up Connor Whigby, they'd be asking him again. And she knew he wouldn't hesitate to tell them about her.

"Tell me what you found."

He sighed, as if he knew he couldn't dodge her questions any longer. "Connor Whigby has a clean record, not even a DUI. He's worked for Senator Macintosh for several years now. You know she's on an intelligence committee?"

"I heard that."

"They have oversight responsibilities, and they review the intelligence budget submitted by the president, and—"

She interrupted. "Stop the Wikipedia information. What's Whigby's involvement?"

Arnie opened his mouth, then closed it, swallowing before he spoke. "Macintosh would have access to classified intelligence. Whigby's a senior aide, so who knows how much he knows about what's going on."

She arched an eyebrow. "That sounds clandestine. What do the feds want with him? Is the senator involved?"

"How the hell would I know that? And if I did, I wouldn't be talking about it."

"What else did you find in Whigby's files?"

He tilted his head. "Have you heard the name Irena Garin?"

"No." It meant nothing to Jo.

The hard stare came again. "That's the truth?"

"Yes, Arnie, it is. Who is she?"

"The file didn't say. It was about that time that someone came in my office. I got the third degree—why was I looking at Connor Whigby, what was I working on now and how did it tie into him. I kept explaining that his name came up in a different search I was doing, that it wasn't a big deal, but he didn't believe me." He let out a heavy sigh. "Now *I'm* going to be scrutinized more closely, and for who knows how long. You got me into a heap of trouble."

"I'm sorry."

She genuinely meant it. Arnie hadn't given her much, but the fact that someone had come down so hard on him was significant. If nothing was going on with Connor, Arnie wouldn't have gotten that reaction from some higher up.

"Was there anything about Whigby's daughter, Brooke?"

Arnie uncrossed his arms and glared at her. "Is this what that's about? Something with his kid?"

An interesting response. "What did you read about her?"

"Not much. She'll be a senior at Middlebrook. It's a great private school. She gets excellent grades, and she's on the swim team. She's pretty good, and she might be up for some scholarships."

"Has she been in any kind of trouble?"

He shook his head. "Not that I could find." His eyes surveyed her. "What's she involved in?"

Jo dodged the question. "Was there anything to indicate that Whigby might be abusive to her?"

Arnie held up his hands. "Is that what this is about? Some kind of domestic thing? If you know, you better tell me."

A woman in a tan business suit paused nearby, and Jo eyed her, waiting for her to move on before she spoke. "Arnie, if you're worried about people wondering why you were looking into the Whigbys, you don't want any more details."

For a second, he almost smiled. "That was a good non-answer. I'll give you this. If you're looking for more on the daughter, I didn't see anything. The Whigbys look like your typical upper middle-class family, no problems, nothing going on."

"Except that if someone had that reaction to your looking into them, then something *is* going on."

"Sure seems that way." He glanced at his watch. "I need to go." Arnie scrutinized her, and his face softened a little further. "I don't appreciate that you've gotten me involved in something, but be careful. Whatever it is, it can't be good."

Jo didn't say anything. She'd apologized once, and that was all he was going to get. He pushed back from the table and got up, turning around without a word and walking away from the restaurant. He moved at a good clip down the street toward the Metro, his shoulders squared, that military bearing. Then he vanished into the crowd.

CHAPTER SIXTEEN

Jo sat and assessed her conversation with Arnie as she watched people hurry along Hayes Street. Someone had him alarmed, and that was hard to do. Was it the feds, or somebody else? Arnie hadn't wanted to tell her, which made her nervous. She needed to know more about Connor Whigby and his association with Senator Macintosh, and she needed to find out who Irena Garin was.

She was about to google the name when she spotted a man across the street, watching her.

She hadn't noticed at first. He was trying to be subtle, acting as if he were looking in a department store window. But he'd been doing that for too long, and he hadn't moved on. The guy was tall and thin, with a shaved head that glistened in the sun. It had to be hot in the suit he was wearing.

Jo swore under her breath. Had Arnie pointed her out, told someone that he was going to meet her? It would've been just like him to do that, but if he was spooked, maybe he hadn't had a choice. Right now, it didn't matter. She had to deal with the man watching her. Jo didn't know if he—or anyone else who might be around—knew about her rental car, but she wasn't going to lead them to it.

She got up, made a full pass of the area with her eyes, and slowly headed down Hayes Street. The good thing about Washington, DC, was that it was a big place, with lots of people. Easy to get lost in. Jo walked with the crowd's flow toward the Metro entrance, watching to see if anyone else was tag-teaming her. No other tail.

Near the entrance, she deliberately bumped into a stocky man and allowed herself to be turned around. The bald-headed man had crossed the street behind her and was walking in her direction. She walked by a bus stop, pretending as if she didn't have anywhere specific to go, certainly as if she had no idea she was being followed. Then she ducked into the Pentagon City station.

She paid for her fare and took the escalator down. The man continued to follow. When she reached the train platform, the crowds shielded her. He stayed at the other end, staring at the railroad tracks. When the sound of the train drew near, he started to shift closer.

Jo went on the offensive as well.

As the train pulled into the station, she walked closer to the man. He was trying to act casual, not looking at her. The train doors opened. People jostled to get on and off. Before the man could react, Jo subtly swiped at his knee with her foot. The knee bent at an awkward angle, and the man collapsed. No one noticed her move—they were too busy getting where they needed to go.

The doors beeped, alerting people to get on now, and Jo hopped on the train. Behind her, a woman bent down to ask the man if he was okay, and he nodded as he clutched his knee. Jo hadn't permanently damaged it, just slowed him down. There was no way he was going to make it onto the train. The doors started to close, and he looked straight at her. She turned away—no reason to give him the satisfaction of a glare. The train began moving, and she relaxed a little.

Her relief was short-lived as she spotted somebody else farther down the car. She'd missed him. A mistake—she was out of practice. The second spotter, a man in a dark suit, was less subtle, staring right in her direction. She turned away. As the train rocked along, Jo thought about what to do. She didn't want to get too far from her car, and she needed to lose these people before she could continue to look into Connor.

At the next station, she exited the train and joined the throng on the escalator going up. The new tail was behind her, keeping close. She reached the top and darted to the left, around a group of teenagers. She dashed for the exit, burst out, and sprinted to her left. She wasn't familiar with the area, but she could still disappear.

After a minute, as she passed an office building, Jo glanced over her shoulder. The tail was on his phone, likely alerting someone else to her location. There were too many of them against her. She turned the corner, and a dark Suburban pulled up, a government vehicle. They were all the same.

Three men hopped out, dark suits and dark shades. She turned the other direction, but the second tail was there. His face bent into a slow, threatening smile as he pulled his coat back just enough to reveal a holstered gun. Jo watched him approach. She wasn't stupid enough to think he would shoot with so many people around, but she was tired of running. If she escaped these guys now, more would come after her.

She turned to the three men near the Suburban. They all looked fit; all seemed ex-military. It was pointless to ask them to identify themselves. With the way security was since 9/11, they more than likely weren't obligated to tell her anything. The one in front had a hand up, a gesture for the man behind her to stop.

Jo looked at the leader. "Will he roll over if you ask him to? Does he do other tricks, too?"

The man didn't crack a smile. He approached, but not close enough to where she might be able to hit him.

"Jo Gunning? Would you please accompany us?"

Ever so polite. "Where are we going?" she asked.

She saw her reflection in his sunglasses. He didn't say anything, just looked at her. One of the men behind her opened the back door of the Suburban. She felt the second tail cutting off any escape. People walked around them, oblivious to the drama. Jo gauged them all one final time, then stepped up to the Suburban.

"Spread your arms," the lead man said.

She did. He searched her and put her phone in a Faraday bag, where the aluminum foil would isolate the phone from Wi-Fi. She wouldn't be able to remote into the phone, wouldn't be able to wipe any data from it before they could get a warrant to search it. *If* they intended to get a warrant. He also took her fake ID, credit card, and keys. One of the other men gestured for her to get into the car.

"It looks like a nice ride," she said casually. "How about we get some dinner and talk?"

The men didn't say anything, but when she was in the back seat, the one who'd held the door slipped in beside her. Before she could even think to go out the other side, that door opened and another man slid in. She was blocked from escape, but that was no surprise. Jo had been expecting it. The lead man got in behind the wheel. He started the Suburban, glanced over his shoulder, and pulled into traffic. Jo saw the tail disappear into the crowd.

"Where are we going?" she repeated.

The three men remained silent. The Suburban had a new car smell, and the man to her right wore cologne, enough to be appealing but not overpowering. The one to her left clearly smoked—probably not much, as he couldn't afford to be out of shape, enough to calm his nerves when he needed it. Jo had never picked up the habit, but she knew plenty who did. It was also a good way to tamp down your hunger when food wasn't around.

The Suburban crossed the Potomac, and she was pretty sure where they were headed. They soon got onto Fourth Street and turned into a parking garage at the FBI field office. They went down below, and the driver parked the Suburban next to glass doors and got out. The man to her right opened the door and got out as well. He was still wearing his sunglasses as he glanced in at her, then nodded for her to exit the vehicle. When she did, the three men surrounded her.

"This isn't the dinner I was expecting," she said.

Still nothing from any of them. They moved as a unit through the glass doors to an elevator, and she couldn't resist them. The lead man punched a button, the elevator doors slid open, and they all got in.

On the fifth floor, when the doors opened, he marched down a hallway, and the two others followed with Jo. They strode along a maze of halls until the lead guy stopped in front of an unmarked door. He opened it and stepped back.

The man wearing the cologne nudged her shoulder, and she walked into the room. It was small—four walls, a table, and two chairs.

"Have a seat," the leader said.

Jo walked around the table and sat in the chair opposite the door. She crossed her arms and looked at him.

"I'll have a pepperoni pizza," she said.

The man's face was impassive as he gave her one final stare. Then he backed out of the room and shut the door.

Jo didn't bother to get up and check the knob. It would be locked. She glanced around the room. At one end was a dark, one-way window. She didn't know who was behind it, but there would be cameras and microphones taping everything she said and did.

So she didn't say anything, and she didn't do anything. She just sat there, waited, and counted the minutes. By her calculations, she'd been in the room for approximately thirty-five minutes when the door opened and a new man wearing a dark blue suit, a white shirt, and a striped tie entered. He stared at her for a moment, closed the door, then pulled out the chair across from her and sat down.

CHAPTER SEVENTEEN

The man had a file folder, and he opened it and consulted some pages. Jo studied him. He was tall, with long arms and legs, his chest thick as a barrel. His full head of steel-gray hair reminded her of her father. So did his stern expression. He finally looked up, his lips pressed together. They locked eyes, and she waited.

"Josephine Ann Gunning."

"Jo," she said pointedly.

He nodded. "I'm Special Agent Hal Stone."

Jo stared at him without a word. The room was quiet, and she couldn't hear anything beyond the closed door. She glanced toward the dark glass and wondered if any of the other agents who had brought her here were behind it. The room had no smell.

Stone was businesslike, polite. His eyes darted to the file. "You have quite the career. Battery Executive Officer in Echo Battery, 1/79th Field Artillery Battalion. Civil Affairs Planner for Special Operations Command Forward in Afghanistan. Special missions detachments. You earned several medals." His head remained down, but he arched an eyebrow. The tone didn't quite reach the level of respect. No matter what Jo had done in the past, she was interfering in something now, and he didn't like that.

He finally looked up. "I need to ask you a few questions."

"Okay," she said.

"Who are you working for now?"

"I'm not working for anybody. I'm unemployed."

Stone's responses came a bit slow each time, as if he was pausing to think, or maybe just trying to unnerve her with his calm. "You live in DC?"

"For the moment."

"You have plans to leave?"

"Maybe."

A pause. "I can't access everything in your file." She kept quiet, and he went on. "That in and of itself tells me a lot."

The man was concerned she might be working for any number of covert organizations, on an operation he might not know about. He glanced at the file, then back at her.

"Why did you leave Civil Affairs?"

"Not my cup of tea anymore."

His expression said he knew there was more. "You're a little young to be retired." She shrugged. "You're just hanging around the DC area."

"Yes."

"Do you know Connor Whigby?"

"No." She kept it short and sweet, no details for him. If he wanted information, he'd have to drag it out of her.

"Fran Whigby?"

"What about her?"

Stone's right eyelid twitched, frustrated. "Do you know her?"

"No."

"If you don't know either of them, why are you asking about them?"

"What makes you think I'm asking about them?"

"You've been looking for information on them."

"If I was, it's a free country. I can do what I want."

"Not from the sources you were using."

Jo swore silently. Arnie led them to her, whether he meant to or not. She forced a smile. "Okay, lesson learned. May I go now?"

The pause was longer this time. "What do you know about Connor Whigby?"

"He works for Senator Macintosh."

One of Stone's eyes twitched a bit. "That's not common knowledge."

She shrugged. "I must've read it somewhere."

That was a slip on her part. She shouldn't have said anything. He pounced on that.

"You say you don't know Connor Whigby, but you had contact with him."

That confirmed what she had suspected, that the feds had eyes on the front of the house. They'd seen her talking to Connor.

"I can talk to somebody without knowing them," she said.

"What did you and Whigby discuss?"

"The weather."

She picked a random topic to see if he knew anything more about the conversation with Connor, but he didn't seem to. If the Whigby house was bugged, they hadn't picked up her conversation.

Stone's expression was not amused. "I would appreciate if you would be straightforward with me."

She shook her head. "Again, it's a free country. I can talk to who I want to, and I don't need to tell you what my conversations are about."

"Did he discuss Senator Macintosh?"

"Who?"

"Connor Whigby."

"No."

"What do you know about the senator?"

"Nothing."

For some reason, he didn't push it. "Did you ask Whigby why he wasn't at work yesterday?"

"No," she said.

"Why?"

"It's none of my business."

"I'll ask again. Who are you working for?"

"No one."

"When you talked to Connor Whigby, did he give you anything?"

"No."

"Did you give him anything?"

Jo shook her head again. "No."

"Did you see Fran Whigby?"

"No."

"Did Connor say anything about her?"

That was an interesting turn in the conversation. "No," she answered once more.

Stone exposed his teeth, not in a smile, but in frustration. Like the eye twitch. He was fishing, but he wasn't catching anything.

"What are you hiding?" he asked.

Jo put her hands on the table. "Nothing. What are you hiding?"

He ignored that. "Someone who isn't hiding anything doesn't run from federal agents."

She smiled without humor. "Why would federal agents be after me?"

"One of my agents might have a damaged knee." Stone ran a hand across the file.

"I didn't do anything that severe. I just stopped him from following me."

It was interesting he hadn't brought up Brooke. With all their information, they had to know that Connor and Fran had a daughter. Jo wondered if they had any idea that Connor had potentially locked her up in a safe room. She debated telling him about the girl. Jo didn't really care what was going on with Connor; the teenager was her real concern. But distrust was in her nature, and at the moment she couldn't tell if the feds were the good guys or not. By telling Stone about Brooke's predicament, there was the possibility she would be putting her in danger. And Jo still wanted to find out if Brooke had been telling her the truth.

She decided to do some fishing of her own.

"How's Connor's daughter?" she asked.

"Brooke?" He knew the name. "She's out of school for the summer. You know her?"

"In a manner of speaking." They didn't seem to know that Brooke had run away, or that Jo had talked to her.

"Where were you born?" he asked.

Jo kept her face straight. Where was this new line of questioning was going? "I was born in Alabama."

"You grew up there?"

She stared him in the eye. "My dad was a mechanic. Times were hard, and we moved around."

"Where all did you live?"

If he had a file, he had the answers. But she gave them

anyway.

"Florida, New York, Washington State. We ended up in Colorado."

"And your mother?"

"She's dead."

"I'm sorry." But he wasn't. "What happened?"

"Cancer."

"It must've been horrible to see her suffer through that."

Jo hadn't, in fact, seen her suffer through anything. She had been overseas when her mother had gotten sick, and she hadn't come home. Her father hadn't forgiven her for that. It was one of the reasons why she resisted going back to Colorado.

"And you have a younger sister?"

"Yes."

"She's a lot younger than you."

Jo nodded. "Ten years."

"And you went to college where?"

"UConn."

"In Connecticut. Same as Yale," he mused. "Were you in any clubs, any extracurricular activities during that time?"

"I did the usual things." Now it made sense. He was digging to see if she knew Connor or Fran sometime in the past.

Stone tapped the file. "But you were interested in a military career. You speak several languages fluently."

"Yes."

He rubbed a hand across his chin, another tell that he was growing impatient with her. That might lead to mistakes on his part.

"I'll ask again—why were you talking to Connor Whigby?"

"It was a private conversation," she said.

He consulted the file folder, but it was just for show. He wasn't getting anywhere with her and he knew it. Finally, he closed it and contemplated her. His eyes were cold.

"We're done here," he said. "Do you have plans?"

She shrugged. "I don't know."

"You say you're hanging around." Stone leaned forward. "I suggest you leave. Find somewhere else to go. Somewhere safer. Away from the Whigbys." She was about to say that it was a free country again, but he held up a hand. "Spare me anything about your rights. Stay away. If you're not working with anybody, stay away."

"I'll take that under advisement."

Stone nodded and stood up. When he opened the door, Jo saw the driver of the Suburban standing by it. Stone stepped back, and she walked into the hall. Neither man said a word to her, and the driver led her to the elevators. They rode in silence down to the lobby, and he walked with her to the front door, where he held out a bag with her keys and cash.

"My phone and ID?"

He just held the door, and she went outside. When she turned back to say something more to him, he was gone.

It would've been nice if they'd given me a pizza, Jo thought wryly.

She took a moment to get her bearings, found the closest Metro station, and started walking there. She didn't think she'd given Special Agent Stone anything to go on, and he probably thought he hadn't revealed much, either. But he'd given her enough. There seemed to be something going on between Connor Whigby and Senator Macintosh. And they had no idea where Brooke or her mother were. That was interesting as well.

CHAPTER EIGHTEEN

The closest station was Judiciary Square, where the National Law Officers Memorial was located. Someone would be following her now, and Jo didn't want anybody to find out about the rental car, so she had to make her next moves carefully. Since she'd spotted the surveillance the last time, the feds would be much more careful now.

She sat on a short retaining wall in the park for a while, never seeing anybody specifically watching her. But someone was there.

After a few minutes, she started meandering around the park, looking at the curved marble wall inscribed with the names of law enforcement officers killed in the line of duty, making her roundabout way to the Metro station.

She took a crowded train back to Pentagon City, and as she stepped off, she thought she saw her tail, a man of average height in jeans and a black T-shirt, that telltale bulge at his ankle. She was pretty sure she'd seen him near the park.

Jo rode the escalator up to the street, near where she'd

met Arnie Evans. After a couple of cars drove by the curb-
side pickup area in front of the mall, she darted between
them and hurried into the mall, glancing back toward the
entrance once she was in. The man in the black T-shirt was
approaching the doors.

The mall was crowded, with plenty of people escaping
the heat, so Jo had lots of cover between her and the fed.
She walked through the concourse to Macy's, pausing occasionally at a storefront to glance behind her. The man held
back, but he was definitely tailing her. As she neared the
Macy's entrance, she rushed into the store, started down an
aisle, then stood behind some shelving at the end.

A moment later, she saw the fed walk past. He paused
farther down the main aisle, where she could barely see
him. He was clearly wondering where she'd disappeared to,
but he also had to be careful. After a moment, he moved on,
and she ducked down and snuck past some clothes racks,
then peeked around them. She didn't see him. He must've
gone down one of the aisles.

Jo took the opportunity to dash out of the store, back
along the concourse, and outside. She didn't go directly to
her rental car, though. Instead, she walked farther down
Hayes Street and around the south side of the mall. She
crossed the street and hid behind some bushes near an
apartment complex. She waited, but she didn't see the man
who had been following her, or another tail either.

Leaving her hiding place, she walked farther south, and
finally made her way to where she'd parked earlier in the
day. She didn't approach right away, watching the car for a
few minutes first. A woman in a business suit went to a
nearby BMW, got in, and drove away. Another couple got
into an SUV and drove off as well.

When Jo was satisfied that nobody was watching the

rental, she approached it, got in, and left. She still wasn't sure she was safe, and she drove north, darting in and out of traffic, turning on a whim and changing directions, trying to see if she was being tailed. Finally satisfied that she was in the clear, she changed directions and drove away from Pentagon City.

When she crossed into Crystal City, she didn't go directly to her motel. Instead, she found a Target store and bought a prepaid phone with another credit card she'd taken from the bank safety deposit box. Back in her car, she sat with the air-conditioner on and programmed Dack's number on speed-dial. She'd memorized Brooke's prepaid number, and she entered it as well. Then she entered her father's and sister's, although she was rarely in contact with either. No other numbers she needed to worry about.

Jo wished now that she'd used a fake card to buy her original phone. At the time, she wasn't involved in any clandestine activities, and there'd been no need to keep her identity a secret. But now, if the feds tried to track her phone—and she was sure they would—they'd see Brooke's prepaid number. Only they wouldn't know who owned it. The feds didn't seem to know what was going on with her, but at this point, neither did Jo.

Her mind went to Brooke. If the girl had access to her phone, at some point she would've been in touch with Jo. She thought of something else, and she grabbed the burner phone with the tracking device and turned it on. The target didn't register. The feds had swept the car and found the device.

Whatever Connor was up to, she'd now gotten herself involved too. She still didn't know if Brooke was okay, and whether her story of being locked in a safe room was true. A plan formed in her mind on how to check on the girl. It was risky, but it would answer some questions.

Jo left the Target and headed west. Traffic was heavy on I-395 as she drove back to North Springfield. She was much more cautious this time as she made her way into the Whigbys' neighborhood, checking cars on the street as she approached the cul-de-sac entrance. When she was certain there were no FBI vehicles around, no one watching from this distance, she parked and trained her binoculars on the house. The front door was closed, and it was hard to tell if anyone was home.

She wondered what equipment the FBI was using to spy on the Whigbys. Equipment these days was sophisticated. They could easily have placed a fake sign on the street. A crew dressed to look like the local electric company could install a box across from the house that would have cameras and even listening devices pointed toward it. The feds would know whether the Whigbys were home or not without vehicles and teams watching nearby. Jo didn't have those options, so she had to hunker down in the back seat until she saw someone.

Keeping her eyes on the house, she shut off the car and rolled down the window, then pulled the prepaid phone from her pocket. She got on the internet and studied the nearby geography, researching what she was going to soon do. Then she typed in "Irena Garin." After several minutes of looking, she didn't find anything. If Irena was a real person, she didn't have an identity on the internet. It sounded like it could be a Russian girl's name. Googling the surname "Garin," she found several genealogy sites that detailed its history. It could've been French or German, but also a Russian patronymic derived from the first name "Garasim," which meant "elder" or "guardian."

Jo sat back. Why would a Russian woman's name be in a file related to Connor Whigby? What was his association with this woman? His name hadn't come up in her search of Irena Garin, so what was their connection? Jo didn't have the resources to do more research on the woman. She wanted to contact Dack again, but she wasn't going to ask him yet. No sense in pulling him into all this if she didn't have to. Whatever *this* was.

She pocketed her phone and looked at the cul-de-sac. A couple of the Whigbys' neighbors came home from work. Eventually, a silver Lexus turned into the cul-de-sac, and the Whigbys' garage door slid up. She snatched up her binoculars and focused on the car. Connor was at the wheel, and he was alone. The car pulled into an empty garage, and the door closed.

Jo had a plan to get Connor—and his wife, if she was home—out of the house. She pulled out her phone to enact the first step. She was going to order a pizza in the Whigbys' name, then stop the driver before he delivered it to them. She'd pay him to let her to put a note in the box that would say, "We need to talk, but you're being watched," along with instructions to meet at a park that was a half hour's drive away. The Whigbys would likely take the bait. Then Jo would enact the rest of her plan.

Only she didn't have to call anyone, as the Whigby garage door opened again, and the silver Lexus backed into the street. Connor was still behind the wheel. He wore dark sunglasses, an apprehensive look on his face. He didn't look toward Jo as he drove away.

CHAPTER NINETEEN

Jo scrambled into the driver's seat and started the car. She drove in the opposite direction from Whigby, through the neighborhood to the road on the other side of the wooded area behind the house. She spotted the white minivan parked near the spot where she'd first seen it when she was spying on the blue minivan earlier in the day. The FBI, still listening to the Whigby house. She drove around a bend in the road where she wouldn't be seen, parked her car, and pocketed the knife and the tiny bug transmitters she'd bought earlier.

No one was around as she struck out through the trees.

Jo jogged toward the Whigby house, and when she neared the fence where the hidden camera had been placed the other night, she paused. Once she was sure that no one was around, she moved up to the fence and saw the camera still in place. Using the knife, she carefully pushed against the camera until it faced the ground. It wouldn't be long before whoever was monitoring it noticed, and someone would come check. But for now, she wouldn't be seen.

Kids were playing in a yard farther down the cul-de-sac,

but no one was out back on either side of the Whigbys' house. Jo hauled herself over the fence, then crouched and listened. Nothing happened, so she ran across the grass, past the deck chairs at one end of the pool, and approached the sliding glass door. A security camera watched from an eave. She would be on surveillance video, but she didn't care. By the time the Whigbys checked the video, she would be gone. And it didn't matter if Connor recognized her. He'd never be able to find her.

Jo used the knife to jimmy her way into the house, then slid the door closed behind her. No alarm sounded, but there was the possibility of a silent one. She called out, and no one answered.

Looking around, Jo saw an open kitchen with cherry cabinets, stainless-steel appliances, and an island surrounded by bar stools. No panel with buttons to disarm an alarm, no sign of whether their security system would alert the police. If a signal was sent to law enforcement, she figured she had five or six minutes. Probably a little longer than that before the feds would come to check their camera. Whigby had been gone about ten minutes or so. It had taken her that long to drive away from his street and walk through the woods, then break in. The security system had probably alerted him on his phone that the back door had been compromised. If he turned around right away, it'd be about that long before he returned.

Her internal clock began.

Jo quickly walked through the rest of the main floor—living and dining rooms, a family room, a home office—but didn't see anyone. The house was decorated in rich tones, dark hardwood floors with area rugs, expensive furniture, and walls painted in a variety of colors. A faint flowery smell lingered in the air. A large painting of an abandoned barn hung above a fireplace in the family room. She stuck a transmitter behind the frame, then another behind a photo of Brooke hanging on a kitchen wall. The girl's burner phone was on the counter, but Jo left it alone.

The garage was empty. If Fran Whigby was around, Jo would've expected another car. She shut the door and went to the stairs. Listening, she didn't hear anything, so she ascended to the second floor. The master suite was empty. She quickly placed a bug behind a picture of a sailboat that hung over the bed, then checked a spare bedroom. Empty. The last bedroom was obviously Brooke's—a swim poster of Michael Phelps on one wall, photos of a boy band Jo didn't know on another. Some of her clothes were strewn about the floor.

Jo didn't waste any time, heading back to the main floor and down to the basement. The main room had a pool table, a TV, and a couch. A fancy bar took up an entire wall. The room was empty. She looked around. If there was a safe room, where was it? She didn't have long to search, maybe another three minutes or so.

Standing in the middle of the room, Jo tried to calculate the size and position of the basement compared to the layout of the main floor. She walked to a wall that had dark paneling and momentarily studied it, then began pushing on each section of it. The third panel slid back, exposing a small hallway and a door.

The safe room.

Jo stepped up to the door. It was metal and sturdy, likely soundproofed. She tried the knob. Of course it was locked. There were two other bolts on it, which was probably only part of the locking system. No safe room would have a door that could be easily opened. Jo put her ear to the metal and listened. Nothing. She banged on it anyway, then stepped back. Was she hearing something, or was her imagination playing with her? She put a hand to the door. Did she feel the faintest of vibrations?

Time was running out.

She walked back to the bar area in the main room and opened cabinets and drawers. If Connor wanted quick access to the room, would he have left keys around? She searched everywhere, but didn't find any.

Jo ran a hand over her face, wiping away sweat. No sign of Brooke, but there was a safe room. Was she in it? At this point, she assumed the girl had been telling the truth, and she was locked inside.

Jo couldn't do any more in the basement, so she put another transmitter behind a picture, then hurried back upstairs. She went to the home office and glanced around, then tried desk drawers. The clock in her head kept ticking. Nothing in the files she found seemed significant. A bear figurine sat on a shelf, and she placed a transmitter on it before hurrying back into the kitchen. As she checked the drawers there as well, she heard a vibrating sound. The garage door was opening.

Jo swore in a whisper. Connor had gotten back sooner than she expected. She raced to the sliding glass door, let herself out, and closed it again. Having been a track star in high school was still helpful, and she leaped over a deck chair as she ran around the pool and to the back fence. She climbed it and hopped over, then crouched down, breathing hard.

She peeked through a slat in the fencing. Connor Whigby was standing at the sliding glass door. Jo remained still as he looked into the yard. When he turned away, she ran until she reached the edge of the woods. The neighborhood was still quiet—no one was around. She hurried to the

rental car and got in. She wasn't familiar with the neighborhood, so she used the GPS to take a different route back to
the cul-de-sac entrance. Parking in a different place, she
scrambled into the back and checked the Whigby house
with her binoculars. Then she turned on the listening
devices. Silence.

Jo looked back at the house. The police hadn't shown,
but the silver Lexus was parked in the driveway and the
garage door was open. A moment later, Connor came out to
the front porch. He put his hands on his hips as he looked
around, then crossed the street to talk to a balding man in
shorts and a T-shirt. Then Connor returned to his house
and disappeared inside, the man waving after him.

The house was quiet again. Jo could picture him going
through the house, looking to see if anything was missing, or
if anyone was there. She didn't think he'd find the transmitters. At some point, he would check his surveillance video
as well, and he would recognize Jo. However, he would still
have no idea who she was. He would be in a panic about it,
though.

Then she heard a phone ring.

"Yes, Senator," he answered. "I'm on my way." A pause.
"I know this wasn't the ideal time, but the media will be
waiting on the Capitol steps, and everything is set up for the
press conference. I'll see you soon."

She heard Connor swear, and then nothing.

CHAPTER TWENTY

When Brooke awoke, she didn't know where she was for a moment. Then she remembered.

The little twin bed hadn't been too uncomfortable to sleep on, but it wasn't *her* bed. She eyed it ruefully, hoping she wouldn't have to sleep there again. A foul mood washed over her. She yawned and stretched, but it didn't change how she felt. The room was cool and air-conditioned. At least there was that. She couldn't imagine what it would be like in the safe room otherwise. It might stay cool, it might not.

She surveyed her wrinkled shorts and blouse. She hadn't wanted to take off her clothes, in case her dad came back and she needed to leave quickly—although she couldn't figure out why she'd have to hurry. Regardless, she'd slept in her clothes, and they were now a mess. Brooke sniffed an armpit. Ugh. She went into the bathroom, stripped down, and got in the shower. The warm water washing over her felt good. A trial-sized shampoo and conditioner sat on the ledge, and she used both. When she got out, she found a hairdryer in the sink drawer, and after using it she felt a little better.

As she dressed in the same clothes, she wondered if her dad had even thought about clothes. Maybe because he hadn't put any in the safe room, he didn't intend to keep her locked up for very long. That gave her some hope.

Brooke walked on bare feet into the kitchen area, grabbed a bowl, and filled it with Cheerios. Her dad had put almond milk in the refrigerator, and that could last for a while. She shook off the thought. Surely she wouldn't be in here for *that* long.

She took her bowl to the couch, turned on the TV, and ate while watching a morning news show. It was just after seven. She normally slept later, but nerves had awoken her. After a minute, she glanced toward the door. Where was her dad?

As if on cue, the locks in the door rattled, and the door opened. She put her bowl on the coffee table as Connor stepped into the room. He wore a blue pinstripe suit, his tie neatly knotted, but his face was drawn, as if he hadn't slept at all.

"How're you doing?" he asked, looking her up and down.

"How do you think I'm doing?" she snapped. She gestured at the bed. "That's not my bed, you know."

He glanced at the coffee table and the cereal bowl. "I see you got something to eat."

Brooke nodded. "How long are you going to keep me in here? This is a pretty crazy punishment."

"I need to go to work, and there's some stuff I need to take care of."

Brooke threw up her hands. "Why don't you let me out of here? I can hang out by the pool just as easily as I can be cooped up in here." She jammed a finger toward the TV. "That's all I have to do, all day long. Watch TV. There aren't even any books in here."

Her dad frowned. "That's not the end of the world."

She stood up. "You can't do this to me. I won't go anywhere if you let me out." She took a couple steps toward him, and he lost it.

"Stay right where you are! I don't have time for this."

She rarely heard him angry like that, and it sank her right back onto the arm of the couch. His nostrils flared, and her ire deflated.

"Dad, I'm sorry for running away. It won't happen again."

Connor took a step toward the door. "I'll be back to check on you later."

Just as quickly as her anger had dissipated, it returned.

"If you're going to keep me in here like this," she said, her voice dripping with sarcasm, "I'm going to need more clothes. I can't wear the same shorts and blouse all the time. You didn't think of that?"

He surveyed her as if it truly hadn't occurred to him before. "I'll get you something."

"And how about some books?"

But he was already opening the door.

"Don't leave me here!" she yelled, and leaped to her feet.

Her dad slipped out, and the door closed. Brooke ran over and grabbed the knob, but it was already locked. She yelled obscenities at him, but she knew he couldn't hear her. The futile effort made her feel slightly better, though. She banged on the door a few times for good measure, then went back to the couch, where she sat and rubbed her hand, the TV droning on in the background.

Finally, she ate the rest of her Cheerios, but they were soggy now. She was tempted to throw them out, but decided not to. She didn't know how long her father intended to keep her here. Based on what he'd just said and done, it could be a while.

Brooke couldn't figure out what was going on with him. Keeping her in the safe room seemed to be about more than punishment. What was coming next? Her dad never acted like this, and it frightened her. She thought about her mother. Fran was sometimes gone for long periods, and if that was the case this time, Brooke had no hope of rescue.

She went back to the bar and washed the cereal bowl, left it in the sink, and returned to the couch. Flipping TV channels for a while quickly grew boring, so she got up and looked around the room again. Nothing more than yesterday. The place was a fortress, with no way out. She sighed as she flopped onto the couch. She zoned out to some TV, napped, and then ate lunch.

Time dragged on, and she was dozing on the couch again when she heard the locks on the door. She sat up as her dad came into the room. He had shorts, T-shirts, and undergarments in his hands, and he set them on the bar.

"Here you go," he said.

There was something in his face, some tenseness, and she stayed still, making no attempt to move toward the door.

"I'll be back to check on you again," he said. "I have to work late."

He didn't even try for niceties this time, just shut the door before she could say anything. The locks clicked into place. Brooke moved to the bar and picked up the shorts and T-shirts. He'd just grabbed stuff, not necessarily matching things. She snorted. Not like it mattered—no one was going to see her.

The TV was off, and she stood in the bar area and snacked on a granola bar. She was staring into space when she thought she might've heard something. Had someone pounded on the door? She moved to it and listened. She couldn't tell if there had been a noise or not. The isolation was getting to her. But if someone was there, and she didn't do anything, she was missing an opportunity. She raised a fist, pounded on the door, and yelled as loud as she could.

"Help!" she repeated it, then yelled, "I'm locked in here!"

Nothing.

Pent-up frustration got the best of her, and she pounded furiously on the door with both fists. She cursed her father, cursed her mother, cursed the entire world and her situation, all the while beating on the door. Then she ran out of steam and stepped back.

Nothing.

Brooke drew in a deep breath, her lip trembling. Her shoulders sagged as she walked over to the couch and plopped down. Burying her face in her hands, she wept uncontrollably.

The hopelessness returned.

CHAPTER TWENTY-ONE

Connor panicked when he received a text that the back sliding door had been opened. There was no way Brooke could've escaped the safe room, which meant someone had broken into the house. He sped home, screeched to a halt in the driveway, and sprinted into the house. At first glance, nothing looked awry. He hurried through the kitchen and down the hall to the front door, where he checked the locks, but they didn't look tampered with, so he went to the back sliding glass door. It was closed but not locked. Looking out, he didn't see anybody.

His heart thumped as he locked the door, then raced through the main floor and upstairs. Nothing out of place, nobody around. He hurried down to the basement. The game room was empty, and the paneling on the far wall didn't appear disturbed.

Connor approached, slid the middle panel back, and looked at the safe room door. Closed. He checked the deadbolts, and they looked untouched. Then he laughed at himself. In the short time he'd been gone, it would've been impossible for someone to get the door open to let her out. He breathed a sigh of relief.

Standing in the little hallway for a moment, he ran a hand through his hair. The alarm system wouldn't alert the police, just his and Fran's phones. So no one would know about Brooke. Then a thought struck him, and he dashed to the kitchen. That morning, he'd plugged in Brooke's burner phone. She'd received a couple of calls, but he was scared to call back, so he'd left the phone alone. It was still there.

Thinking about his daughter, he shook his head. She was certainly pissed off at him. On the one hand, he didn't blame her. But what he'd told her was the truth. He couldn't afford to have her get out, couldn't afford to have her tell anybody what was going on. She could hate him all she wanted; right now, he didn't care. He'd gotten her some clothes, and she had plenty of food. She'd be fine in the safe room for quite some time, and she'd have to deal with it.

So Connor went to work as he had to, acting as if things were normal, but the whole time his mind was on home. He still hadn't heard from Fran, and he wasn't sure what that meant. And all that was going on with Senator Macintosh and the Intelligence Committee only added to his problems. Since the last election, the committee had faced more scrutiny, which added pressure. Connor snorted. If the public only knew what went on behind the scenes. There were hearings coming up, and the senator was gathering analysis on individual terrorist cells operating in Eastern Europe and their connections to Russia. She was also worried about some heckling from some others in her party about the plausibility of those threats. Lord, if she only knew.

Heading back upstairs, he went into the office that he and Fran shared. Nothing appeared missing from the desk drawers, but he couldn't be sure none of the files and papers had been disturbed. He checked the security system software, and his heart skipped a beat as he saw a familiar woman approach the sliding glass door. It took him a second, and then he remembered who she was. The woman who'd helped Brooke. What was her name?

Connor sat back on the desk chair and wiped sweaty palms on his slacks. Had she broken into the house to look for Brooke, or for something else? He stared at the desk for a moment, not sure what to do. Then he got up, went out to the front porch, put his hands on his hips, and looked around. The neighborhood seemed normal, and he recognized all of the parked cars. He saw his neighbor across the street, and walked over.

"Hey Glenn," Connor said. "How're you doing?"

"Pretty good," Glenn said. "How about you? Fran out of town again?"

He grimaced. "Yes, she is."

They exchanged a few pleasantries, and then Connor said, "Have you seen anyone around today? Maybe a woman with shoulder-length, blondish-brown hair?" Glenn was retired and generally home all day. If anyone had seen her, it'd be him.

The man cocked an eyebrow. "You mean like someone who shouldn't be here?"

Connor nodded.

He shook his head. "It's been quiet, as far as I know." He laughed. "Are you getting paranoid? With your government work, you think someone's after you?"

Connor returned a forced laugh. "No, nothing like that. Sorry to bother you. I've got to get back to work."

Glenn raised a hand in goodbye as Connor crossed the street and walked back into his house. Then his phone rang. Senator Macintosh. He spoke briefly to her before she ended the call. Macintosh was always curt. And demanding.

He took one final look around the main floor, ending up back in the kitchen. Then he glanced at his watch. The meeting awaited. He'd have to deal with the rest of this later. He went back outside to his car, closed the garage door, and drove out of the neighborhood. His mind kept going over the same thought.

Things were getting out of control fast.

CHAPTER TWENTY-TWO

W hen the silver Lexus backed out of the driveway, Jo scrambled behind the wheel of her SUV, tailing Connor out of the neighborhood.

He took a main road and soon headed into DC. As he turned into a lot near the Capitol, she peeled away and drove around until she found a metered space. Then she ran back to the Capitol steps. A small gathering of press were assembled near some of the iconic marble pillars, along with a group of bystanders and curious onlookers. A few minutes after seven, Senator Macintosh approached the press, followed by Connor and a few other people. The senator paused in front of the crowd. Jo found a place at the back where she would be inconspicuous, and watched as the senator began talking.

"As you know, there will be a hearing next week regarding threats to the national security of the United States, particularly in Eastern Europe. It is important that we understand the threat against us before we send valuable resources overseas . . ."

As she droned on, Jo watched Connor. He stood behind

the senator's right shoulder in a blue pinstripe suit, his hands clasped in front of him. He nodded a time or two at the senator's talking points, seemingly a subconscious gesture. Jo scanned the crowd. There was the security around the senator, but she knew there also had to be feds watching Connor. A man in black jeans and a green polo shirt at the other end of the crowd was gazing intently at him. She couldn't be sure if he was a fed, though.

She turned her attention back to the senator.

"In regards to Afghanistan, we are monitoring the situation. It's important to know the success of our intelligence relies on an incredible amount of resources and hours of analysis . . ."

As she went on, Connor looked into the faces in the crowd, and then his eyes suddenly grew wider. His body stiffened. Jo followed his gaze. He'd seen the man in dark slacks and green shirt. The guy was big, solidly built, with a short, military haircut, and he continued to stare at Connor, not flinching from his stare. After a moment, he put a hand to his chin, then pointed toward the podium. Some kind of signal. Jo's gaze darted back to Connor. His mouth was slightly open.

"As such, we will assess the situation after the committee meetings are concluded," the senator was saying.

Connor didn't move, and neither did the man in the crowd. As Macintosh wrapped up her remarks, a smattering of applause filtered through the crowd. The senator smiled, thanked everyone, and backed away from the podium. The crowd began to disperse, but Jo continued watching Connor. As Senator Macintosh turned around, he approached her and put an arm on her shoulder. They walked side-by-side up the Capitol steps. The senator said something to him, and he shook his head. She spoke again, her brow furrowed, making angry gestures. Connor nodded as they continued up the steps. The others in the group followed them to the Capitol door, and they all disappeared inside.

Jo scanned the crowd, looking for the man who had signaled Connor. He was gone. She took a few steps back and walked around the Capitol, looking for him, but there wasn't a sign. It was now after eight, and even the tourists were in shorter supply.

She didn't know if Connor had left the Capitol, but she assumed he would go home at some point, so she drove back to his neighborhood, parking where she could see the front of his house. It was dusk, slightly cooler. A couple of boys were playing basketball with their dad two houses down from the Whigbys'. She listened to the bugs, but the house was quiet. Was he home and just didn't have the TV or anything on? Jo couldn't see lights on in the front of the house.

Then a phone rang. She sat up and pressed the earpiece in.

"Yes?" Connor said.

A pause.

"Yes, I saw you." Tension laced his voice. "Why does she want to meet me?" Now fear. "The Hotel Clarion? Okay, I'll find it." Another pause. "Noon? What do I tell the senator?" He sighed. "Fine. I'll figure something out."

He quit talking and sighed again. Then footsteps, as if he were pacing. A rumbling sounded, and something clinked on glass. He must be making a drink. When he was finished, it grew quiet again.

As the sky deepened to a dark blue, Jo continued to listen. More footsteps, muffled, away from the bugs. Then noise in the bedroom. Connor was getting ready for bed. Finally silence.

She started the car and returned to the neighborhood on the other side of the wooded area behind. As she drove down the road, she didn't see any vehicles that might be feds surveilling the house. They'd probably gone home for the night.

Home. That was where she ought to be. But she didn't have a home, just an impersonal motel room. Still, it was better than listening to a silent house all night.

She drove away from the neighborhood, then maneuvered in various directions and turned down some side streets, all to make sure that she wasn't being followed. Finally, she got on a main road headed east. She hadn't eaten much all day, so she stopped at a Firehouse Subs to grab a sandwich. Jo sat by herself in the lobby, ate, and assessed what she'd learned so far. She was almost certain Brooke was locked in the safe room. If she wasn't there, she was missing.

Jo frowned. Whether the girl was in the safe room or not seemed immaterial. She needed to find out what had happened to her, and she wouldn't let it go until she knew Brooke was okay.

Connor appeared to be in over his head as well. The senator was angry with him. A one-time occurrence? And who was he meeting at the Hotel Clarion tomorrow? He was cooking up something, and whatever it was could be putting his daughter in danger.

She finished her sub, wiped her hands on a napkin, then gathered up her trash and threw it away. Leaving the restaurant, she drove back to Crystal City, but she didn't park her rental car in the motel lot, instead finding a garage a few blocks away.

It was late as she approached the motel, and she did her usual assessment. She didn't see anyone around the building, so she tiptoed down the walkway toward her room door. Then she stopped. The small piece of paper that she'd tucked between the door and the jamb was gone.

Jo took a couple of quiet steps backward, then whirled around and dashed down the walkway. She heard footsteps from behind as she raced around the corner. Running across the street, she leaped behind a pickup truck. When she looked back, two men were standing on the sidewalk in front of the motel. They listened, then ran in the opposite direction.

Jo jogged down a block and to the next street over. No one was after her. She took extra precautions anyway, walking half a mile out of her way, all the while making sure she hadn't been followed. Then she finally made her way back to the parking garage and her car.

The motel had been compromised, which meant she needed to find a new place to stay. She wouldn't miss anything that she'd left in the room. The clothes were irrelevant to her, and she didn't have any other belongings. She'd known the feds would figure out where she was staying. It was the speed that surprised her. She was a bigger threat to them than she'd realized, and that was disturbing.

Jo drove out of Crystal City and found a small motel off I-395, nothing fancy, but it had a kitchenette. She paid with a fake credit card and asked for a room on the first floor at the back.

The kitchenette turned out to be particularly small but functional, and there was only one window by the door. She nodded in satisfaction, locked the door, and put the towel around the door stopper and the chair under the doorknob. She peeked through a crack in the curtains. The parking lot was still. After watching for a moment, she closed the curtains tight. Then Jo went into the bathroom, took off her clothes, and washed her undergarments in the sink.

She hung them over the back of a chair near the air-conditioner, took a shower, and crawled naked under the covers. She would get new clothes tomorrow. For now, it had been a long day, and she was exhausted. For a few minutes, she listened to the darkness. Then she closed her eyes and was fast asleep.

CHAPTER TWENTY-THREE

Jo arose early the next day, and since she didn't have any food in her new motel room, she ate a large breakfast of bacon, eggs, and pancakes at a nearby café, along with a strong black coffee.

After she finished eating, she stopped at a Target for new clothes, undergarments and toiletries. She also found a Washington Nationals baseball cap. She took all her purchases back to the motel, then changed into new jeans and a short-sleeved polo shirt. She placed the scrap of paper, locked the room, and drove to North Springfield, where she found a park near the house. Turning on the surveillance receiver, she put the earbud in, then rolled the window down.

All was quiet at the Whigbys'.

She waited a few more minutes and still didn't hear anything, so she left. Traffic was bad as she drove into Arlington, where the Hotel Clarion was located, but she still made it with plenty of time before Connor's noon meeting. She circled around the building, then parked in a lot across the street from the hotel, where she could scope the front. The building was curved, nine stories high, and many of the rooms had balconies. A long, circular drive surrounded by trees led to a covered entrance. The hotel was busy, with cars coming and going and a steady stream of people entering and exiting the hotel.

Jo scanned the entire block with her binoculars but didn't see any telltale signs of the feds. They had to have overheard Connor's phone conversation. Somebody would be tailing him, and they'd likely have a person positioned inside the hotel as well.

She donned the baseball cap she'd purchased at Target, then checked herself. The hat gave her a tomboy look. She got out and walked to the corner. Dark clouds loomed overhead, a harbinger of things to come. As she crossed the street, she checked for anyone following her, then went partway down the block and into a side entrance of the hotel. She smelled chlorine as she passed a swimming pool. A few people were in the gym next door. She eyed expensive shops as she entered the main lobby. To the left was a long counter, where clerks were busy assisting guests. To the right, two sitting areas held chairs, couches, and tables. Past those were two sets of revolving doors that led to the front driveway. A Starbucks near the entrance had a line of people waiting. Banks of elevators lined a wall across the lobby and down an alcove. A few signs pointed patrons in the direction of rooms where conferences were being held.

Jo got in the Starbucks line and surveyed the lobby. No feds as far as she could see, but she was early. Once she got her coffee, she sat down at a round table and sipped it. As she waited, she mulled over who Connor might be meeting and why. She had a gut feeling but no way to confirm it.

Her gaze roved around the lobby once more, and she froze.

The man she'd spotted in the crowd at the previous night's press conference had just walked in through the revolving doors. He was still wearing black jeans, but he'd switched the green polo shirt for a dark short-sleeved button-down shirt, untucked. She studied him, sure that he had a gun hidden under it. As he walked to the elevators, Jo slid off her chair, her coffee almost untouched.

One of the conferences was on break, and people milled around wearing lanyards with name tags and the conference logo on them. She pulled her cap down, blended in with the crowd, and moved toward the elevators. The man in the dark shirt waited for the car to arrive, and when it arrived, he got in by himself. She watched the lights above the doors. His elevator stopped at the seventh floor.

Jo stepped away from the elevators and searched for the stairwell, then hurried up to the seventh floor. She opened the heavy metal door and peeked out before starting to walk down a long, empty hallway. She turned the corner, and at the end of another hallway, she saw a woman in slacks and a yellow blouse. The woman wore a lanyard from yet another conference, and she had a file in her hand.

"Excuse me, ma'am?" Jo asked. "Have you seen a man in black jeans and a dark shirt on this floor?"

The woman shrugged. "I don't know. I just came up to get something for the conference."

Jo shrugged. "I was supposed to meet him, but I'm not sure what room he's in."

"It's crazy around here. I got in last night, and there's at least three conferences going on. I heard the hotel's full. It's packed everywhere you go." The woman smiled. "Maybe try at the front desk?"

"Sure."

Jo rode the elevator with her down to the lobby. The

woman smiled again as she joined some other people, and Jo headed to a chair in the seating area, away from the elevators, partially shielded by a pillar. She got out her phone and pretended to be on the internet, remaining alert all the while.

Shortly before noon, Connor Whigby entered the hotel. He was in a gray suit with a white shirt, black tie askew. His face was tight. As he started to cross the lobby, the man in the dark shirt materialized behind him. He touched Connor on the shoulder and said something in his ear. Connor stiffened and gave a slight nod. The two walked toward the elevators together. Jo glanced the other way and saw another man in jeans and a blue shirt. He stood near the revolving door, talking on his phone, but he glanced toward the other two. She had to be careful. She'd been questioned, and they knew she was somehow involved with Connor. They'd be watching for her as well.

She glanced back toward the elevators. Connor was staring at the floor. His companion scanned the lobby, momentarily meeting the eyes of the fed near the entrance. Then he looked into the seating areas. Jo locked eyes with him, then signaled him in the same manner that he'd signaled Connor the previous evening. The man was good, his expression barely changing. But he'd noticed the gesture.

The elevator doors opened. Connor and the man got on with a few other people. Jo watched as the fed moved to the chairs in the Starbucks lounge and sat down. When he was looking the other way, she rose and walked down the hallway to where she could still see the elevators, but not the fed. She paused near an entrance to bathrooms and waited.

Fifteen minutes later, Connor emerged from an elevator. His mouth was pinched, his posture tight. A different man was with him, and he said something to Connor as they moved away from the elevators. Then he held back as Connor walked across the lobby by himself. Dashing into another elevator, the man was quickly gone.

Jo moved to the edge of the lobby. Connor headed out the door, followed by the fed who'd been waiting at the Starbucks. She looked back at the elevators and spotted two other feds, both in dark suits, telltale bulges under their armpits. They disappeared behind the sliding doors. Leaning against the wall, she prepared to wait again.

A few minutes later, the two feds exited the elevators with disappointed looks on their faces. They marched up to the counter and began talking to a clerk. She typed on her computer, then shrugged and shook her head. Jo had a pretty good idea what was going on. The feds had known that Connor had met somebody on the seventh floor. They, unlike Jo, had resources to figure out which room he and his associates had been in. But when the feds had gone up there after the meeting, they'd discovered no one there. Whoever Connor had met had given the feds the slip.

It wasn't that hard to do. They would have left their room as soon as Whigby got on the elevator, having paid for a room on another floor using a different name. They'd wait there while the feds searched for them. Eventually, the feds would give up and return to the lobby, to wait and watch again.

And that was exactly what the feds did. The two agents took up positions on either side of the lobby, scanning the crowds. Jo was just as patient. An hour later, they gave up and left, clearly realizing they'd been thwarted.

A minute after they walked out the doors, Jo slipped back into the lobby and sat down in the same chair she'd occupied before. She glanced at the time and knew she wouldn't have to wait long. One of the conferences must've been on lunch break. The lobby grew busier, the din of conversation louder. Jo scanned faces but didn't see any other feds. A few minutes later, the man in the dark shirt exited the elevator. He moved into the lobby and glanced around. She knew he'd seen her even though he didn't show it. He stepped out through the entrance, but a moment later, he came back inside and turned toward Jo.

CHAPTER TWENTY-FOUR

The man approached and looked down at her.

"Who are you?" His voice was deep, with a trace of an accent she couldn't define.

She looked up at him. "I could ask you the same thing."

The man seemed to know better than to ask the question again. He stared at her for a moment, trying for intimidation.

"What do you want?"

She gambled with a supposition, putting pieces together. "Irena Garin. I want to talk to her."

His face gave away nothing. He stared at her for a moment, then gestured. "Come with me."

Jo followed him to the elevator. She knew he wouldn't make a move in the lobby. Too many people around, too many risks. And he was curious about her, just as she was about him. They got onto the elevator with a couple who were obviously tourists, both with brochures in their hands, discussing what they'd seen that morning. The man punched five, and the other couple pushed six. Putting his back to the wall, his hands at his sides, he stayed silent, but glanced down to assess whether she had a weapon. The other couple chatted, completely oblivious.

The elevator stopped at the fifth floor, and the man got out. Jo followed him down a hallway and around the corner. He stopped at room 501 and tapped on the door. It was opened by another man with a similar build, though he was wearing a suit. Jo stepped into a short hallway, and the man in the dark shirt held up a hand.

"I need to search you."

She nodded. His search was quick and effective.

"No weapon," the man in the dark shirt said.

The second man nodded and led Jo down the hall, which opened into a spacious suite with a couch and loveseat, coffee and end tables, and a large-screen TV mounted on one wall. The news was on, muted. Room service with coffee and cups sat on the table. The man motioned for Jo to sit down.

Already on the couch was a beautiful woman with dark hair and bright blue eyes. She was on the thinner side, with long legs, that belied her height even in her seated position. She wore little makeup and no perfume to mask a slight odor of cigarettes. Her gray business suit fit her perfectly. It didn't appear that she had a weapon, but her men certainly did. They also stayed in a natural stance, as if unprepared for any danger. This was common in Systema, a Russian form of martial arts. Maybe they'd been Russian paramilitary at one time?

Jo sat down and looked at the woman. She contemplated Jo for a moment but didn't say anything. The two men stepped back, observant but quiet.

"You signaled my associate," the woman said.

Jo nodded. "I figured it was a good way to get a meeting with you."

"You know who I am?" Her voice was soft with a pleasant lilt.

Jo didn't let her know how little she actually had, and a guess at that. "You're Irena Garin."

"And you are?"

"Jo Gunning."

Jo didn't see the point in hiding her name. She had no association with the government now, and anything sensitive in her past would be classified. The woman's expression told Jo the name meant nothing to her.

"Why do you want to meet with me?" Irena asked.

"Because you met with Connor Whigby."

She nodded. "And what organization are you with?"

"None," Jo said.

"You have no job?"

"Not at the moment."

Irena pondered that. "And you know Connor how?"

"Through his daughter." It wasn't a lie, but it wasn't exactly the truth, either.

"And your interest in this matter?"

Jo relaxed subtly in her seat. It was a game of chicken, to see who would flinch first. Irena smiled at her, and Jo smiled back. Then the woman pointed to the coffee.

"Would you like some?"

Jo nodded politely. "Please."

Irena poured a cup and handed it to Jo with a saucer. Jo pretended to sip as she looked over the rim of the cup at Irena. The wait continued as she put the cup and saucer down, and Irena glanced at the man with the dark shirt, who gave a subtle shrug. Finally, Irena looked back at her.

"Do you know someone named Yuri Orlov?" Irena began.

Jo shook her head. "No, I don't."

That was the truth. The name was obviously Russian, but beyond that, she hadn't heard anyone, from Connor Whigby or Arnie Evans to the feds, mention the name.

Irena sat back and let out a deep sigh. She studied Jo for a minute, maybe more. The two men stood, legs apart, hands clasped in front of them. The room remained quiet. Then Irena tipped her head, a decision made.

"What I'm about to tell you is confidential," she said. Jo nodded, and Irena went on. "Mr. Orlov is a Russian businessman. He has done quite well for himself over the years, and he is quite wealthy. Houses around the world, a yacht. Whatever he wants, he gets." She leaned slightly forward, focusing in on the point of her story. "Unfortunately, Mr. Orlov is also missing. My associates and I"—she gestured to the two men—"have been hired by Mr. Orlov's daughter to find out what happened to him. Our search has brought us to the United States."

"How long has Orlov been missing?" Jo asked.

Irena pursed her lips. "Mr. Orlov travels a lot, and we've pieced together his itinerary. It's been over two weeks that his whereabouts have been unaccounted for. As you can imagine, his daughter is quite upset. She is sparing no expense to find out what happened to him."

Jo gave her a blank stare. "How does Connor Whigby relate to this? Does he know Orlov?"

"That is what we are trying to assess. It's why we talked to Connor."

Jo crossed her arms. "What did you find out?"

"According to him, he does not know anything about Mr. Orlov."

The tone indicated that Irena didn't believe this. Although Jo herself didn't know about a connection between the two men, it was certainly a possibility.

Irena pressed the issue. "Did Connor mention Mr. Orlov?"

Jo shrugged. "Not that I'm aware of." She wasn't going to let Irena know that she'd had only the briefest contact with Connor. "What is Mr. Orlov's business?"

Irena sat back and crossed one leg over the other. "He's an investor, and he owns several businesses." She droned on a for a minute, and Jo knew the story. A man made rich by confiscating a part of Russia's natural resources: coal, natural gas, oil, nickel, and aluminum. Crony capitalism. "He's traveled all over the world, and he's never run into any issues. Until now."

Jo arched an eyebrow. "Anything illegal?"

Irena frowned. "No, nothing like that. I know that is an assumption when someone disappears, but any number of things could've occurred."

"Like what?"

"Somebody could be after him for his money."

"Is Orlov being held for ransom? Have you received a note, anything like that?"

Irena shook her head. "We have very little information to go on as of yet."

"Except for whatever Connor Whigby knows," Jo pointed out.

"That appears to be a dead end," Irena said. She tilted her head. "How well do you know Connor?"

How best to navigate this? In her previous work, Jo was good at intelligence gathering, good at getting information without revealing any. She had a play here, though. A common connection. She was worried about Connor's daughter, and Orlov had a daughter who was worried about him.

"Connor has a daughter," Jo finally said.

"Brooke."

"How much do you know about her?"

"I believe she's a teenager, right?" Irena said.

Jo nodded. "She's worried about her dad."

She didn't reveal anything about her conversations with Brooke or the possibility that the girl was locked in a safe room. Better to see what Irena would give her.

"Connor and I discussed her, as well as his background. He went to Yale, studied political science and history. He's traveled around some. He'd been working in Washington DC for quite some time, and he's been with Senator Macintosh for several years. Do you know her?"

Jo shook her head. "I stay away from politics when I can."

Her lips formed a slight smile. "Probably a good move. How much does Connor associate with her? I would imagine it's quite a bit."

"I don't know."

"She tells Connor things?"

"I don't know," Jo repeated.

"He must have a high level of security clearance in his position."

"You'd have to ask him."

"You know Connor's wife, Fran?"

"I haven't met her." Jo remained careful not to reveal anything beyond the direct question Irene was asking.

Irena scratched her nose. "Daughters worrying about their fathers."

"Yes," was all Jo said.

Irena took another long moment before speaking. "And you just happened to be at the press conference last night? You just happened to see a signal my associate sent to Whigby?"

Jo noted the switch to calling Connor by his last name. Irena was displaying her irritation with Connor, and also her distrust of him.

"Something like that," Jo said.

The woman evaluated her with shrewd eyes. Jo wasn't going to give up any information, and Irena knew it. She uncrossed her legs and stood up.

"We need to continue our investigation," Irena said. "I'm sorry you were not able to help us."

Jo stood up as well. "Yes."

Irena reached into her pocket and pulled out a business card.

"That has my phone number. If you hear of anything that would help us with Mr. Orlov, I would be most grateful if you would give me a call. It's very important that we find him."

Jo took the card and glanced at it. It was simple, Irena's name and a phone number below it, nothing else. Jo pocketed the card, and Irena walked her to the suite door and held it open. As Jo stepped into the hall, she glanced back, but the door was already closing.

Walking away from the room, she had two things on her mind.

Irena's story could've been a lie. It also could've been the truth. She had to figure out which it was.

CHAPTER TWENTY-FIVE

As Jo walked toward the elevator, she noted that none of the men were escorting her. It didn't matter. Irena was sure to have her followed.

Jo pushed the button for floor three and rode the empty car down. When she got out, she found the stairs and hurried to the parking garage. Stepping out, she heard voices to her left, so she went right.

The garage was dim and smelled of engine exhaust. Jo meandered through cars, finally making her way to an exit. Out on the street, she took great pains walking around the neighborhood to lose anyone who might be following her. Good exercise, too, and the movement kept her alert. Then she went to the rental car and took the same painstaking maneuvers.

Finally, she drove back toward Connor Whigby's house.

She parked in a different place than before, popped the earbud in, and listened to the bugging devices for a few minutes. The house was still silent. She needed time to think, and time to talk to someone in private.

Getting back on the highway, she drove to a grocery

store, where she bought some food, coffee grounds, and water, then returned to her new motel. Jo drove by her room. She looked hard and saw the tiny scrap of paper still in place in the upper corner of the door, so she parked away from the room and lugged her groceries inside. Nothing had been disturbed. She put her groceries away and fixed a turkey sandwich. She took a bite, poured a glass of water, and sat down at a little table in the kitchen. Then she texted Dack from the new phone.

He wouldn't recognize the number, and like her, he was suspicious by nature. He would check to see if it'd been tapped before he would respond. Jo had finished her sandwich by the time he finally texted back and asked her to video-chat with him. She hesitated. With video, he would be able to see her face, and she didn't want that. Dack would be able to tell how worried she was.

The video call came through before she could reply. Jo sighed and answered it.

Dack's face appeared on her screen. He eyed her and began typing, and they carried on a text-to-voice conversation.

"What's with your phone?" he asked. As always, she imagined she heard his voice, not the impersonal computer sounds. "I've called several times but no answer."

She looked at him for a second, then shrugged. His face held concern.

"I lost the other phone," she said simply.

Dack stared at her for a moment. She couldn't fool him. His gaze went past her, then he sneaked a peek behind her and typed.

"You're in a different room. Does that mean you left DC?"

She shook her head. "No."

"What's going on?"

Jo glanced away and sighed. So much had happened in such a short time—she didn't know where to begin. Dack was studying her closely when she looked back at the screen.

"You look like hell," he said.

She smiled. "Thanks a lot."

"Are you going to tell me what's going on?"

She couldn't put anything past him. She never could; she never would. He used her own tactic against her, waiting her out. Finally, she began, telling him everything that had happened since their last conversation. He nodded periodically and never interrupted, just kept looking at her.

When Jo finished, he put a pensive finger to his lips. Then he began typing, and she heard his voice.

"The feds talked to you?"

She nodded. "It wasn't a big deal."

"Yes, it was. And they wanted to know why you'd talked to Whigby, and what you know about him."

"Yes."

"Given what you *do* know of him, and that his daughter claims he locked her in a safe room, do you think he's a pedophile, doing something kinky to his daughter?"

Somehow, she hadn't thought about that possibility. Jo considered that for a moment, then shook her head. "I don't think so. If he *is* doing something to her, I'm not sure what else I could've done. I talked to Connor, and I tried to get the police involved." She frowned. "Brooke didn't seem abused in any way, didn't show any signs of that kind of trauma. She's confused, maybe, but I don't think her father's abusing her. And in his position, he'd have gone through a thorough background check. If he's doing something like that, you'd think they would've caught it."

Dack shrugged. "If he was doing something online, sure. If it was just with his own daughter, in the privacy of his own home, how would they know?"

She grimaced. "Good point."

He typed. "But after going into his house, you do think Whigby locked Brooke in a safe room."

She nodded.

"Is it possible Whigby sent her somewhere, or she ran away again?"

"I doubt it. She would've called me from that phone if she could have. I think Connor got the phone and charged it. On the one hand, he wants to know who's been calling, but he's scared to answer."

"You tried again this morning?"

"Yes. It rang a few times and went to the canned voice message. I've been by the house, too. It's quiet. And since I broke in, the feds'll be watching for me."

Dack frowned. "That's true." He stared at her for a moment, deep in thought. "Something's going on if the feds are watching Whigby, and if this investigator from Russia talked to him as well."

"What's the connection with Orlov?" Jo asked. "There has to be one, or why would Irena Garin want to talk to Connor?"

"Orlov wants Brooke?"

Jo shuddered. "If that's the case, what kind of sick thing is Connor up to?"

Dack didn't answer that. "Go over what Irena said again."

When Jo had finished recapping it, she added, "I'm dealing with somebody who has a lot of money and resources." She tapped the table with a finger. "Think about it. Irena and her men were at the Clarion, an expensive hotel where there were plenty of conferences, plenty of people around, and full occupancy. And yet they knew ahead of time that they would need at least two rooms on different floors, in case they had to shake the feds or somebody else. That takes planning and money."

Dack nodded. "I was thinking the same thing. What do you know about Irena Garin?"

"I couldn't find anything on her."

"Hang on."

He looked away from the screen and began typing. Jo sipped her water. Dack's jaw remained firm as he worked at the monitor. With his job in security, he would have access to more databases and information than Jo did. Not as much as someone in the government, but enough. As he typed, she looked at his profile. A faint scar ran from his ear and along his jawbone toward his cheek. It seemed to be lighter than before, a visible injury that was fading with time. She frowned. His other injury would always be with him; he would always be mute. Regardless of what anybody said, including Dack, that was her fault.

He turned back to her.

"I can't find anything on her, either."

Jo shook her head. "I don't have access to websites in Russia, though."

"It would take me longer to look at that, and I will. But I wouldn't count on finding anything."

"That's troubling," Jo said, stating the obvious. She thought back to her conversation with Irena. "She was digging for information from me, too, and she was careful with her story about Orlov."

"Let me see what I can find on him."

He came back after a minute. "I found a few Yuri Orlovs. One does seem to have the wealth that Irena referenced, but I can't find much about him. You know her whole story of Orlov could all be a cover."

As happened so often, he voiced what she'd been thinking.

"She's not a private investigator," she said.

"Right."

"Am I dealing with FSB, Russian state security? Or Russian spies?"

Dack nodded slowly. "If that's the case, they'd have the resources you mentioned. But what do they want with Connor Whigby?"

Jo thought about that. "Irena was asking a lot of questions about Senator Macintosh and Connor's connection to her. And the FBI is spying on him."

A troubled look swept across Dack's face. It took him a moment to respond.

"Whigby's a senior aide to Senator Macintosh, who's on the SSCI?" Jo had told him that Macintosh was the chairwoman on the Senate Select Committee on Intelligence. He continued to type. "That would mean the senator has access to highly classified information."

Jo nodded. "How much information could the senator's aide get? Would Connor know what she knows?"

Dack shrugged. "He should have high clearance. In theory, the senator would be extremely cautious with what she shares with him. But that doesn't mean he couldn't get information anyway. We supposedly have moles all throughout the intelligence community, and people have sold information to our enemies in the past. What if Whigby's selling intelligence to Irena Garin?"

"If we're correct, and Irena is working for the Russian government, what is this guy doing? Is he working for our government or against it?" Jo asked.

Dack nodded. "And how much would the senator know about what he's doing?"

"Given her position, you would think a lot." Her mind raced. "On the other hand, it's possible the FBI hasn't told the senator anything yet, but who knows?" She raked her fingers down her face. "I would need to talk to her, but how would I do that?"

Dack tipped his head. "You get close to her."

Jo threw up a hand. "I can't just get close to her. What about security?"

Now he smiled. "Only a small number of top-ranking senators are assigned security details. Everyone else has to pay for their own security, and how much they have depends on how deep their pockets are." He was getting into territory that he knew. "Some of the senators have spent upwards of 50K for a consulting firm. A few senators even more than that."

"How do they pay for it?"

"Exactly. Paying for private details can be costly, which poses a problem for senators who don't have a lot of money. However, following the shooting of Gabby Giffords, the FEC eased restrictions so that they can use campaign funds for security. But you have to have the funds. Hold on a second." He turned away from the phone again and typed. Then he looked back at her. "Macintosh has hired a private security firm, but it looks like she has just one ex Secret Service agent assigned to her." He glanced at the monitor and typed again, then gave her an address. "That's where she lives. You ought to be able to find out her day-to-day routines and then approach her. If you want, I can help you with that."

Jo was already shaking her head before he finished the words. "You're too involved in this as it is."

Dack pursed his lips, then typed. "Jo, I don't want anything to happen to you."

She stared at him. "Something already did happen to you, and it was my fault."

He slapped a hand down on his desk, surprising her. "Stop saying that. You can't keep blaming yourself. And you need the help now."

She moved closer to the screen, enlarging her face in the view. "Dack, I know you mean well, but you can't do this. The feds are involved, and possibly Russian spies. This is big time, and I need to do it alone. If you help and get caught, who knows what it would do to your career. You have a good thing going, and I don't. I have nothing to lose. Let me take care of this."

He stared at her and blinked a few times, his jaw working. Then he nodded.

"Okay, but you promise me that you'll be careful. And you promise me that you'll keep in contact, let me know what's going on."

"I will. I'll see what I can find out about the senator, and I'll let you know what happens."

He stared at her for a moment longer, then nodded again and told her goodbye. Jo reached out and touched the screen, and he was gone. She sat back for a minute, her nerves on edge.

What had she gotten herself into?

CHAPTER TWENTY-SIX

J o sat at the table, going over everything she and Dack had discussed in her mind. They were making assumptions about Connor Whigby, but she felt they were pretty good assumptions. She didn't like the idea of tracking down the senator and talking to her, but she knew she had to do it.

Using the phone's internet, she researched Senator Macintosh's address. As Washington, DC, had grown more expensive, it had become more difficult for congresspeople to live in the area. It wasn't well-known, but many members of Congress slept on cots in their offices at the Capitol. Others lived in semi-communal settings, where they had individual quarters but shared a common living space. Senator Macintosh lived in the Kalorama neighborhood, a politically packed area where a number of DC elites lived, at one time even former President Barack Obama. The senator must've been doing fairly well, as the neighborhood was expensive. Jo studied a map of the area. Once she was familiar with it, she had to figure out when Senator Macintosh was home.

Jo left the motel, drove to the Capitol, and parked as close as she could get to the building, which was still blocks away. Security was so tight, she had no hope of getting inside, so she found the main number for the Senate offices and called. The only thing she was able to find out was that the senator was in the building. That was enough. She camped outside in the heat. While she waited, she googled Macintosh and read about her.

Soon, Jo stumbled upon a website that said the senator liked to eat at a local restaurant nearby. At five o'clock, she saw Senator Macintosh leave with a small entourage, including Connor. They walked a few blocks to the restaurant and went inside.

Jo had time, so she jogged back to her car and drove to the restaurant. She pulled in down the street and waited. Almost two hours later, the senator emerged with a tall, stocky man who had the telltale bulge under his armpit. Her one-man security detail. A black SUV pulled up to the curb and they got in. The vehicle pulled into traffic, and Jo followed the senator to the Kalorama neighborhood, parking down the street from her home.

The area was even more beautiful than what Jo had read, with several stately homes and row houses along tree-lined streets that provided ample shade. Security would be here, probably a lot of doorbell cams and other surveillance devices around these homes.

She decided not to use her binoculars. Instead, she donned her baseball cap and sank low into her seat. The SUV was parked in front of Macintosh's row house. Several steps led up to the front door, and a window to the left looked onto the street. The SUV sat for a moment before the senator and her bodyguard got out. He stayed a couple of feet back as they walked up the steps. The SUV remained at the curb, the driver still inside.

The senator unlocked the door and they disappeared inside, and Jo wondered about overnight security. But then the door opened again and Macintosh emerged with a Pekingese on a leash. She and the bodyguard headed down the steps in the opposite direction from Jo. The senator was on the phone, walking fast, and the man held back, alert, his head swiveling to and fro as if it were mounted on a post. The dog's excitement showed as it strained on the leash.

The senator disappeared around the corner, and ten minutes later, she appeared on the street nearest Jo. She was off the phone now, but her bodyguard still held back. She turned the corner, and a couple came out of a nearby house. The senator stopped and briefly talked to them. The couple moved on, and Macintosh walked back down the street and up the steps of her row house. She stood on the porch with the bodyguard for a moment, talking, and he smiled. Then she unlocked her door and stepped inside. The bodyguard stood on the stoop for a moment, then walked down the steps and got back into the SUV. It drove off in the opposite direction.

It appeared the senator was in for the night, so Jo drove out of the neighborhood and went back to Connor Whigby's neighborhood. She again pulled over in a new place, put the earbuds in, and listened. The TV was on, the latest political news, a panel debating how much inflation was impacting the economy. Jo thought she heard dishes clinking, and then the TV suddenly cut off.

"Hey." Connor's voice had an edge to it. "No, everything's okay on my end. Don't worry." His voice grew stronger as he neared the bug in the kitchen. "Yes, it's a burner phone, just like you told me to get."

Who was he talking to? Irena? Had she told him to get it?

"No, I don't know about that. Elaine's asking more questions. I think she's suspicious. Yeah, I have to be careful."

Footsteps sounded on the floor. He was pacing.

"I'll see what I can do." A pause, and he repeated, "I'll see what I can do. Yeah, I got it, but you have to give me a little more time."

Jo squinted. It sounded as if someone were giving him instructions.

"You still haven't seen Orlov?" His voice grew angry. "What do you think I'm supposed to do? The senator's getting suspicious. Something's going on with her, so I have to be careful." He sighed. "Don't start with that, okay?" Something under his breath that sounded like a curse. "You really think that's happening? Okay, hold on."

The footsteps faded away, and so did Connor's voice. Jo heard a door opening. He'd gone outside. She stared out the windshield. Finally, some confirmation. The man was definitely up to something with the senator.

CHAPTER TWENTY-SEVEN

It had been a long day for Brooke.

Her dad had come in first thing in the morning and woken her up. He'd brought a stack of books from her room. He set them down on the bar counter, asked her how she was doing, and before she could even get out of the bed, he'd left.

The whole short time, he'd been cold and distracted. She hollered at him as the door closed, but it didn't matter.

With almost nothing to do, she rolled over and slept again. When she finally got up, she ate a bowl of cereal and then showered and dressed. She lingered with every activity, making them take as long as they could. She watched some TV shows that she used to love, but now with nothing else to do, they'd lost some of their allure. She checked out the books. Connor had gathered some of the Harry Potter series, not even in order. She laughed. She'd read all of them several years ago, and really wasn't in the mood to again. He'd brought a couple of his David Baldacci thrillers, and she picked one up and began reading it. It was all about a hitman who had witnessed a bombing in DC. After reading through a few chapters, she tossed the book aside.

As the day wore on, Brooke had grown more and more discouraged. She ate a bologna sandwich and chips for lunch, then worried about all the carbs. She hadn't been able to swim, and that bummed her out. In the small space, she did some stretching and running in place, even some yoga. It should've calmed her down, but it didn't. Too anxious.

How long did her father plan for her to stay here, and what was he up to? Keeping her in the safe room had gone beyond just punishing her for running away. She couldn't figure out why he hated her so much, why he wanted to do this to her. She tried to remember when her mom was coming home, but she couldn't. He had to be giving her excuses for why Brooke couldn't come to the phone. Given how distant her mom had seemed of late, how distracted, Brooke wondered how much she would care.

At dinner time, Brooke fixed another sandwich, this time peanut butter and jelly. She was already getting sick of sandwiches. What she would give for a really good salad, or possibly splurging on a hamburger and a chocolate shake. Her mouth watered.

She expected her dad to come check on her, but he never did. As she watched more TV, her hopelessness grew. No one was going to rescue her, certainly not Jo. She had no idea where the woman had gone, and regardless, she probably didn't even know what was happening. Brooke was on her own.

Then something popped into her mind.

So far, Connor had checked on her each morning. She needed to take advantage of that. He was a big man, formidable, but maybe she could figure out a way to outwit him, just like the spy in the Baldacci book outsmarted his foes. She'd have to be awake early, be prepared when he came into the room the next morning.

Brooke was still thinking about her plan as she shut out the lights and crawled into bed.

CHAPTER TWENTY-EIGHT

Putting his phone back in his pocket, Connor walked down the street. It had never occurred to him that the house could be bugged. How stupid could he have been? He swore, then quickly put on a fake smile and gave a wave as he realized one of his neighbors was watching.

Connor hurried back into the house. He locked the doors and shut all the blinds, then spent several minutes looking around, trying to find any listening devices, with no success.

He swore to himself again.

He wasn't a spy, didn't know how to do all of this. Still, he should have been more careful. He fixed a stiff drink and sat at the kitchen island, thinking for a few minutes. Something was going on with the senator. She was asking too many questions, and she was angry with him. He had to be more careful.

Connor gulped down the drink, but it didn't calm his nerves. Today had been awful. He'd never been so nervous in his life as meeting with Irena Garin. The woman had asked so many questions, too, wanted so much information, and he didn't have answers yet. But he was going to have to get them.

Pouring himself another drink, he went into the living room. He set the glass down on the coffee table and sprawled on the couch, sipping as he stared up at the ceiling. Brooke barely crossed his mind. All of his focus was on what he had to do next.

CHAPTER TWENTY-NINE

Jo heard Connor and she figured he was searching for bugs. He couldn't have known about her planting any, but he never discovered hers. He made a drink, and he never got on the phone again. It grew late, and she finally decided to leave.

When she reached the motel, Jo found her room undisturbed. She fixed herself another sandwich, ate an apple, and drank a lot of water. Then she stripped down and went to bed.

She spent the next day following Senator Macintosh's movements as best she could. The senator showed up at the Capitol building around nine and was inside for most of the morning. At twelve thirty, she emerged with her security guard and two other people Jo didn't recognize, along with Connor. They got into an SUV and drove away. Jo took the opportunity to get a hot dog from a street vendor and was back by the Capitol when the senator returned an hour and a half later. Macintosh was inside for the rest of the afternoon.

While Jo waited for her to emerge, Dack called.

"I found a little info on Yuri Orlov. Basic stuff—his business profile, family history—but I'm suspicious. It's like it's too clean."

"Like maybe it's been set up, a cover," she said.

"Right. What're you doing?"

"Watching Macintosh. I may be able to get to her tonight." She told him about her activities.

"If you talk to her, is it time to be blunt?" he asked when she was finished. "Mention Orlov and see what she does?"

Jo thought about that. "Maybe."

"You think she has any idea that Whigby has his kid locked up?"

"Doubtful."

"You need to be prepared for anything. If she calls for backup, you might find yourself being interrogated again. And they'll sweep the neighborhood for your car."

"Good point. I'll plan for that."

"Keep me posted."

"Will do."

She ended the call, then snacked on some mixed nuts she'd brought with her.

At six, the senator was again picked up by a dark SUV, and this time no one was with her except her bodyguard. Jo had managed to find a place close enough to the parking lot that she was able to follow the senator as they went to another restaurant popular with DC elites.

Jo figured the senator's dinner would last a while, so she drove to a spot a few miles from the rowhouse. She put her fake IDs and credit cards in the glove box, left the car in a paid lot, and took the Metro back to the Kalorama neighborhood. She waited at the end of the block, and as she expected, a dark SUV soon parked in front of the senator's home, and Macintosh and her bodyguard got out. They went up the steps, disappeared into the house, then came back outside with her dog. The only change from the previous night's routine was that the senator walked in Jo's direction, and this time she was ready.

Jo moved toward the corner. As she approached, the senator looked up with a forced smile. The security guard held back, but he was eyeing Jo warily. As Jo drew closer, she spoke.

"I need to talk to you, Senator."

"I'm afraid I'm busy right now," Macintosh said. She had a deep voice and sounded slightly tired and a little put off.

Jo tried to block her way, and as the senator was about to sidestep her, the bodyguard stepped between them. He was deceptively quick.

"It's about Yuri Orlov," Jo said.

The bodyguard was closer now, a hand reaching under his coat. The senator surveyed Jo for a moment, then held up a hand to the man. He stopped, but his hand remained under his coat.

Macintosh sighed. "Let's talk."

CHAPTER THIRTY

The senator walked for a minute in silence. The
Pekinese trotted up ahead, sniffing everything in
sight, oblivious to the tension in the air. The bodyguard
held back, but Jo was keenly aware of his presence. Across
the street, a couple walked casually hand in hand. Otherwise, the neighborhood was quiet, the heat of the day
fading.

Macintosh wore a pantsuit, but she'd switched heels for
a pair of tennis shoes. She was a few inches shorter than Jo's
five foot eight, with high cheekbones and heavy makeup.
Her brown hair was perfectly coiffed, and she carried
herself in a self-assured manner. She looked at Jo with tired
eyes.

"Who are you?"

"Jo." No reason to give her any more. She didn't know
how much time she would have with the senator, how much
she could ask.

The woman glanced at her. Her eyes narrowed as
several things seemed to occur to her, including who Jo was,

and that the feds had recently spoken to her. Macintosh spoke in a clipped tone.

"I presume you're with one of the many agencies that our government has?"

"Given your resources, you should know that I'm not."

The senator considered that. "I don't know *everything* that goes on with the government."

They walked a little farther.

"You're with the other side?" the senator continued.

"No," Jo said. "I'm a concerned third party."

"Who hired you?"

"Nobody."

The bodyguard kept pace with them. Macintosh never glanced back at him. Clearly, she trusted he would react if and when he needed to. And Jo knew it, too.

"How do you know the name Yuri Orlov?" Macintosh asked.

"It came to me in passing."

The senator slowed down. "What is your interest in Orlov?"

Jo had thought a fair amount what she would say in this conversation, if it occurred. Her only real concern was for Brooke, but she had to be careful. By talking to the senator, she'd just taken things to a new level.

"As I said, his name came up. I need to know about him."

They stopped at the corner, and the senator appraised her.

"You think I would be able to help you?"

"You're the chairman of the SSCI. That means you're privy to highly classified information."

Macintosh gave a slight headshake. The Pekinese

pulled on the leash, and the senator started around the corner.

"If you know so much about me," she said, "you would know there's no way in the world I could tell you anything about Orlov, even if I do know about him, which I don't."

She was telling the truth and telling a lie at the same time. Jo pointed back toward the senator's home.

"You stopped when I mentioned the name. You want to know why I know."

A dark-colored Mercedes drove by, and although the senator paid it no mind, the bodyguard did. He was watching everything.

"I'm sure whoever you are, you have your reasons for coming to me," Macintosh said. "You're hoping I'll give you some kind of information." The senator glanced at Jo out of the corner of her eye. "I'm sure you're very good at what you do. If I had to guess, you're with some clandestine organization, but of course you won't tell me." She paused. "You're ex-military?"

"Yes."

Macintosh nodded. "You're taking a very big risk coming here."

"That's true," Jo agreed. "Tell me about Connor Whigby."

They rounded the next corner, sidestepping a man who jogged past. The senator gave him a nod as if she knew him, and they walked on.

"What's your interest in him?" Macintosh asked.

"He's your senior aide, and he's been with you for several years," Jo said.

"You're telling me things I already know."

"Do you trust him?"

"Of course." Her tone changed with words, much more cautious now. Suspicious.

Jo was sure that was another lie.

"You haven't looked happy with him lately," Jo said. "I saw an angry exchange on the Capitol steps."

Macintosh's posture stiffened. "You've been watching me."

Jo avoided that. "You know his family?"

The senator nodded, then slowed as the dog began sniffing intently at a particular bush.

"I've met Fran at several functions. She's a lovely woman."

Something again in the tone, as if she didn't really care much for Connor's wife. "They have a daughter, too. Brooke. I understand she's in high school. I have two daughters. That's a tough age—so much to deal with, so many emotions."

"You know about Brooke?" Jo asked.

"What about her?"

The senator had no idea what was going on with Connor's daughter. Jo had to proceed carefully. "Has Connor mentioned her?"

"Not recently."

They reached the end of the block, and Macintosh stopped. The bodyguard still maintained his distance. The senator turned to Jo.

"You've been asking about certain individuals."

"Irena Garin."

"What do you know about her?"

"Orlov is a Russian businessman who's gone missing. Irena was supposedly hired by his daughter to find him."

"And you don't believe that?"

"No," Jo said.

Macintosh glanced at her watch, then looked Jo in the eyes. "You want me to be frank with you, so I will. I can't tell you anything about Yuri Orlov, and anything that goes on with my staff is private as well." She smiled. "This is as far as I go with this conversation." She glanced toward the sound of an oncoming vehicle. "Perhaps you'll be more forthcoming with these gentlemen."

The senator waved a hand as another dark SUV careened around the corner and double-parked nearby. Jo glanced at the bodyguard, who'd raised an eyebrow at her—he'd called in reinforcements.

"A very good trick," Jo said. "The feds are at your beck and call."

The senator shook her head. "We're beyond the feds." Her face grew hard. "And we need to know what you know."

Jo looked at the senator. She'd been stalling to give whoever had been called time to show up.

Four men got out of the SUV, all big, all wearing dark suits. They carried themselves with a practiced assurance, separating into two pairs and spreading out to flank her. With the bodyguard behind her, it was impossible for Jo to escape in any direction. One of the suits approached her.

"Would you come with us?" His voice was deep, lacking any tone.

Jo glanced at Macintosh. "We'll have to cut our conversation short."

An amused look leaped into the senator's eyes. "Of course. I know you have information, and I hope you'll cooperate with these gentlemen. You have a nice night."

Gentlemen, Jo thought. Right.

Two men escorted her to the SUV, one signaling the other what to do. She asked them who they were, and the lead man didn't answer directly, instead citing the Patriot Act. Jo didn't bother pushing for more information. It would only lead to more quoting of the Act.

They searched her for weapons, took her cash, then nodded toward the SUV. Four agents against her. They didn't bother with restraints. As she got in the vehicle, she looked back. The senator had continued down the street with her dog, the bodyguard nearby. But her shoulders were slightly stooped, as if she was carrying a lot of weight on them.

And she probably was.

CHAPTER THIRTY-ONE

J o sat in the back seat of the SUV, shoulder to shoulder between two of the men. The car was clean, with an antiseptic smell. None of the men said anything as they drove out of the neighborhood. Daylight had faded, and the traffic had eased considerably as well. Jo finally spoke.

"Am I being arrested?"

Nothing from any of them. She tried a different tack.

"You can't just take me somewhere without any cause."

The one in the passenger seat turned to look at her. His brown eyes were cold.

"We can do what we need to do." Then he went on about government security and the Patriot Act, more stuff she'd heard before. She listened and kept her mouth shut. Arguing would do her no good, and she was curious about where this was headed.

They drove darkened streets through the city, past the monuments and across the Potomac River. None of them spoke a word. Jo thought back to her conversation with Senator Macintosh. She'd missed something amid it, but she couldn't put her finger on exactly what. And in her present circumstances, she couldn't ponder that.

Once in Virginia, they drove through Arlington, then picked up Highway 50. Here, the houses were fewer and spread out. The driver turned down a long road with no streetlights. Jo had no idea where they were. She didn't panic, though. If they'd wanted to kill her, they would've by now. The vehicle turned and drove on, then finally slowed in front of a darkened building.

When they got out, the air was fresh, as if it had rained. The men escorted Jo inside. As they walked down a hallway, Jo noticed nothing hanging on the walls, no pictures, posters, or logos to give away a clue as to where they were. They ended up in a windowless room with gray paint on the walls, a rectangular wooden table and chairs the only furniture. Cameras were positioned in the upper corners, the typical one-way glass on one wall.

Unlike the feds, where only Agent Stone had interviewed her, this group didn't leave her. All four men came into the room, and the driver sat down across from her. They locked eyes, and Jo waited until he spoke.

"You have no ID."

She shook her head. "No."

"How did you get to the senator's neighborhood?"

"I walked."

She expected a deep voice, given his stocky build and thick chest. Instead, his voice was higher, probably not the threat that he hoped to convey.

His lips twitched. "From where?"

"Around."

"Why were you harassing the senator?"

"I wasn't harassing the senator," she said. "We were having a pleasant conversation. It's not against the law to talk to somebody on the street. In fact, the senator told me we could talk. Nothing harassing about that."

He stared at her. "What did you want with her?"

She shrugged. "Like I said, just to talk. There's no law against that."

"She obviously didn't like it."

"Sorry," Jo said.

"You were pushing the senator for information, but you know she can't tell you anything."

Jo nodded. "It was worth a try."

"No, it wasn't."

"Am I under arrest? If not, I'd like to go."

He shook his head slowly. "We both know you're not going anywhere."

"Who are you with? CIA? NSA?"

"We can't say."

"How about a name?"

He stared at her. "Borland."

Not a chance that was his real name. Jo sat back and crossed her arms. "Well, Mr. Borland, what do you want?"

He laced his fingers together and rested them on the table. "You had an outstanding military career. Some intelligence gathering operations in Syria and Afghanistan." He rattled off some details about her deployments. "Quite impressive."

She was wary. He had more than the feds, access to classified information.

"So?"

"You're not with the military anymore," he said. "You're not with any organization that I can find. Yet you're interfering in things."

"What things?"

His eyebrows jerked. "We know the feds talked to you, but you didn't tell them anything."

"There's nothing to tell."

His eyes went dark. "But there is, and we're going to find out exactly what."

She glanced at him, then at the other three. None seemed overtly threatening. The one to her right looked nervous, maybe a little uncomfortable with the interrogation. She pegged him as green, new to all this. A rookie.

What would they do if they didn't get what they wanted? She'd been in worse situations before, though, and she stayed calm, looking back at Borland. "What's going on with Connor Whigby?"

He was smooth. "What makes you think there's anything going on with him?"

Jo smiled. "Let's not play this game. I've run afoul of government agencies since the moment I started asking questions about him. It doesn't take a genius to know something is up."

He didn't answer that, just asked some of the same questions that Stone had asked her: How did she know Connor Whigby, why was she in contact with him, and had he given her anything?

She gave Borland the same answers. Then she turned things in a different direction.

"Why is your organization so scared?" she asked.

He shrugged. "What makes you think anyone's scared?"

"You're sure giving me a lot of attention."

"What's it to you, if you're not with any organization?"

Jo glanced around the room again, considering her answer. She didn't trust him or the other men in the room, but they were getting nowhere with this line of questioning.

And time was running out for Brooke, if not for Jo. Finally, she made a decision.

"You know the Whigbys have a daughter?"

He nodded. "Brooke. She's sixteen."

"With all of this running around you're doing, looking into Connor Whigby, wondering what he's up to, have you asked yourself this? Where's Brooke?"

She watched Borland closely. He stayed composed, but there was something in his eyes, curiosity mixed with caution, as if he were wondering not only why she was asking the question, but wondering what he'd missed.

"I assume she's at home," he said.

It was a mistake. A tiny one, but still a mistake. He didn't know as much as he thought he did.

"You assume?" She didn't hide the sarcasm in her tone. "Which means you have no idea where Brooke is."

His face communicated nothing, but the subtle shift in his chair did. The man was uncomfortable now. This was not where he envisioned the conversation going.

"She should be at home with her father," he said.

Jo raised her eyebrows. "Do you know that for sure?"

His lips parted slightly. He had to be running through a ton of different scenarios right now, wondering why they hadn't picked up on where Brooke was and who had missed that critical piece of information. They'd been so focused on Connor Whigby that they weren't thinking about what else should have been going on in his household, or where his daughter was.

Borland cleared his throat. "Maybe she's with a friend."

She would've expected better from him, but she'd caught him off guard. However, he quickly recovered and glared at her.

"You know something, and I suggest you tell us now. The life of Whigby's daughter may be at stake."

That was the very thing she'd been worrying about, the safety of Brooke. It was what had led her to this point, what kept her going in the midst of all of this mess. She was troubled that Borland had no idea if Brooke was in danger, either from her father or from somewhere else. But beyond his hard exterior and embarrassment about missing something, there was the tiniest hint of concern.

"Tell me what you know," he repeated.

"I'm not with any organization," Jo said. "I ran into Brooke the other day. She'd run away from home."

He listened as she went through what she'd done since first seeing Brooke in Rawlins Park. She told him about Brooke calling her to tell her that her father had locked her in the safe room. Jo left out a lot of details, including that she'd been in the house and planted bugs there. She didn't tell him that she'd met Irena Garin or any of that conversation, either. When she finished, Borland studied her.

"That's why you were looking at Connor Whigby?" He seemed to know she wasn't going to give him everything. That kind of perceptiveness was necessary in this line of work.

"When I couldn't get hold of Brooke again, I wanted to know what was going on. For all we know, Connor Whigby could be a pedophile. I was trying to find out."

He kept staring at her, assessing what she'd told him.

"You're a female Lone Ranger, out to help the little guy. Or gal."

"Brooke was in trouble. I wanted to help."

There was a long silence. Borland seemed to be examining whatever he knew in a different light.

"How can I verify this?" he finally asked. "You could be slinging a line of BS."

"Talk to a pimp called Leroy Doherty," she said. "He lives near the U Street Station. He's got a crew of kids working for him near the park where I met Brooke." She described the area in detail. "You ought to be able to find some of those kids, and they'll tell you Brooke and I were there. You also should be able to get her phone number—not the prepaid phone, her main one." She glanced at the others. "You guys can do that. Find out if she answers, find out what's going on."

"I know that," Borland grunted.

He went over the same questions again, and she gave him the same information. He tried to trip her up to see if she was lying, but she stuck to her story. He ended with Leroy Doherty and the teenagers that Brooke had been talking to in the park.

Borland stared at her. "And if I can't find them? If I can't verify what you're saying?"

"Then you've wasted a little time," she said. "Regardless, I'm no threat to you."

He contemplated her for a long moment. "We'll see about that." His chair scraped loudly against the floor as he scooted back. With a quick nod to the others, they all left the room. Jo thought they would be gone for a few minutes, that they'd make a few phone calls and then come back to her.

As time dragged on, she realized that she might be in for a long night.

CHAPTER THIRTY-TWO

Jo didn't know how long had passed—certainly hours—but she'd had plenty of time to think. The room was deathly quiet. Finally, Borland and the three other men came back in. The man's expression was hard to read.

"What did you find out?" Jo asked.

Standing across from her, he put his hands on his hips to expose a Glock 9-millimeter automatic pistol. It was good, reliable, and she got the threat. She also had no way out. If she attempted to leap over the table, she wouldn't get very far. And even on the incredible off-chance that she made it past the four of them and into the hall, where would she go? It was a big building, had to have many other people about. She did have an asset, though, even though she had no weapon. Something that she had learned in all her years in Civil Affairs. She could communicate well. And she put that skill to use now.

"You have more questions for me?" she asked, keeping her voice even. "I've cooperated with you so far, and I have nothing to hide." That last part was a lie, but she couldn't give them everything. "Did you find Leroy Doherty? I'm sure you could've found a way to get him talking."

"You need to come with us," Borland said. His tone was neutral, but his expression was not. It said that if she were to try anything, it would go badly for her. Jo glanced at the other three. As if on cue, they showed their weapons as well. If she resisted, she didn't think they'd shoot her, but they'd certainly disable her somehow. She decided to cooperate.

"Sure," Jo said, standing up. "Where're we going?"

She headed around one side of the table, and the agent there stepped into the corner to let her pass. Even if she'd wanted to go at him, it would've been difficult to approach him without the others being on her in a second. Borland had already stepped out of the room, and she went into the hallway. He walked ahead, and two agents fell in step beside her while the last stayed several steps behind.

They walked down another dim hallway and around a corner. Jo felt her heart accelerate, and she tried to keep calm. They weren't going to let her go. What would they do to her now? She wasn't stupid enough to believe she wasn't in a perilous situation here. Like it or not, the US had agencies that did a lot of things people never heard about. Right now, there seemed a very real possibility that she was going to be another victim.

They walked another hall, and Borland stopped in front of a metal door, opened it, and gestured for her to enter. She tried one more time to reason with him.

"Borland, we can talk," she said. "Whatever you're thinking of doing, it's not necessary."

The man jerked his head, an impatient motion for her to enter. She sighed and walked through the doorway.

The room was small, with gray walls and no windows.

A small cot sat in one corner, a metal toilet with no lid in the opposite, with a metal sink nearby. A prison cell. The overhead light was bright, and the room felt cool. She turned around to face Borland, who was now standing in the doorway.

"Really?" she said. "How do you justify this illegal imprisonment?"

The trace of a smile crossed his face. Then he pointed at her shoes.

"Take them off and push them toward me."

She stared at him for a moment, feeling her ire rise. But anger would do her no good; it was a distraction she couldn't afford. She slipped off her shoes and kicked them toward him.

"Sit down on the bed," he said.

Jo glanced at the cot that he'd called a bed, then sat and looked up at him. Borland bent down, grabbed her shoes, and backed out of the doorway. He didn't say another word as the door shut. She heard the distinctive click of bolts sliding into place. Silence enveloped her as she looked around again.

There was obviously no way to escape. The room was about eight feet square, the ceiling about the same height. It had a stale smell, probably hadn't been cleaned in a while. She went to the sink and turned on the faucet. Only cold water, which she splashed on her face. Her throat was dry, and she cupped her hands and took a long drink. She had to use her shirt to dry her hands and face. Then she paced the room for a moment and checked for any way out, even though she knew there wouldn't be one. She kept at it, despite feeling discouraged.

Jo wasn't sure of the time, but figured it had to be close

to midnight. Finally, she went back to the cot. The mattress was thin, barely any cushion, covered in nothing but a cheap gray wool blanket. No pillow. She flipped the blanket back, crawled under it, and closed her eyes, then pulled the blanket over her face to block out the light. All she could hear was the sound of her breathing. It was a tad fast, her nerves on edge. She didn't know what to expect, or when to expect it. What would Borland and his agents do to her?

Jo was still thinking about that when she fell into a fitful sleep.

She awoke several hours later, still with no idea what time it was. She had a decent internal clock, and she knew that she rarely slept past six or seven, so probably around then. Sitting up, she stretched for a minute, then went to the door and listened. She couldn't hear a thing. Ignoring her growling stomach, she performed some light exercises. Then she sat down on the cot and waited.

About an hour later, Jo heard the bolts on the door unlock, and the door opened. She remained on the cot. The rookie agent stood in the doorway.

"Stay where you are," he instructed her.

She didn't move, and he bent down and put a sandwich on the floor. Then he rose and shut the door. Once the locks clicked into place, Jo picked up the sandwich. Ham on white bread, no condiments. She sat back down on the cot, ate it, and drank from the sink.

The hours dragged on. The same agent brought another sandwich for lunch, but no one came for a long time after that. Jo counted the minutes. She knew it was late in the evening when the door rattled again.

Borland took a couple of steps into the room, careful to not get too close to her, then studied her.

"You look okay."

She wasn't sure what to make of the statement. Did he think she would've tried to harm herself during the night, or scratch her way out of the room?

"It's an interesting time we live in, isn't it?" she said. "You haven't read me my rights, charged me with anything, or let me make a phone call or talk to a lawyer. But that's the way it goes, huh?"

He stared at her, then gestured with his hand.

"Come with me."

Jo sat on the edge of the bed. "No shoes?"

He didn't say anything, waiting her out. She stood up.

"Lead the way," she said, as if she were the one in charge.

Borland backed out of the room, and when she stepped into the hall, the three agents from the night before were there. She raised her eyebrows at them.

"Working long days," she observed. If they were tired, they might make mistakes.

They surrounded her the same as they'd done the previous evening, leading her back down the maze of hallways to the original room where they'd talked. She sat down at the table and looked at Borland.

"Are you going to tell me why you kept me here overnight?" she asked. "I'm not a threat to you."

"You were told to leave Connor Whigby alone," he said.

"And I did," she replied.

He paused. "I have reason to believe that's not the case."

"I haven't broken any laws," she said.

Jo didn't mention breaking and entering the Whigbys' home or planting bugs there. Those were details they didn't need to know.

"Tell me again about Leroy Doherty," he said.

She did, and when she finished, he stared at her.

"You found him?" she asked.

He nodded.

"And?" she prodded.

Borland still didn't say anything, so she said, "He confirmed my story."

"We talked to Doherty," he finally said.

She didn't bother asking again. Leroy must've had wonderful things to say about her. Borland was trying to figure out what to do next, and what to do with her.

"Tell me what you know about Connor Whigby," he said.

She let out a loud sigh but it didn't faze him.

"I told you, I don't know him," she said. "Did you check into him? Where's his daughter?"

"You need to leave the senator alone, or it won't go well for you."

Jo shrugged. "Fine."

"And you need to stop interfering."

"In what?" She stared at him.

He scowled. "Consider this your last warning."

Jo didn't reply, but her mind raced. He hadn't brought up Brooke. Did that mean he hadn't checked on her? It seemed they were more worried about Connor than his daughter.

Borland contemplated her for a moment longer. His phone rang, and he pulled it from his pocket, frowning at whatever he saw. He nodded at the two agents to Jo's left, then stood up.

"Take her back," he said to the rookie. "Keep your piece on her."

Borland left the room, and the agents led Jo into the hall. The other two turned left, and the rookie unholstered a

Glock 9-millimeter. No restraints again, as if the gun were enough of a threat. He motioned with it as he escorted her down the hall and around the corner.

Jo was alone with him. And she wasn't worried about the threat.

CHAPTER THIRTY-THREE

The TV was on, but Brooke barely heard it. She tapped a foot against the coffee table, completely bored, completely discouraged.

When she'd gone to bed the other night, she'd had a plan. When her dad came in the next morning, she was going to pretend to be sick. She'd lay on the bed and moan. He would be concerned, and he would have to act, would have to get her help. He'd have to let her out of the safe room, maybe even consider taking her to a doctor. She'd even gone so far as to chew up some food and put it on the floor to make it look like she'd thrown up.

But he never came in.

Brooke chided herself as she cleaned up the food mess. She should've known better. He had the room stocked with food, and there was water. Someone could stay in here for a long time. In reality, he didn't need to come and check on her at all. She'd just expected him too. He was her dad after all.

It had now been over forty-eight hours, and she still hadn't seen him. First, she was angry with him. How could

he do this to her? Then she grew worried. What if something had happened to him? Would anybody know to look
for her in here? The thought made her sick to her stomach,
and she almost *did* throw up.

She shook her head. No, that couldn't be the case. Her
mom or somebody would know to look for her, would figure
out about this room. Her dad's parents lived in Florida, and
her mother's in California. They had to know about the safe
room, right? They'd come get her.

If they knew she was here.

Grabbing the remote, she switched channels. She found
a repeat of an NCIS episode and she began watching it. But
soon she grew bored again, staring off into space. Her mind
kept going back to the Baldacci novel that she'd finished the
day before. The main character had outwitted people
several times, but he'd also fought his way out of dangerous
situations. She sat back and crossed her arms. Would she
have to resort to fighting her father? But with what?

Getting up, she looked around the room again, but it
was pointless. No matter how many times she searched, she
didn't find a weapon, nothing could help get her out of this
situation. She couldn't even break a dish or something—
there were only paper plates and plasticware to eat with,
and not a glass bottle anywhere in the room. Brooke opened
the cupboards and drawers again. Canned goods. She
picked up a can of green beans. She could throw it at him,
but would it knock him out, or just make him mad? There
were no cleaning supplies, nothing like that to strike him
with or blind him. And when she thought about it, she
didn't want to permanently hurt him. As she continued
looking around, she found a heavy-duty flashlight in a
drawer. She flicked it on. It still worked. Maybe she could
try to blind him when he opened the door.

She put the flashlight back and returned to the couch.

Brooke was watching TV when she heard the bolts in the door slide back. She stood up as the door opened, all her plans forgotten. Her dad stepped into the room, but he stayed by the door.

"Were you just going to leave me in here?" she snapped at him. "It's Saturday. I want to go out with my friends."

Connor scowled at her. "Not now, Brooke. I've got too much going on."

She'd never seen her dad look the way he did now. His hair, usually neatly combed, was tussled. Dark circles hung under his bloodshot eyes, and he looked haggard.

"What's wrong with you?" she asked.

He glanced around the room before answering. "Are you doing okay?"

Brooke put her hands on her hips. "As well I can be doing locked in this room." She filled her voice with sarcasm.

He looked at her for a moment, then said, "Okay, as long as you're all right."

It was as if he hadn't heard anything she'd said. Suddenly, she saw red.

"You can't keep me in here! This is child abuse! As soon as I get out of here, I'm going to report you to social services and whatever other agencies I can. I'll call the news, too. They'd *love* to hear about this!"

"Shut up," he said.

She kept yelling. "Where's Mom? I want to talk to her."

Her dad sighed. "This will all be over soon." He took a step toward the door, and she ran toward him.

"Let me out of here!" she yelled.

As she approached, he turned, raised his hand, and slapped her. Brooke stopped dead in her tracks, stunned.

His eyebrows formed an angry line as he glared at her. Her cheek burned, and she placed her palm against the spot he'd hit.

"How could you do that?" she said.

His face contorted. "Don't make more trouble for me."

Before she knew it, he was out the door. It slammed shut, and the bolts locked into place. Brooke was alone again.

She went to the bed, curled up in a ball, and cried. After a long time, she stopped, rolled over, and sat up. She looked around the room, thinking about her dad. She'd never seen him like that. He seemed unhinged, and it scared her.

After a minute, she went into the bar area and ate a granola bar. Then she opened the drawer and stared at the flashlight. Picking it up, she found that it was heavier than she'd thought. She looked toward the door. Her dad would come back again, at some point. And Brooke was going to have to do something now, something serious. Even if it meant hurting him.

CHAPTER THIRTY-FOUR

The rookie agent turned another corner, and Jo slowed down as they neared her holding cell. He didn't notice, and she stepped back onto his foot. It wasn't enough to hurt, especially with her feet bare, but it was enough to distract him, just for a second. He glanced down, and the Glock wavered. She spun to her left, then chopped the palm of her hand against the side of his neck. A brachial stun, a blow with just enough force to knock him out for a few seconds. His eyes went up in his head, and he dropped to the floor, his gun nearby. She grabbed it and whacked his head harder. Now he was out cold.

Her breath came in quick gasps as she dropped to a knee, the Glock aimed down the hall. No one seemed to have heard the disturbance, but she didn't have much time. He'd be expected back at any moment.

Jo quickly searched his pockets. His driver's license identified him as Joseph Lockwood. He had no other badge or ID. He was wearing a Suunto tactical watch that had GPS capabilities. She knew the brand—watches were popular with law enforcement, and with military and

Special Forces personnel. Even in a less-than-ideal location, people knew good watches. Rolexes and the like. A good watch could be an operational gift, something toward building rapport and earning trust. A watch had perceived inherent value, and many brands were recognized worldwide. They could be traded for information, or even shelter, a ride, or a vehicle.

She slipped the watch off his wrist and glanced right. Another hall, which she took. She passed a couple of closed doors, checking both. Locked. Tiptoeing on bare feet to a heavy-duty door at the end of the hall, she tried the knob. It turned. Jo bent down and opened the door. Clear night air greeted her. She slipped out and crouched down, looked around, and listened.

Nothing.

The structure she'd just exited was in a clearing surrounded by woods. Faint shadows danced from moonlight slipping through huge trees. A breeze whispered in the leaves. She let her eyes adjust to the darkness, then scanned the small clearing. She couldn't tell if there were video cameras around, or if someone might be watching from inside the building. If she ran, she could be seen. But she also knew she couldn't stay where she was. It would only be a short time before somebody found the agent she'd taken down.

Risking exposure, she ran across the clearing and darted into the trees. No shots came as she crouched down again behind a large oak. It shielded her as she looked back to a long, single-story structure with dark siding and blacked-out windows. Nearby was another small building, probably a garage. Nothing else, and no movement. A road led away from the building.

Jo had no idea where she was, just west of the DC area.

Whoever had taken her wouldn't want to be away from their resources, and from Connor Whigby. Regardless, she was on foot with no shoes. For her, it was a long way to go.

A gust of wind rustled branches as she moved quietly into the woods. She checked the watch for her bearings and began jogging. The road that led to the building was nearby, and she ran parallel to it, staying in the shelter of the woods. She scanned in all directions. Her ears were alert. She ignored the occasional sharp footfall on her bare feet, but with every step, she was afraid she was making too much noise.

After a minute, Jo stopped and looked back. The building had vanished from view. She hurried on, her heart racing. When she'd covered about half a mile, she paused again. As her breathing evened, she heard something. Ducking down, she listened.

Movement behind her. Had they discovered the fallen agent and realized she'd escaped?

Jo snuck forward in a crawl and tried not to make any noise. She came across a rock outcropping and crept around it, then looked back. At first, she saw nothing. Then a well-built man clad in black moved stealthily around a tree. He was good, barely noticeable. Her gaze swiveled back and forth, but she didn't see anybody else. When she looked for the man again, he was gone.

After a few minutes of silence, she started to move but thought better of it. Might reveal her position. The night was deathly calm. Then she saw the slightest movement, closer now. The man was within feet of her, a gun in his hand. He saw the rock outcropping, squatted down, and approached. She thought about taking a shot at him, but the gunfire would alert any others to her location. Pulling back, she waited.

As the man rounded the rock, Jo leaped out, grabbed his wrist, and twisted his arm away from her. He grunted and dropped the pistol. He was fast, and he threw himself on her. She dodged a fist, but as she stepped backward, his foot hooked her leg, and they tumbled to the ground. He was bigger than her, but that didn't necessarily mean he had the advantage. She was trained in martial arts, and she was good. Better than good.

They struggled silently for a moment, and then Jo adjusted. She threw her left leg around the man's neck as he tried to hit her. In another quick motion, she threw her right leg over her left, trapping his arm against his body. Then she squeezed. The man gasped and struggled. He mumbled something that sounded like "not yet," but she kept the pressure on. Finally, he stopped resisting and went still.

Jo kept holding him, wary that he might be faking. When she was sure he'd passed out, she released him and quickly pushed him away. He'd be out for a while. She got to her feet and listened. Were those voices? She couldn't be sure. If he'd come from the building, there had to be other agents searching for her.

She bent down and felt through her assailant's pockets. He had a car remote key fob on a ring with other keys and some change in his right front pocket. She stuffed it into her jeans, then found his phone in his other front pocket. Jo took that as well.

She pulled a wallet from his back pocket and opened it. An ID and a credit card, both in the name of Kent Jacobs. There was no badge from any government organization. She checked his watch. A gold Vostok Komandirskie. Jo stared at him for a second. Was he with whoever had held her? She shrugged, memorized the address on the ID, then took the cash in the wallet and tossed it aside.

Using his own shoelaces, she tied him up, then ripped his shirt and stuffed a piece of it into his mouth. Finally, she took a moment to study his appearance. He had short-cut blond hair and a narrow face. She hadn't seen him before, but she wanted to know more about him. If he wasn't with the feds, who was he working for? Nothing about him answered that question yet.

Without wasting any more time, Jo dropped to one knee and pulled off his shoes and socks. He had bigger feet than her, so she rolled up the socks and stuffed them in the toes of the shoes, then put them on. It wasn't the best fit, but it would work.

She peeked around the rock outcropping and saw no one. For the moment, the woods were quiet. She found his pistol, a Sig P220 with a suppressor, stuffed it in the small of her back, then jogged toward the road, ignoring the discomfort in her feet. She made good progress, keeping to the edge of the trees, and had gone another half mile when she saw a fork in the road. Following it to the right, she eventually came upon a dark, four-door sedan that she assumed belonged to Jacobs. No other cars were around.

Jo approached carefully, holding the Sig P220 low. She waited and watched, and when she detected no movement in or around the car, she used the key fob and unlocked it. The sound brought no reaction, so she walked up cautiously and got in. She rifled through the center console and glove box but found nothing. The car started smoothly, and she put it into gear and headed down the road.

Her sigh of relief was short-lived.

As she passed the fork in the road, a dark SUV with tinted windows pulled in behind her. There'd be men inside, perhaps the ones who had interrogated her, and they would no doubt be armed.

Jo didn't panic, didn't hit the gas and immediately try for an escape. Instead, she gripped the wheel and thought about her best move. It was almost pitch black, and the road was deserted—no cars, houses, or other buildings around. She glanced in the rearview mirror. The SUV was closing the gap, headlights bright as it neared her sedan.

She slammed on the brakes. Tires screeched as the SUV shuttled toward her car, but before it hit her, it veered to the side. She punched the gas, and the sedan shot forward. Jerking the wheel to the right, she collided with the front side of the SUV. It careened off the road, hit a guardrail, and flipped into a ditch with a loud crash. She righted the sedan, pressed the gas pedal to the floor, and sped away.

A few miles ahead, Jo turned on the car's GPS system, then pulled up Kent Jacobs's address, in Falls Church, Virginia. She headed in that direction, but she knew whoever had interrogated her would be looking for the car now. When she passed a Metro station, she abandoned the car, but not before memorizing the license plate number.

She put both pistols in her waistband and covered them with her untucked shirt, then went into the station and purchased a fare to take her to Falls Church. The few people around didn't pay her much attention. As she waited for the train, the cell phone she'd taken from the man in the woods buzzed with a number she didn't recognize. She was tempted to answer, but then whoever was on the other end would know that Jacobs had been compromised. She put the phone back in her pocket and boarded the next train.

She had to transfer a couple of times, and when she reached her destination, she took extra precautions to make sure no one was following her. Jacobs's phone buzzed again, the same number. Again, she ignored it. Once she got her bearings, Jo walked the few blocks to the three-story apartment building where Jacobs apparently lived. She didn't know how long it would be before he returned, whether he'd even been found in the woods yet, so she hurried.

The building had a small lobby with a security door. She perused the bank of intercom buttons, found Jacobs's apartment, and pressed the buzzer. When no one answered, she tried again, then pulled out the keys she'd taken from him. One opened the door. A musty smell greeted her, but no alarms went off.

Jo walked quietly down a hallway, found a stairwell, and climbed to the third floor. She opened the door carefully and peeked out. The hallway was brightly lit, and empty. She walked down to Unit 301, trying keys again until she found one that fit the doorknob and deadbolt.

Opening the door, she slipped inside.

CHAPTER THIRTY-FIVE

Jo pressed herself against the wall, held up the Sig P220, and listened.

The apartment was quiet, and she smelled nothing. Light filtered in through a window. The living room was sparsely decorated with a couch, a coffee table, and a TV sitting on a small entertainment center. When it remained quiet, Jo quickly checked the small kitchen, bathroom, and a bedroom. No one was around, so she went back into the living room. She didn't know how much time she had before Kent Jacobs or someone else showed up, and her heart thumped as she closed the window blinds and turned on her phone flashlight. She began searching for anything that might tell her more about Jacobs.

Moving to the couch, she checked under the cushions but found nothing. The only thing on the coffee table was the TV remote. Jo glanced around the room. Not a single painting or picture hung on the walls, and the entertainment center was empty. There were no photos, souvenirs, or knick-knacks of any kind.

She checked the kitchen cupboards and drawers. Some

prepackaged oatmeal, boxes of granola bars, and a few canned goods. Coffee grounds and powdered cream sat in a cupboard above a coffee pot on the counter next to the refrigerator. Jo opened the refrigerator and looked inside. Bottled water and Gatorade. The freezer had a few packaged meals and nothing else. Why did Jacobs have so little to eat? Was he just a bachelor living alone?

Jo shelved that thought and moved on. One drawer held some silverware, and another cupboard had dishes, not even a full set. She opened the dishwasher, and a musty odor emanated from that. Checking under the sink, she found only a few paper bags and a single bottle of dish soap and a rag. As she glanced around, blank white walls loomed back at her. It felt more like an abandoned office than a home.

Hearing a noise outside, she tiptoed to the window and peeked between the blinds. A fire escape led to a parking lot below, but Jo didn't see any movement, and no more sound came. She turned and checked the table. A power cord was plugged into the wall, but there was no sign of the laptop that it seemed to go with. Not even a mouse or mousepad.

The bathroom was next. The usual stuff—washcloth, aspirin, some Band-Aids—but two toothbrushes. Drawers in the sink cabinet held shaving cream and a razor, men's and women's deodorant, a comb and brush, flower-scented lotion, pink nail polish, and nail polish remover.

Did a woman live here as well?

The cell phone in her pocket vibrated again, the same number. She debated answering, then silenced it and tiptoed to the bedroom. A mattress on a box spring was centered against the wall opposite the door, a cheap dresser standing against one of the side walls. A few clothes, nothing else. A black duffel bag sat on the floor, and she bent down and opened it. Inside were a flashlight, men's jeans, a dark T-shirt, tennis shoes, and socks.

Jo stood up and turned back to the room. As expected, nothing on the walls. She looked down at the bed. The sheets were rumpled, but there was no comforter, no throw pillows. Did a human being actually live here? The place seemed like nothing more than a flophouse for Jacobs. And given the few feminine items in the bathroom, possibly a woman as well. Jo frowned. Who was she dealing with?

After a last look around, she returned to the living room, got down on her hands and knees, and peered under the couch. Nothing. She stood and studied the room. She'd found nothing to tell her who this man was. But he lived sparsely, and that was telling.

Her thoughts were interrupted by the faintest sound. She looked toward the door. Someone was slipping a key into the lock.

Jo quickly moved to the side of the door, Sig P220 at the ready, and held her breath.

CHAPTER THIRTY-SIX

Connor Whigby stood in his kitchen, feeling utterly hopeless and terrified. Things were unraveling fast. He was planning his next moves, but he had to be careful. At some point, his lies would be exposed. He frowned. If he could only stay one step ahead of everyone, they'd be okay. Right?

He stared into space for a moment, and then his worries were interrupted by his ringing phone. He glanced at the number, let out a huge sigh, and answered.

"Hello, Senator. How are you?"

"I'm sorry to bother you so late, Connor." Her voice was smooth, the apology insincere. She was used to getting what she wanted, when she wanted it.

"It's no problem."

Macintosh asked a couple of questions about a few meetings for the upcoming week, then said, "Is everything all right with you?"

Connor wasn't sure how to respond. "Of course. Why would you ask that?"

"You seem a little stressed lately."

He took another beat. "I'm fine. I just . . . haven't slept well the last few days."

"Are there any problems at home?"

That was direct. Connor gulped.

"Of course not, Senator. Thank you for asking, though."

Macintosh rarely asked about his personal life. There were too many other things for her to worry about.

"Well, you have a good night. I'll see you tomorrow."

"Right."

Connor ended the call and set the phone down next to the burner that he'd purchased after his meeting with Irena Garin. She'd told him to get it, and she had more instructions for him. He'd tried to placate her, but he wasn't sure how much she believed. How long could he hold her off before she suspected him of lying to her?

The senator was suspicious, too, and that was a huge problem. Especially now that things had taken the turn that they had. Macintosh was asking too many questions. Connor was answering as best he could without letting her know what was really going on, but she was no fool; she hadn't gotten to the position she was in without knowing a thing or two.

He touched the burner phone. If the senator knew about Garin, she still wouldn't know what he'd told her. He'd been careful, had only used the burner phone to contact the woman, only called her when he was outdoors and away from other people.

Connor glanced around the kitchen. There had to be bugs in here, somewhere, but he didn't know where. They were listening. At some point, they would come to ask him questions, to find out where Fran and Brooke were. What would he tell them?

Brooke. He hadn't checked on her in a couple of days.

He couldn't face her, and the guilt about that . . . he shook his head. He was going to have to do something about her. That fight, how angry she'd been—Connor hadn't meant to hit her, but she didn't understand what was going on, how she *had* to stay in the room. It was truly the only safe place for her right now.

After a few more minutes of staring into space, Connor went upstairs. He lay down on his bed, but sleep didn't come. His mind kept racing.

He had to resolve things, and fast.

CHAPTER THIRTY-SEVEN

The apartment door opened, and a sliver of light burst into the room. Jo remained perfectly still, the Sig P220 ready. The light grew, along with the shadow of a person in the doorway. Jo counted a beat, but nothing happened. The person, about Jo's height and size, moved a couple of steps into the room, holding a gun up.

Jo held her breath.

The figure stepped forward and closed the door, and the room plunged into shadows. A faint cigarette smell drifted in the air. As the person moved, Jo lashed out and knocked the gun away, then swiped the person's legs. The person hit the floor hard. Jo kicked the gun away and stared into the shadows.

"Irena Garin," Jo said.

Irena got to her knees, and Jo studied her. Instead of a business suit, she wore black khakis and a black long-sleeved shirt. Her dark hair was tucked into a baseball cap.

"Stay down and keep your hands where I can see them," Jo ordered her.

Irena held her arms away from her sides, staring at Jo.

She kept the Sig trained on Irena, then stepped to the door and listened. Nothing. She locked it and turned back to the woman.

"Turn your pockets inside out," Jo said. "Carefully."

Irena eased one hand into her pocket, pulled out a phone, and dropped it to the floor. She had money in another pocket, and she tossed that away as well. Jo nodded, and Irena slid the phone toward her. The room was quiet, just the sounds of their heavy breathing.

"Get up slowly," Jo said. "Hands where I can see them."

Irena carefully got to her feet, keeping her hands out in front of her.

"Back into the kitchen."

Irena did as she was instructed, and then Jo had her sit in a chair in the corner, with the table between them. That way, Irena couldn't get a straight lunge at her. The woman put her hands on her thighs.

"You weren't expecting me," Jo observed, keeping her gun trained on Irena.

"Where is Kent?" Her voice was thick with anger.

As Jo looked at her, she was putting the pieces into place. Jacobs and Irena Garin had a connection; they were probably working together. And if Jacobs knew that Jo had been taken by the agents to that house in the woods, that meant he'd likely been following her since she'd left the Hotel Clarion after first talking to Irena. Jo chided herself for her own carelessness. She'd been so focused on Connor Whigby and who had been tailing him, and making sure she wasn't followed by those same people, that she'd missed being followed by Irena's people. She wouldn't be so careless now.

Irena glanced around. "What have you done to him?"

Jo's mind raced. Irena hadn't heard from Jacobs, so she'd

come here. But did she have backup? Probably, which meant Jo didn't have much time.

"Jacobs works for you," Jo said quickly.

Irena nodded. "Not too hard to figure out."

"You're not a private investigator." Irena didn't answer. Jo thought about the feminine items in the apartment. "You live here, too?"

Irena gave only a tiny smile, and Jo knew she'd guessed wrong.

"Who are you?" Jo asked.

"You know my name."

She kept thinking fast. "Jacobs was way too skilled to be just someone helping a private investigator. And he wore a Russian military watch."

"So?"

Something else occurred to Jo. "He said something about 'not yet.' Or maybe it was 'nyet.'"

Irena stared at her.

Jo waved a hand around to encompass the apartment. "This place is almost empty. No personal effects, nothing to indicate a permanent residence, or roots being put down. That's the behavior of a spy."

Irena sniffed again. "'Spy' has such a negative connotation."

"What would you prefer?"

"Spies deal in information." She smiled.

Jo narrowed her eyes. "Jacobs is Yuri Orlov."

Irena didn't hide her irritation. "Where is he?"

"Jacobs?"

"Orlov," Irena finally said.

"I don't know."

"Who are you working for?" the woman asked.

Jo shook her head, ignoring the question. "You

concocted that story at the hotel, that Yuri Orlov was a businessman who was missing, because you wanted to see if I'd heard of him."

"I had to find out what you knew." Irena's eyebrows turned down in anger. "But I obviously couldn't tell you who he was."

"You have now."

Irena shrugged. "It doesn't matter."

"Are you with FSB?" She didn't answer, and Jo went on. "What's your interest in Connor Whigby?"

"He works for Senator Macintosh."

Jo stared at her. "And he's selling you information, correct?"

Another small smile. "Possibly."

"Why were you following me?" Jo asked.

Irena blinked at her. "We have to know what you know."

She shrugged. "I don't know anything."

"I find that hard to believe," the woman said. "You've been far too involved, and you are far too disruptive, to have such simple motives."

Irena hadn't asked about Brooke. Jo's brow furrowed.

"Why haven't you made a move on Connor Whigby?" she asked.

"We will when the time is right," Irena replied.

Another puzzle piece fell into place. Connor Whigby hadn't given this woman what she needed.

Irena's phone rang in the living room, and she glanced that way. "If I'm not heard from soon, people will come to handle the situation."

Jo knew the "situation" was her.

Irena spoke, her voice eerily calm. "If we don't get what we want, Whigby's daughter is dead."

Something else clicked into place.

The phone stopped ringing.

"Where's Fran?" Irena asked.

Jo looked at her. "Connor's wife? Why do you want to know about her?"

Irena glanced away, then said, "You have no idea who you're dealing with. It's only a matter of time before we get what we need, and we'll disappear without a trace."

Something wasn't right. Irena was giving her information too easily. It was the same as at the hotel. Irena was hoping she would slip up, and she also figured Jo wouldn't be a threat. And Jo had given her one thing, too. She didn't know where Fran Whigby was.

Jo was about to ask about Fran, but she stopped. They heard it at the same time—a noise at the door. Someone was trying a key in the lock.

Irena yelled something in Russian as a man burst through the door. He saw Irena on the chair, then Jo. But Jo was too fast. She opened the kitchen window as he raised a gun with a suppressor, and went out headfirst. A bullet chased after her, hitting the windowsill. She tumbled onto the fire escape, and the Glock that was in her waistband clattered away. Righting herself, Jo raced down the ladder. She glanced up and saw the man at the window. He aimed at her, but she knew he wouldn't risk another shot. Bad line of sight, and a body on the fire escape would draw unwanted attention. Plus, Irena didn't have what she needed just yet.

His head disappeared from view. Jo reached the second floor and dropped lightly to the ground. She aimed the Sig up toward the apartment window, but no one was there. She sprinted around a corner to the back of the building and crossed the street. Voices sounded on the other side, drawing nearer. She cut between two houses, scaled a fence, and ran through a back yard. Pausing by a gate, working to even her breathing, she listened.

A car in the distance, then nothing.

Jo opened the gate and snuck along the side of the house to the front. The street was quiet, but she waited a while, then disappeared into the night.

CHAPTER THIRTY-EIGHT

I t was almost two in the morning when Jo found her way to an overpass where several homeless people had camped out. A few people gave her cautious looks and avoided her, but most were already asleep. She was aware of the irony, her telling Brooke that she didn't want to end up on the streets, and here Jo was. But she couldn't go back to the rented SUV. If it hadn't already been towed, Irena and her people would at least have known about it and possibly searched it. And if not the Russians, Borland and his people may have found the car by now. Borland also would've had time to trace calls from Jo's prepaid phone. If he'd found her fake IDs and credit cards, he would've found her new motel room as well, so there was no way Jo could take a chance on going there, either. She could have found a cheap motel, one where they didn't care if you paid cash, but she wanted to hang on to the rest of the money that she'd taken from Yuri Orlov's wallet.

Something else was on her mind as well. Her surveillance equipment was in the rental car, so she would no longer be able hear what was going on at the house. She swore to herself at that unfortunate turn of events.

It was hot and humid, even this late. Jo found a spot away from the other people and rested her back against a concrete pillar. She had the Sig P220 tucked in her waistband, and she made sure her shirt covered it. Then she closed her eyes. She slept fitfully, wary of her surroundings, alert to both immediate dangers and the possibility that Irena and her people might be after her.

When the sun came up, Jo crept out from under the overpass. Making sure she hadn't been followed, she walked to a Metro station and got on a train. She hadn't showered in a couple of days, and she knew she smelled, but there was nothing she could do about it at the moment. She was careful that no one saw the gun as she rode to Crystal City, an area she was well-familiar with.

Jo had to wait a while for stores to open, but she found a Starbucks and went inside. It was crowded, but the bathroom was free. She spent a few minutes cleaning up as best she could, then got in line and ordered coffee and a ham and cheddar croissant. Taking a seat at a table outside, she ate ravenously. Then she walked to a Walmart, which had just opened, and used the last of Orlov's cash to buy another prepaid phone.

When it was all set up, she walked a few blocks to make sure she hadn't picked up a tail, then used the video calling.

"Where have you been?" Dack's blue eyes filled with concern, and she imagined his voice full of worry.

"Everything I have has been compromised," Jo said.

"What's going on?"

The sun was warm on her back as she stood on a street corner and told him what had happened since the last time they'd talked.

"You know what I missed?" she said. "Fran Whigby isn't around. Brooke said that she was out of town, that she's out of town a lot. But when I talked to Senator Macintosh, she asked about Connor and Brooke, but she didn't bring up Fran. Why?" Dack let her work out her reasoning. "She works at the Department of Defense, so she must have top-secret clearance. And Irena Garin brought up Fran as well. Was it just to see what I'd say?"

"She was fishing for information?"

"Yes. And when I didn't have any, she clammed up." Jo thought again. "What information Irena gave me came too easily. She wanted to see what I would say."

"You don't know who picked you up at the senator's house and took you to that building in the woods?"

Jo shook her head. "It wasn't the feds. Maybe the CIA, or someone more covert."

"Whoever it is, they've been trying to trace this number," Dack said.

She stared at him. "You're sure it's safe?"

He waved a hand, then typed. "Yes. You don't have to worry about that." He looked at her. "You're okay?"

Jo nodded and pursed her lips. "Brooke's in danger. Irena threatened her." She felt her eyes grow wide. "What if Connor put her in the safe room not to punish or harm her, but because he's trying to protect her?"

Dack thought about that and nodded. "If so, he's gotten himself in way over his head." He studied her. "This isn't just about Brooke anymore, is it?"

The man knew her too well.

"They kept me locked up overnight," she said. "I'm pissed, and I want to get to the bottom of this."

"Of course you do."

"In order to do that, I need money. And I need a new ID. Can you help with that?"

"You know I can," Dack said. "I can get you cash, a new ID, and a credit card."

"How long will it take?"

He smiled. "I've got a guy. He's good. I'll contact him as soon as we get off the phone. You can be up and running within an hour."

"That's great."

"Do you want other guns?"

Jo shook her head. "I'll stick with what I have."

"You need to rent another car."

"Yes."

Neither one said anything for a moment.

"What are you going to do next?" Dack finally asked.

She'd been thinking about her next move ever since she'd left Orlov's apartment.

"I need to talk to Connor Whigby, but I can't call him or go to his house. They're watching him, and I'm sure his house has other bugs, not just mine. They've got to be tracking his phone calls, too. I'll probably have to follow him in a disguise, then approach him carefully."

"It's Sunday. He won't be at work."

Jo considered that for a moment. "I don't know what he'll be doing today. He'll have to go to work tomorrow, though. He can't risk anything not seeming normal."

"Let me help you."

Not a chance. "You've risked too much already. Just help me with the money and ID, and that'll be enough."

Dack's eyes crinkled with humor and irritation. "You are one stubborn woman."

She stared at him. "And that's served me well."

He hesitated, then typed slowly. "I know."

She shouldn't have said that. He knew what she meant. Jo had gotten them into the situation that had almost cost him his life, that had cost him his speech. But her stubbornness was also what had gotten him rescued. She looked at him, and her face softened.

"Call me back when I can get the ID and money."

Jo ended the call before he could argue with her. She walked the streets until she found a park, then sat on a bench in the shade. While she waited, she googled the nearest car rental agency.

Just under an hour later, Dack called back.

"Where are you?"

She told him, and he nodded.

"Stay there. In about twenty minutes, you'll see a white SUV. My guy'll have money, a credit card, and an ID for you. He can take you to a rental car place."

Jo shook her head. "I'll get there myself."

He knew better than to argue. "Let me know how it goes."

She nodded. "When it's safe, I will."

Dack ended the call with a smile. The screen went blank.

As promised, about twenty minutes later, a white SUV pulled to the curb at the far end of the park. Jo watched for a minute, then walked up to it. The passenger window rolled down, and a man in dark clothes and matching sunglasses held up a small bag. Jo took it without a word.

She stepped back, and the window rolled up and the SUV drove off.

When the car turned the corner, she checked the bag. Dack had given her several hundred dollars in cash, a few IDs with her picture but different names, and credit cards to match each one. She stuffed them all in her pockets and tossed the bag in a nearby trash can. Then she took the Metro to a Hertz Rent-A-Car and got another SUV.

Once on the road, she drove to a Walmart for new clothes, toiletries, and binoculars. From there, it was on to a sleazy motel where no one would question her paying cash for a room.

Feeling refreshed after cleaning up and changing clothes, she stopped at a café for a quick but big lunch, then headed to the Whigbys' neighborhood, where she spent the day watching the house. She didn't have the burner phone to listen to the bugs, though, and she decided not to risk sneaking to the back. It was likely being watched still, and she couldn't afford to get caught. She was stuck, though, without knowing if Connor was at home. The afternoon dragged on, and she fought boredom. Finally, later in the evening, his silver Lexus drove up and went into his garage. She sighed. A day wasted.

But tomorrow was Monday, and she knew he'd have to go to work at the Capitol Building. At some point, he would leave, and she would be waiting for him. He had explaining to do, because everything pointed to one person.

Fran Whigby.

CHAPTER THIRTY-NINE

On Monday morning, Jo followed Connor from his house to the Capitol, watching all day for a chance to talk to him alone.

The opportunity presented itself that evening. A little after five, Connor, Macintosh, and a few other people left the Capitol and walked to the senator's car. Jo was parked nearby and followed as the SUV drove to the same expensive restaurant that she'd visited before. The bodyguard that Jo had encountered with the senator was with the group, and she took evasive measures to make sure he didn't spot her.

The group pulled up to the valet stand, and Jo found a metered space around the corner, where she could still see the restaurant. The group was seated near a window. Jo pulled out the binoculars she'd purchased at Walmart. They took their time eating, and when the meal was almost over, Connor got up and headed toward the front, where the restrooms were located.

Jo hopped out of the vehicle and dashed across the street. She entered the restaurant lobby just as he disappeared into the men's room. Smiling at the hostess, she indicated she needed to use the facilities before being seated. Jo tried the door.

Locked.

She faced away from the men's room and counted the seconds. She glanced over her shoulder, hoping Connor didn't exit. Suddenly, the women's restroom door opened and a woman walked out. Jo darted past her into the restroom, then peeked out the door. When Connor emerged from the men's room, she opened the door, grabbed him by the shirt, and yanked him in to the women's restroom. It all happened so fast, he didn't have time to say a word. She locked the door and stared at him. Now he was blustering.

"What're you doing?" he said, a panicked look on his face.

His brow furrowed as he seemed to realize he'd seen her before, but he couldn't place where. She pressed him up against a wall.

"Who are you?" he asked.

"Shut up!" she hissed. "You need to listen to me, and listen fast. I know about the trouble you're in, both with the feds and with Irena Garin."

His jaw dropped, and he squirmed against her grip. "Please don't do anything to me."

She clamped a hand over his mouth.

"We don't have much time, so listen to me!" she repeated. "Go to Folger Park at nine o'clock tonight and wait on the corner of D Street and Second."

Someone tried to open the door. When they found it was locked, they started pushing on it. Connor glanced toward the door.

Jo shook him. "Are you hearing me? Folger Park at nine o'clock. Walk there, don't drive. Leave your phones at the

office, and don't wear your suit jacket. Empty your pockets.
I need to make sure you're not bugged."

He stared at her, eyes wide. She shook him again.

"Why should I believe you?" he asked.

"Irena threatened your daughter."

Connor went pale, and he tried to say something.

"Do you understand me?" she said. "I'm here to help
you."

The door rattled again, and someone knocked. Connor's
lip trembled.

"If you want Brooke to live, don't say a word to anyone.
Okay?"

Jo moved her hand, and he opened his mouth. She
tensed, wondering if he would cry for help. He searched her
face and nodded.

"I won't say a word," he whispered.

"Good."

She let go of him, unlocked the door, and opened it. A
woman in a blue dress looked at them in surprise, then
frowned. Connor adjusted his tie and walked out of the
bathroom.

"Well I—" the woman started to say, indignation in her
voice.

Jo ignored her and stepped out of the bathroom,
glancing around the corner. The senator's bodyguard stood
near the table, watching. Connor was sitting down at his
table, and he forced a smile as the senator spoke to him. Jo
waited until the senator and the bodyguard looked the other
way before slipping out of the restaurant. She ran back to
her car and watched until the senator's party left. Connor
glanced around nervously, but he didn't spot Jo. When the
SUV pulled away from the curb, she left as well.

She had time to spare, so she drove away from the Capitol. She was almost certain she wasn't followed, and when she reached a quiet street, she got out and switched her license plates with some she'd stolen from a car in Crystal City that morning.

Jo found a street vendor and bought a hot dog, then drove to Folger Park. She had to drive around for a few minutes before a parking space freed up where she could see the corner of D Street and Second. Pulling in, she ate the hot dog while she waited.

A few minutes before nine o'clock, she saw Connor Whigby walk down D Street. He'd made the decision to meet her, but she didn't know if he'd told anyone about their encounter in the restaurant bathroom. That was a chance she'd have to take.

He crossed Second and stood near the street corner. Jo studied him through the binoculars. He wasn't wearing his coat, as instructed. He had sweat stains under his armpits, and his mouth was twisted up. It appeared as if he was trying to act casual, as if nothing was wrong, but his spine was stiff, and one hand opened and closed nervously.

Jo swept around with the binoculars. She didn't see anybody following him, but she was sure someone was there. She started the vehicle but kept the headlights off. After a few cars passed, she drove quickly to the corner. She braked hard, leaned over, and opened the passenger door. Connor looked at her in surprise.

"Get in!" she snapped.

He hesitated.

"I'm the only hope you've got," she snarled at him. There was no time for his reluctance. "If you want to stay alive, and you want your wife and daughter to stay alive, you'll listen to me."

He took a quick look around, then jumped into the car.

She sped off down the street, careened around the corner, then raced down another street. At a stoplight, she got into the left lane, and right before the light turned green, she hit the gas and shot through the intersection. A car in the oncoming lane turned after her. Jo glanced in the rearview mirror. No one was tailing her.

"You don't have your phone?" she asked.

Connor shook his head. "My pockets are empty. I don't even have money for Metro fare."

She snorted. "Don't worry, I'm not going to strand you."

"Who are you?" he asked. "What agency are you with?" He pressed himself into the door, as far away from her as he could get.

Jo glanced at him. "That seems to be what everybody's asking."

She drove farther away from the park, and when she was sure she hadn't been tailed, she pulled over on a side street and hopped out, quickly switching the license plates again and discarding the stolen ones in the grass. If someone had gotten the plate number when she was at the park, they'd be looking for a different car and owner.

"You didn't answer my question," Connor said when she got back in.

She spun the wheel and drove away. "I just happened to be at the wrong place at the wrong time." She laughed bitterly. "Or the right place at the right time, to keep your daughter safe."

"My daughter's okay."

She shook her head. "I know you have her locked in your safe room. And now I know why you did that."

"I'm not trying to hurt her." His voice choked up.

"I know," she said softly. "You're trying to protect her. But you're in a lot of trouble."

Connor stared at her. "You're not with an agency?"

She shook her head. "You wouldn't be here if you thought I was."

He closed his mouth and sat with that for a moment. "What do you know?"

"Where's Fran?"

"My wife? She's out of town," he said dully.

"Where?"

He took a long time before replying. "Up north."

"Irena Garin's looking for her, and so is everyone else. And until they find her, no one's making a move on you."

He nodded.

"Why do they want her?" she asked.

Connor bit his lip and stared out the windshield. Jo pulled into a shopping center parking lot, cut the engine, and turned to look at him.

"I need you to tell me everything."

He ran a hand across a creased forehead and stared at her with tired eyes. Then he drew in a deep breath. "I don't know how it all went so wrong."

CHAPTER FORTY

"My wife has been selling information to the Russians," Connor explained.

"I wondered about that," Jo said. "Everyone, from the feds to Irena Garin, has been avoiding asking questions about Fran. It's like they don't want to draw attention to her, to let me know anything."

"You talked to Irena?"

She nodded. "I saw how one of her men signaled you at Senator Macintosh's press conference the other night, and then I heard about your meeting with her. I was at the Hotel Clarion when you were there."

His eyes widened. "You knew about that? How?"

"I bugged your house."

"*You* broke into my house." He jabbed a finger at her.

"I had to know what was going on."

Connor didn't say anything for a moment. Jo checked the side and rearview mirrors, but she didn't see anyone suspicious. He looked down, thinking.

"How are you going to help me?" he finally asked.

"I need to know everything."

"Who are you?" He surveyed her. "You say you're not with an agency, but you seem to know exactly what you're doing. You've got . . . skills."

"I used to be in the Army, and I was with Civil Affairs. I've been on plenty of missions overseas." She spread her palms. "You can trust me, or you can face whatever's going on alone. Your choice."

He glanced away. "What did Irena say?"

"She concocted a story about how she was working with the daughter of a Russian businessman who'd gone missing. I didn't buy it."

"Smart."

"You've heard of Kent Jacobs?"

He grunted. "Don't you mean Yuri Orlov?"

"So you also figured out they're one and the same."

Connor nodded, but he looked so weary it seemed like an effort. "That man destroyed our lives."

"Tell me about it."

He fiddled with the seatbelt. "It all started a couple of years ago. We're having marital problems. I worked too much, and I was at the senator's beck and call. At least that's what Fran said." He threw up a hand. "Fine. That's all true. I haven't been around a lot, and I've been busy, both then and now. Fran complained, and then it seemed she got busier with her work, and she started going out of town on business."

"I know she works at the Department of Defense, but what does she do?"

"She's an analyst." He shrugged. "I know that's vague, but she can't say a whole lot, even to me. You know, top-secret clearance." He laughed, but it held no humor. "Whatever it was, it shouldn't have meant her needing to go out of town, but I bought it anyway. I didn't question it, in part because I was so busy, too. I didn't have time to think about her or what she was doing. Anyway, things went on like that for several months. We were both around for Brooke's activities, but we weren't there for each other."

He let out a heavy sigh. "Things came to a screeching halt about six months ago. Fran was supposed to be out of town for a few days, but she came home early. She was distraught, not herself at all. She'd snap at me, and she'd yell at Brooke. One night when Brooke was at a friend's, Fran and I had a huge fight. Everything came out then."

"Fran was having an affair with Kent Jacobs."

Connor gave a single nod, defeated. "If only it were just that, it'd be okay. We could've dealt with that. But she said she'd also been giving him top-secret information. I couldn't believe it. That wasn't like Fran at all. She'd always been so trustworthy. At least I thought so. And then she found out Kent Jacobs was really Orlov, and that he was a Russian spy."

"Fran really didn't know that Jacobs and Orlov were one and the same when she began the affair with him?"

It took him a second, but he shook his head. "No, and I believe her. She said it all started one night when I was working late. Brooke was with some friends, and Fran had gone out to dinner by herself. Orlov was sitting at another table, and he caught her eye. Have you seen Orlov?"

Jo nodded. "I saw Kent Jacobs's driver's license photo. He's good-looking."

Connor smirked. "Yes, he is. He was a charmer as well. He started talking to Fran, and she said he sensed that she was lonely and wanted someone to talk to. She said it was as if he knew everything about her, the right questions to ask, the right things to say, to get her talking." He tapped the dashboard. "I don't know how, but I'm sure the Russians knew to go after her, knew her position at the Department of Defense. Anyway, he played her well. At first, he just seemed to appear whenever she was out alone, and he told her it was because he worked at the Department of Defense as well. One thing led to another, and before she knew it, they ended up back at his apartment one evening." His voice was choppy and uneven as he talked about the affair. "She loved the attention, loved that someone thought she was special. It was everything that she wasn't getting from me." His shoulders sagged.

"When did she start giving him information?"

"A few months into the affair. Initially, he asked about her job and talked about his. They had to be careful, because according to him, they both had top-secret clearance. Like I said, he was a charmer. He worked her, first with general questions about her work, but then he got her to be more detailed. He steered her to conversations about terrorist cells in Eastern Europe, said he was curious, and she fell for it. A few weeks later, his questions grew more pointed, and she became concerned. Then he asked her something about the details of a mission in Belarus, things he shouldn't have known. She got a friend in the department to do some checking around, and she found out that Kent Jacobs didn't work there." His voice grew quieter. "That's when her world, and mine, fell apart. She spent days not knowing what to do. Things were so bad at home. She withdrew. Then we had that terrible fight, and I found out about the affair and everything with Jacobs." He ran a hand over his face. "I was stunned. It was bad enough to know that she'd had an affair, but then to find out she'd been giving away information . . ."

Jo checked their surroundings. No suspicious cars. "And then what?"

"It gets worse than that. You know I work for Senator Macintosh, right?"

She nodded.

"The senator is on the Senate Select Committee on Intelligence. She has access to all kinds of classified information about operations we have going on all around the world. Things that most Americans would be shocked about, if they really knew. There's a particularly dicey situation going on in Afghanistan right now. A little town that the Russians want to move in on."

"The senator mentioned Afghanistan the other night on the Capitol steps."

He cocked an eyebrow. "That's right, you were there. She couldn't get into any specifics, but suffice it to say, there's a lot more going on there than she said, has been for at least a couple of years. I'm privy to more information than you probably realize."

She shrugged. "That doesn't surprise me."

Connor collected his thoughts and went on. "When Fran and I argued about the affair and what she'd been telling Jacobs, I found out she had access to some of the same information as I had, that her work involved the US's particular dealings in Eastern Europe and Afghanistan. When she told me that, I couldn't believe what I was hearing. She was jeopardizing my career. If anybody found out what information the Russians were getting, it wouldn't be a stretch for them to think that I had given away those secrets. I was furious with Fran about that, that she'd threatened my career on top of our marriage."

"The senator is suspicious of you," Jo observed.

He nodded. "I don't know how, but she is. I've tried to deflect her questions, get her to trust me, but she doesn't."

"Does Macintosh know that you talked to me in the bathroom?"

He shook his head. "No. She's got some big meetings tomorrow, and she was too focused on that. She did ask me about you the other day."

"What did you tell her?"

"I told her I didn't know anything about you. I didn't know for sure if you were the same person that had come by my house, so it wasn't an outright lie."

"You know that you're being followed and your house is bugged by someone other than me?"

He reddened. "I probably should have figured that out sooner than I did, but I've been so focused on Fran and figuring out what to do that I missed that."

Jo considered everything for a second. "She ended the affair right then?"

Connor looked out the window, as if trying to focus on something else. "No, but there's a reason." His face contorted in anguish. "You have to understand, even with her admitting an affair, I loved her. I still do. I don't want anything to happen to her. And we knew that something would, both with our own government, and the Russians, if anybody found out. We talked through a bunch of options, and none of them seemed good. If she suddenly stopped seeing Jacobs, the Russians would know she'd found out about him, that he was a spy, and we didn't know if they would try to kill her. If our government found out what she was doing, she'd face prison and who knows what else. We finally came up with the plan." He shifted in his seat. "As much as it pained me, Fran would keep seeing Jacobs, but she would feed him false information. That would keep the Russians off our backs. In the meantime, we'd figure out a way for her to end the affair, and see about her transferring to another department."

"She still could've been caught by the feds, or someone else."

"Yeah."

"But your plan didn't work."

"No. Fran kept seeing Jacobs, and one time she overheard him talking on the phone, and heard someone call him Yuri. She was giving him false information, but the Russians must've figured that out. Yuri was irritated with Fran. He wasn't the charmer that she first met, and she was worried that he might kidnap her, or worse. She also suspected that someone at the DoD was checking into her, monitoring what she was doing. She was sure she'd be called in, that she'd be questioned, and certain she was being followed. We decided she needed to leave town."

"When was this?"

"The day before Brooke ran away. I withdrew money from the bank and gave it to Fran. She also took our handgun. She went to work like normal last Monday, and at the end of the day, she left her car in her usual place and took the Metro to a Greyhound bus stop. She bought a ticket to New York, but I know she didn't go there."

"Where'd she go instead?"

He sighed. "We used to vacation in a little town called Easton. It's on the eastern shore, across the Chesapeake Bay. Hot in the summer, but it's a quaint town. We haven't been there in a couple of years, but we figured it would be a good place for her to go. She'd get off the bus along the way to New York and hitchhike there. We knew people don't hitchhike much anymore, but Uber and Lyft don't take cash, and we weren't sure about cabs, or if a cabbie would drive her that far. Anyway, once she got to Easton, she'd stay at one of the little hotels."

"Do you know if she made it?"

Connor nodded. "We'd gotten prepaid phones to use, and she called me Monday night to let me know she was heading east." His voice cracked. "But I haven't heard from her in the last couple of days. I don't know what happened."

"If she was smart, she wouldn't use the phone anymore." He looked at her with a blank expression, so she explained. "You have who knows what federal agencies after you, and they have the resources to trace calls. They'll eventually figure out the burner phone number and pinpoint where she is."

Connor grimaced. "I hope it's just that, and that Yuri hasn't found her."

Jo again checked their surroundings to make sure no one was watching them. "Irena contacted you because she wants to know where Fran is?"

"Yes. She first contacted me the morning after Fran left and told me that if I didn't deliver Fran to her, that something would happen to Brooke." He sucked in a breath and let it out. "You have no idea the terror I felt when I came home Monday night and Brooke was gone. I thought the Russians had gotten her. I was so relieved when she showed up the next day, but I couldn't have her leave again. That's why I locked her in the safe room."

"That makes sense now."

"Does it?" he asked, his voice accusatory, but Jo could tell it was aimed at himself.

"What else did Irena ask you?"

"I told her that I needed time, that Fran was going to contact me soon. She threatened me, but she didn't do anything."

"She's hoping you'll lead her to Fran."

"I guess. Irena kept asking me questions about the terrorist cell in Afghanistan, too. It was like she wanted to verify what Fran had been passing along." He shuddered. "I don't know much, and I tried to placate her. I was so scared when I left that hotel room. She also gave me a prepaid phone to communicate with her, and she kept calling, asking me to tell her where Fran was. It's been horrible."

"Does Brooke suspect any of this?"

"She only knows something is going on between Fran and me, and in typical teenager fashion, she was letting us know how unhappy she is." He coughed. "Brooke is furious with me. And I . . . lost my temper with her. I slapped her."

Jo stared out the windshield. She'd been worried about Brooke and the possibility of abuse.

"Just the once?" she asked.

His chin jutted out. "I don't hit my daughter." He choked up. "It was just that time."

She believed him. "Stress makes people do funny things. And when she finds out that you were only trying to protect her, hopefully she'll understand."

"You don't know teenagers." He smiled sadly.

"I only know she was going to be in big trouble if she stayed in that park."

"Tell me what happened."

Jo told him about when she'd first seen Brooke with the other teenagers. "All I wanted to do was help her, and now I've been drawn into this mess."

"How could you possibly help now?"

She checked the mirrors again. "First thing we need to do is get you and Brooke to a safe place. Then I need to talk to Fran."

"I don't even know where she is."

"I'll find her."

"And then what?"

She locked eyes with him. "I know this isn't what you want, but the best thing is for her to turn herself in."

Connor shook his head. "She doesn't want to go to jail."

"That may be the least of her worries. She did break the law. If she's lucky and cooperates, maybe she can get a reduced sentence." Jo put a hand on his shoulder. "You know that's better than her ending up in the hands of the Russians."

Connor clenched his teeth and nodded. "I tried to tell her that, but she didn't want to listen. She thinks there might be another way, that somehow if she can help our side catch Yuri, then she can cut a deal." He was gripping his hands so tightly together, the knuckles had turned white. "I know she and I were drifting apart, but hearing about the affair was like a gut punch. I love her, but I'd just gotten so busy. Everything with the senator . . . I wasn't available for Fran then, but I am now. I have to help her make things right."

"By doing what?"

"We'd get Irena to believe Fran was gone. And then we were going to leave the country, start somewhere new. I don't want Fran to end up in jail, and I don't want Brooke to see her mom like that."

It was an unrealistic hope, but Jo could see how they'd want to try.

"What do we do now?" he asked.

"We need to get Brooke out of the safe room."

He shook his head. "She's furious with me. If I go down there now, she might try to run. And then what would I do?"

"I'll go with you."

"You think she'll cooperate with you?" He didn't hide his skepticism.

Jo tipped her head at him. "I helped her before, and she called me when you first locked her in the safe room. She was looking for me to rescue her."

"She trusts you," he muttered.

"Yes." Jo narrowed her eyes. "Now we have to figure out a way to get me into your house without anyone knowing."

"How are we going to do that?"

She started the car. "I have a plan."

CHAPTER FORTY-ONE

Brooke paced across the room.

One, two, three . . .

She kept counting as she walked from one wall to the other. The whole time, she stayed alert for any noise from the door.

She'd long since lost interest in TV. It seemed so mundane, so pointless. She hadn't eaten much either, and she knew that she had to fight the boredom. It was the enemy. She couldn't let apathy take over.

The anger she'd felt toward her dad had dissipated some. She was still mad at him, but clearly something was going on, something bigger than she'd realized before. Her dad wasn't himself. As she paced, she put a hand to her cheek. Her dad had never hit her before.

Never.

They'd had fights in the past, usually over something that she'd done wrong. But Connor had also been reasonable, willing to listen to her. At least until a couple of years ago. Things had gone downhill then. Her parents had grown distant, had hardly seen each other, and when they were together, they barely talked. They weren't happy.

She wondered if they were going to get a divorce. Brooke wasn't stupid. She could tell that things were wrong between them. However, even with all that, both her parents had come to her events, supported her at school, and never once had either one hit her. Something was definitely wrong.

Brooke had a lot of friends whose parents had divorced, and it had affected some of them. One friend had started drinking more; another had started eating and purging. She shook her head. If her parents divorced, that would mean shuttling between different homes. Would they have to leave this house? She liked it here, with her big bedroom and the pool. And her friend Val was close by.

Brooke continued to pace, count her footsteps, and listen. She had realized since she'd found the flashlight that she was going to have to do something she never would've imagined. She was going to have to hit her father, hopefully knock him out, and then escape the safe room. If she got out, she could call for help, not just for herself, but for him, too. She could find out what was really going on, what was really bothering him. And what had prompted him to keep her in here.

She kept pacing, and the time dragged on. Periodically, she rested on the couch, but nerves would take over, and she'd pace again. Finally, she heard keys in the deadbolts. Brooke raced to the door, shut off the light, and stood to the side. When her father came into the room, she would be hidden behind the door. And she would be ready.

Raising the flashlight, she tried to calm her nerves.

CHAPTER FORTY-TWO

"So what's your plan?" Connor asked as Jo drove out of the parking lot.

"Listen to me closely," she said. "I'm going to drop you off close to the Capitol. Whoever's involved in all this is going to be pissed that you evaded them, but I don't think they're going to act just yet. They still want to know what you know, and they'll hope you're going to lead them to Fran. You go inside, get your phone, your coat, and whatever else you need, and go to your car. Once you're there, you'll need to lose whoever starts following you. Do that by taking a series of right turns." She coached him on the rest of how to lose a tail. He listened carefully and nodded. "Once you're sure you've lost any surveillance, drive to Garfield Park. Wait near the corner of Third and South Carolina Avenue. I'll be waiting there. Turn off your headlights when you get close, pull up to the curb, and stop. Make sure the doors are unlocked. I'll hop in the back seat, and then you drive away."

He took it all in. "Won't someone start tailing me again?"

Jo nodded. "That'll happen. I just need long enough to hide in the back seat. Then you'll drive home, park in the garage, and no one will see us."

"You think that'll work?"

She let out a heavy sigh. "I hope so."

She wasn't going to tell him she wasn't at all sure if her plan would work. A lot of things had to go right. If not, they'd be exposed, and she wasn't sure what that would mean to him. Or her.

Connor lapsed into silence, his hands balled into fists on his lap. Jo stared out the windshield. She wasn't sure he could lose a tail, but he had to try. What else could they do?

Jo remained careful as she drove back toward the Capitol. As they neared First Street, she pulled over.

"I don't want to pick up a tail, so walk from here."

He put a hand on the door handle. "What happens if someone questions me?"

She stared at him. "Lie like you've never lied before. If you don't show in an hour or so, I'll leave the park. Then we'll figure out something else. Now go!"

Connor looked sick as he opened the door. She didn't wait to see what he would do, pulling right into traffic and driving away. She headed to Garfield Park, left her car on a side street, and walked through the park to a wooded area near Third and South Carolina.

She darted behind some trees and hid herself in bushes where she could watch the street. The clock in her head paced what Connor would likely be doing. Minutes later, his silver Lexus drove up, headlights off. He pulled to the curb but kept the car running.

Jo looked around and didn't see any other cars, so she emerged from the bushes and ran to the Lexus. She hopped in the back seat, closed the door, and crouched on the floor.

Connor hit the gas and turned the corner. Once he was away from the park, he turned on his headlights.

"Look straight ahead, pull out your cell phone, and act like you're talking to someone," she said.

He nodded and put his phone to his ear. Now they could talk.

"How'd it go?" she asked.

"Nobody was around my office. I saw a security guard and a few other people, but they barely paid any attention to me. I did have a tail when I drove out of the lot, but I did like you said, and I lost it." He glanced in the rearview mirror. "I don't see anybody just yet."

"Someone will pick up your car," she said. "It's just a matter of time."

"That's what I'm afraid of," he said.

His shoulders were stiff, and he gripped the steering wheel hard. His gaze kept darting to the rearview mirror.

"Don't worry about surveillance," she said. "Just drive home like you always do."

"What do I do when we get home?"

"Park in the garage and shut the door before you get out. Go inside and make sure all the blinds are closed, and that no one's there."

"Someone might've broken in?" Panic filled his voice.

"I doubt it, but you need to make sure. Turn the TV on loud, then come get me. But don't say anything."

"Don't worry, I won't."

"I'll walk with you down to the basement. You'll unlock the safe room door, then go back into the game room. I'll talk to Brooke, make sure she's calm, and then you can see her."

"Why not let her out?"

Jo shook her head. "Not yet. It's the only place in the

house that isn't bugged, the only place where we can talk in private."

She also knew she would have to be careful of him. He was acting as if he wanted her help, but it was possible he was trying to set her up. Jo had to make sure he couldn't lock her in the room as well.

"What do I say to Brooke?" he asked. "There's so much she doesn't know."

"You need to decide if you're going to let her know what Fran was doing."

Connor shook his head. "Fran didn't want to tell Brooke anything."

"I'm not sure you'll be able to shield her."

His gaze drifted off into the distance, and he didn't respond. "I'll be glad when this is all over," he finally said.

"This" encompasses a lot, Jo thought, but all she said was, "Just follow my instructions, and everything will be all right."

He nodded and put his phone back in his pocket. They drove to the neighborhood in silence. Connor kept his eyes straight ahead, and Jo watched as lights flashed by. She stayed huddled on the floor.

As he slowed down to turn onto his street, he said, "I think someone's following me."

"Don't worry about it," she said. "Drive into the garage like I told you."

He turned the corner and pulled into his driveway. He parked in the garage, and the door hummed closed.

"Ready?" he asked, his hand still on the wheel.

"Go on inside."

Connor got out and shut the door. Jo remained crouched in the back seat as he entered the house. A few minutes later, the door opened again. He stepped into the garage and shut the door behind him without a word. He signaled her, and she quietly opened the car door, stepped out, and eased the door shut. Then she followed Connor inside.

Jo kept in step with him as he crossed the kitchen and opened the basement door. They went downstairs, their footfalls in unison. Connor headed straight to the dark-paneled walls and pushed the section of paneling aside. He pulled out his keys as he crossed the short hallway, but paused at the safe room door and glanced at Jo. She nodded. He unlocked the deadbolts and stepped back into the game room.

She opened the door. The safe room was dark, and as she took a step in, she sensed that something was wrong.

CHAPTER FORTY-THREE

J o ducked instinctively, and she felt something pass by her shoulder. Light from the hall shone into the room, and she saw the outline of a figure nearby. She swept to her right where she knew Brooke was, connecting with the teenager's legs. Brooke fell to the floor, and Jo pounced on her. The girl let out a little gasp and began struggling.

"Let me go!" she said.

Jo was bigger, and she pinned Brooke's arms at her sides.

"It's me, Jo."

When Brooke recognized her, she quit struggling and burst into tears.

"I thought you'd never come!"

"I'm here now," Jo said.

She got to her feet and flipped on a light. Brooke sat up, still crying.

"I thought you were my dad. He's kept me locked in here, and I knew if I didn't do something, I'd never get out."

Connor came to the door. He hesitated, seeming unsure what to do as he looked down at Brooke. A tear rolled down his cheek. Jo was still wary of what he might do, and she motioned for him to enter the room. He started toward his daughter, and she held up a hand.

"What do you want from me?" she blubbered.

Connor dropped to a knee and enveloped her in a hug.

"I couldn't tell you," he said softly. "But I never meant to hurt you."

As he held her for a moment, Jo flashed to her own father, how he had been when she was growing up. Will was a strong man who kept his emotions to himself. She'd always known that he loved her, but he wasn't one to show it. Unfortunately, that connection had been frayed after her mother had gotten sick and then died. Jo didn't know what would happen if she saw her father now, what he would do and say to her. Would he understand the choices that she'd made, and care about her reasons? She shoved those thoughts to the side as Brooke and Connor stood up.

"What's going on?" Brooke asked as she wiped her cheeks. "Is this something with your job and the senator?"

Connor gestured for her to sit down on the couch, but he remained standing. Jo cracked the door open and stayed near it. He glanced at her for direction, and she shrugged. How much he wanted to tell his daughter was his call.

The man drew in a breath and began. "Brooke, honey, I can't tell you everything that's going on, but your mother is in danger."

Brooke's head jerked up. "What do you mean? What danger?" She looked at Jo. "Are you involved in all this?"

Jo shook her head. "I knew nothing about you until I saw you in the park." She gestured toward Connor. "But I've become involved, and I want to help."

He nodded and looked at Brooke. "Some very bad people are after your mother, and she had to leave. I can't explain everything right now, but the whole reason I kept you in here was because I was worried that the same people who are after your mother might do something to you."

She stared at him in disbelief. "You're kidding. This sounds like something out of a spy novel."

He held up his hands. "It does, and it is."

"What did Mom do?" Brooke asked.

Connor fumbled for words, and Jo came to his rescue.

"Brooke, do you trust me?"

She bit her lip and studied Jo for a moment. Then she nodded.

"You helped me at the park," she said. "I didn't know what I was doing, but I didn't want to end up with those girls. You wouldn't be here if you didn't want to help."

"That's right," Jo said. "And I need you to trust me now. Your father and I can't tell you everything, but I do want to find your mother and bring her home safely. Would you help us with that?"

Brooke fiddled with the hem of her shirt. "Of course I'll help. I don't want anything to happen to Mom."

Connor breathed a sigh of relief. Then he looked to Jo, raising his eyebrows. "What do we do now?"

She pointed to the couch. "Why don't you sit down?"

He took a seat next to Brooke, and Jo was struck by how much they looked alike, both with the same wavy brown hair, and right now both with the same tension in their faces, and how they both bit their lip. She thought for a moment.

"No one has been asking questions about where Brooke is," Jo said. "We'll use that to our advantage. Connor, the feds will be watching the house closely now, wary because you gave them the slip earlier tonight. It's not safe to stay here, both from them, and from . . . others." She was careful about what she said in front of Brooke, although she knew the teen was smart enough to know at least some of what must've been going on. But she didn't want to panic Brooke by talking about spies. "We'll wait here until early in the morning and then leave." She looked at Connor. "We'll take your car, with Brooke in the passenger seat and me hidden in the back. Traffic will be lighter then, and it will be harder for someone to tail you. You're going to have to use the same skills as you did earlier tonight to lose any surveillance."

He grimaced. "I don't know if I could do that again."

"You'll have to," she said.

Connor gulped and nodded.

"Who would follow us?" Brooke asked.

"I can't share that with you," Jo said. She focused on Connor again. "Once you slip any surveillance, you'll take us back to my car. We'll leave your car and take mine. I want to get the two of you to a hotel, and then I'll find Fran."

"Where is she?" Brooke asked.

Connor hesitated. "She did go out of town, but I'm not exactly sure where she is. Somewhere safe."

He was careful not to reveal too much to his daughter. She looked to Jo.

"What do we do now?"

Jo glanced at her phone. It was almost midnight.

"You two get some rest, and early in the morning, you and your dad need to pack bags with clothes for a few days."

Brooke stared at the bed. "Do I have to sleep here again?"

Jo nodded. "Brooke, you and I'll stay down here. We don't want anything unusual happening, and no one can know that I'm here. I know you want to leave, but can you bear with us for one more night?"

She wavered, and then she sighed. "Can we at least leave the door open?"

"If we do, you can't talk," Connor said.

Brooke looked at him, and Jo explained.

"Surveillance bugs."

"Oh," Brooke said.

Connor raised his eyebrows. "And me?"

Jo put a hand on the doorknob. "You need to go upstairs and do your normal routine. I'll check on you in the morning."

As they talked, she'd been watching Connor's reactions and emotions. He had leaned in toward his daughter protectively, and he'd signaled no threat to Jo. At this point, she sensed he trusted her. That was a good thing, because they had a lot left to do.

"Once we get you safely to a hotel, Connor, you and I will figure out how to find Fran."

He nodded and took his daughter's hand.

"I'm so sorry about all of this. And I'm sorry for hitting you." His voice choked. "I only wanted to protect you."

She hesitated, then hugged him. After a moment, he got up and walked to the door. He looked back at her with a small smile, and then asked if they needed anything.

Jo shook her head. "Go upstairs and get some rest. I'll be around to watch things."

"You'll make sure no one knows you're here?"

She smiled. "I know what I'm doing. I'll keep the two of you safe."

He locked eyes with her for a moment and finally gave her a small nod. She stepped aside, and he headed out of the safe room. Jo heard his footsteps on the stairs, and when they faded, she shut the door and looked at Brooke.

"How're you doing?"

She shrugged. "You guys are scaring me with all this. You really can't tell me more?"

Jo shook her head. "It's better that you don't know, and it's better that you just trust me. Can you do that?"

"I said I would." She was back to being a teenager, which was good.

Jo pointed toward the bed. "Why don't you get some sleep. I've got you covered."

"Don't you need to sleep?"

Jo nodded. "I'll get some."

She turned away and gave Brooke some privacy. Jo heard water running in the bathroom. Then she came out and crawled into bed.

"Could you turn out the light?"

Jo glanced around the room, and Brooke smiled at her.

"Good night," she said. "And Jo?"

She had her hand on the light switch. "Yes?"

"Thanks."

Jo nodded and turned out the light. The room was plunged into darkness. Jo eased the door open and sat down in the tiny hallway. She kept the door cracked, so she could hear into the bedroom. Connor's footsteps sounded on the floor upstairs, and then that faded. From the safe room, Brooke moved restlessly on the bed, but that stopped as well, and her breathing evened. Jo googled a few things in preparation for the morning and then sat back. She had trained herself to snatch fits of sleep when she could, but she always slept lightly, and the slightest noise would awaken her. There was no way Brooke could leave without her knowing.

Jo dozed for a while. When she woke up, the basement was still. Brooke breathed evenly from the safe room. Jo tiptoed upstairs and checked throughout the house. The master bedroom door was open, and Connor was asleep. She peeked out a few windows and didn't see anyone. She had no idea who might be watching the house right now. If they were there, hopefully she had fooled them.

She stole back down to the basement and positioned herself in the hall again, listening to Brooke's soft breath until she fell into a weary sleep.

CHAPTER FORTY-FOUR

J o was up before anybody else. She made sure Connor was getting ready, and then she woke Brooke.

"Tell me what's going on with my parents," Brooke said as she sat up in bed.

Jo shook her head. "I can't right now. It's too dangerous. You promise me, though, that you'll listen to your dad and me."

Brooke stared at her, confusion on her face. Then she nodded, rubbed her eyes, and got up.

"Don't let my dad lock me in here again," she said as she went into the bathroom.

"I won't. And this'll all be over soon." Jo spoke with more confidence than she felt.

A while later, they were all ready to go. As Connor walked around the house, he was extremely careful not to say anything that would reveal Jo's presence. He quietly put overnight bags for himself and Brooke in the car, and then Jo snuck into the garage and buried herself down in the back seat. Connor and Brooke got into the front, and he opened the garage door and backed out.

"Drive out of the neighborhood and tell me what you see," Jo said as he pulled into the street.

Connor stared straight ahead and did as she said. After a few minutes of driving and glancing in the rearview mirror, he spoke.

"I think a dark sedan is following us."

"Do what I taught you," Jo said.

He gave a subtle nod and kept driving, taking a series of maneuvers to lose the tail. Brooke started to look over her shoulder, and Jo chided her.

"Act like nothing's wrong."

Brooke sighed and looked out her window.

Connor drove for another minute. "The sedan isn't there anymore."

"You'll probably be picked up by another car. Watch for it, and then do the same thing as you head east."

Connor did as instructed, and soon another car took up surveillance. Jo coached him, and they were able to lose the new tail.

"We're in the clear," he finally said.

Jo shook her head. "It's only for a matter of time. We have to act fast."

Connor got on the highway and drove back into DC, where Jo's car was. They parked a block away, got their bags, and walked to her rental. They hurried in, and she drove away.

"Now what?" he asked.

"They'll still be after us," Jo said, glancing in the rearview mirror.

She was pretty sure another vehicle had spotted them, and she drove around until she lost it. Then she found a cheap motel with a kitchenette that she had googled during the night, pulled around back, and told them to wait. She went to the office and rented a room using one of the fake credit cards that Dack had given her. When she got back to the car, Connor and Brooke both looked nervous.

"Let's go," she said, opening Brooke's door.

Father and daughter followed Jo to a room on the first floor, and she let them inside. The room had two queen beds and a bathroom. Brooke flopped on one of the beds.

"What do we do about food?"

"I'll get you something," Jo said.

"Is there a pool?" Brooke asked.

Connor shook his head. "We have to stay in the room."

Brooke looked at both of them and let out a heavy sigh. "Fine." She grabbed a remote off the nightstand and turned on the TV. "I can't believe this."

Jo studied her for a moment. Brooke was so much like her sister—the teenage impudence, the naïveté that nothing could happen to you, even after all she had already been through. Jo hoped by the time all of this was over that her innocence wouldn't be completely destroyed. She nodded for Connor to follow her into the small dressing area, where they talked in low tones.

"Tell me more about Easton," Jo said.

"It's not very big," Connor said. "We used to stay at the Eastern Shore Inn. It was south of downtown, near the Papermill Pond. That whole area is beautiful. Great restaurants, a cool art community. We have a painting above our fireplace that we got there, an old abandoned barn. We met the artist and talked to him about it, and he took us out there." There was nostalgia in his voice. "I don't know that Fran would go to that hotel, though, because the owners, Sam and Cassidy, know us."

"They still own the place?"

"They did the last time we were there. They always said

that they would own the place until they died." He held up his hands. "It's possible they've sold it."

"Sounds like you're pretty familiar with the town," Jo said.

Connor pursed his lips. "Yeah. We went to the Downtown Café a lot, and the owner, Patty, knew us as well."

"Fran may not stay in Easton if she thought she'd be recognized," Jo pointed out.

The man ran a hand over his face. "Then I don't know where she is."

She took out her phone and googled Easton. It had a population of about sixteen thousand, with plenty of businesses and restaurants, and several hotels.

"It's a tourist town, right?" Jo asked. Connor nodded, and she went on. "It's the middle of summer, and it'll be busy now."

"That might provide the perfect cover for her."

"Maybe." It could also mean there would be too many people around, and it would be more difficult for Fran to spot any feds, or Irena Garin and her people. Jo glanced at Brooke. "I'll get you stocked up."

She left the motel and ran to a Walmart, where she bought a few days' worth of food along with another prepaid phone. She'd also seen the Baldacci book in the safe room, so she bought Brooke some similar novels to read. When she returned to the motel, she gave Connor the phone and had him memorize her number.

"Only call if it's an emergency, and only use the burner phone. Don't use it otherwise. You understand?"

"Yes," he said. He glanced over his shoulder at Brooke, who was thumbing through one of the books Jo had bought. "She's going to get bored."

Jo shrugged. "There's nothing I can do about that. You

need to keep her here. Irena could be anywhere, and you both could be in danger."

He nodded. "I get it."

Jo nodded and told him that she'd be in touch, and then she left.

CHAPTER FORTY-FIVE

She drove to Highway 295, then took Highway 50 northeast. North of Annapolis, she crossed the Chesapeake Bay. It was a beautiful two-hour drive, and some other time she might've enjoyed it, but now her mind was on other things. Jo knew Connor would stay in the motel room, but she wasn't quite so sure about Brooke. The girl was impulsive, and she was tired of being cooped up. Jo had to find Fran and resolve things quickly.

Once she reached the east side of the bay, Jo took Maryland 322 and drove into Easton. Once there, she used her phone GPS to find the Eastern Shore Inn. It was a two-story red-brick building with a covered walkway and arched windows. She parked outside and watched for a minute. A few people sat at tables near a grassy area, and the lot was almost full. Jo didn't see any signs of surveillance, and she didn't see Fran. She finally tucked the Sig P220 against the small of her back, got out, and went into the lobby.

A man with thinning gray hair sat behind a counter, reading a book. Jo approached and smiled.

"If you'd like a room, we only have a couple available," he said, smiling back.

Jo shook her head. "I'm looking for Fran Whigby. She and her husband, Connor, are staying here."

"Oh, the Whigbys." His smile broadened. "Of course I know them, but they aren't staying here. I haven't seen them in quite some time. Nice couple, very friendly. You get to know the good people, appreciate them."

Jo nodded. "You haven't seen either one of them around town?"

His brow furrowed. "I'm afraid not. Is everything okay?"

"As far as I know.

"If they do show, I could give them your name?"

"No, but thank you."

Jo left him with a bemused look on his face. Next she tried the Downtown Café, where Connor had said the owner knew them. She asked to speak to Patty, but the hostess said she wouldn't be in until four. Jo went back to her car and sat for a moment. Easton was small, but not that small. How was she going to find Fran, if she was here? She decided to drive around town, studying people as she did. Easton was a pleasant town, with plenty of small boutiques and art galleries. She saw a lot of tourists, but not Fran Whigby.

At four, she was back at the café, and a woman with short curly gray hair was at the hostess station.

Jo approached her and asked her if she knew where Fran was.

"You know, it's funny you ask that," Patty said. Her lips turned down. "I haven't seen Connor and Fran around the café in a year or so, but I could've sworn I saw her walking on Oxford Road the other night. I live out that way, so I'm on that road most evenings. It was about dusk, so I could have been mistaken. But isn't that the funniest thing, you asking about her?"

"Yes," Jo agreed. "You didn't stop to talk to her?"

"I slowed down, and then she turned onto the side street. I needed to get home, so I kept going. I didn't think much about it." She waved a hand around. "It could've been someone else."

"Are there any motels or inns out that way?"

She shook her head. "Not in that area. There isn't much unless you go farther down to Oxford. There's a few small inns there."

"This was south of Easton?"

"Yes."

Jo smiled at her. "Thanks for your time."

"No problem."

Jo went back outside, got in the car, and looked at tree-lined streets and red-brick buildings. It was a quaint town with a colonial charm. An idyllic place. But it made sense that Fran wouldn't stay in Easton, where at least some people knew her, where she and Connor had frequently stayed. But she could've gone farther south, to a smaller town where she wouldn't be recognized, where she might feel safer.

It was now after five, and Jo stopped for a quick bite to eat before driving down Maryland 333. The land was flat, some farmland, some heavily wooded areas. Not like the crowded streets of DC, or the towering mountains of Colorado. She'd take the mountains any day. She encountered little traffic as she drove into Oxford. It was one of Maryland's oldest towns, situated on the edge of the Chesapeake Bay. There wasn't much there, just houses with white siding, a fire department, and a few stores.

Jo easily found the Oxford Inn, a three-story building with shuttered windows and a long front porch. She inquired about Fran and was told she wasn't there. Jo left and tried another inn with the same results. She stopped last at the Roberts Inn, at the far end of town. She parked in an inconspicuous place across the street and walked over. A young woman with long blond hair was sitting at a small desk, and she looked up when Jo walked in.

"Need a room?" She sounded bored.

Jo shook her head. "Did a woman named Fran Whigby check in?"

The girl stood up. "I can't tell you about the guests."

This was more resistance than Jo had previously received.

"Are you sure?" she pressed.

The girl hesitated and shifted from foot to foot. "Yeah."

Jo didn't believe her. "I need something else."

"What?"

"Information."

"I can't tell you anything."

Jo pulled a fifty from her pocket and set it on the counter. "What about now?"

The girl pursed her lips and reached for the money. Jo pulled it back. "The information. Is Fran Whigby here?"

The girl made a show of checking the register and shook her head. "No one by that name."

"Can people pay cash for a room?"

"Yeah, if they want to. We charge extra because, you know, they could trash the room and leave, and then we don't have a credit card to charge for the damages."

Jo described Fran. "Does she sound familiar?"

The girl glanced away nervously and shook her head again. "I don't think so."

"You work here full time?"

"Yeah, but I was off the last two days."

"You're sure you haven't seen that woman?"

"Yeah," she said, sounding a little put out.

Jo stared at her, and the girl looked down at the money. Finally, Jo slid it across the counter, thanked her, and left. As she went outside, her gut feeling grew stronger—Fran was there.

Back at her car, instead of leaving, she pulled out her binoculars and watched the motel. It was L-shaped, two stories, with stairs at either end. After a while, the girl emerged from the office, carrying a small bag and a soda. She walked up the steps and along the second-floor walkway, then paused partway down. She tapped on a door, said something, then set the bag and the soda on the floor before heading nonchalantly back to the office. Jo followed her, then swung the binoculars back to the motel room door. A moment later, it opened a crack, and a slender feminine hand reached out and grabbed the bag and soda. The door closed.

Fran. She had holed up here, and was paying the motel staff to bring her food.

Jo watched the room. A moment later, the curtains moved. Fran was keeping a lookout.

So what to do? The woman was obviously taking precautions, but she had to be frightened. She also had a gun, which meant she could be dangerous. Did she plan on staying here until someone found her, or did she plan on moving on? Jo didn't have the luxury of waiting to find out. She had to talk to Fran soon. And she would need to take a cautious approach to not frighten her even more. But how?

Before Jo had a chance to formulate a plan, her prepaid phone rang.

CHAPTER FORTY-SIX

"Dad, are you going to tell me what's going on?" Brooke asked.

She was sitting on a chair by a table near the door, and her dad was stretched out on his bed. He looked over at her.

"Mom needs our help, and the best thing we can do is stay here." He glanced at the TV, which was tuned to a news program. "Jo is going to help us, and we have to trust her."

"Did Mom do something wrong?"

His eyes softened. "It's not that simple, honey. Sometimes people make mistakes. What we need to do now is get your mother back, and then we'll talk about everything else."

"But Dad."

"Brooke," he said curtly, "could we not talk about this now? I'm really tired."

"Um, sure."

She grew quiet. Connor put his hands behind his head and sighed. They both watched TV. Brooke didn't care about the news anymore, but her dad seemed interested. She tried to read her book, but her mind wandered. Then she noticed a change in her dad's breath—he had fallen asleep.

She got up and wandered quietly around the room, then went into the kitchenette. Jo had bought bread, meat, and condiments to make sandwiches, and she'd also gotten apples, oranges, and bottled water. Brooke picked up one of the bottles, then set it down with a sigh. She was dying for a Diet Coke. She glanced at her dad. His chest was rising and falling in an even rhythm. He looked exhausted. She wanted to ask him if she could go outside to the vending machine she'd seen to get a soda, but she didn't want to disturb him, and she also knew he'd say no.

But would it really harm anything? she asked herself. It was just at the end of the building.

His wallet was sitting on the nightstand, and she tiptoed over and picked it up, shoving a couple of dollars into her pocket before putting it back. His eyes stayed closed. She moved to the door and quietly turned the knob. Her dad continued sleeping.

She eased open the door and slipped outside, then squinted against the bright afternoon sunlight. Traffic sounds surrounded her as she walked to the end of the building. Two vending machines and an icemaker stood in a small covered area. Brooke paused in front of a soda machine and looked for the Diet Coke button, then got the money out of her pocket.

She was about to feed a bill into the machine when she heard movement behind her. As she started to turn around, a hand with a sweet-smelling rag clamped over her face, and rough hands pulled her arms behind her. Brooke tried to scream, but the rag muffled any sound. It smelled funny, and she realized too late that it must've been soaked with some kind of drug. She tried to yell, but then everything went black.

CHAPTER FORTY-SEVEN

"Brooke's gone!" Connor said in a rush. "Oh man! I don't know how—what do I do?"

Jo gripped the phone hard. "What happened?"

"I don't know where she is."

"Just tell me what you know."

He calmed down. "We were in the room, and I had the news on. Then I guess I . . . I dozed off. I'm sorry."

"Forget sorry," she said. No time for patience right now. "Brooke left the room?"

"Yes. I think I was asleep for about half an hour, and when I woke up, she was gone. I went outside and couldn't find her. I checked the room again and noticed she'd taken a couple of dollars from my wallet. When I looked outside again, I saw a dollar bill on the ground by the vending machines. Who took her? The feds, or Irena?"

Jo thought fast. "The feds wouldn't do that. It has to be Irena and her people. But I can find out."

"How?"

"I have Irena's number. I'll text her."

Jo put him on speaker, then texted the number Irena

had given her, which she'd memorized. She chose her words carefully. On the off-chance Brooke had run away again, she didn't want to let Irena know this.

"Do you have something of mine?" Jo typed.

A reply came almost instantly. *We have the girl.* Jo swore.

"What?" Connor asked.

Jo read the reply aloud.

"Oh no!" Connor's voice cracked. "Are they going to kill her?"

"That won't do them any good. Irena will use her for leverage. It's Fran they want."

As if on cue, she received another text.

"The girl for Fran," Jo read aloud again. She didn't reply to Irena.

"Fran will give herself up," he said, "but we don't know where she is."

Jo stared up at the motel room door. A small, insignificant motel in a beautiful, remote area. "I found her."

"Where?"

"I can't tell you that, but you'll need to speak with her, tell her to listen to me."

"She doesn't answer her phone."

"I'll get her to talk to you, and you need to convince her to work with me. If she does, I'll keep both her and Brooke safe."

"How?"

Jo was already thinking ahead. "Any idea how Irena found the motel? Did you see anybody suspicious around?"

"No. I've been watching out the window, and there's hardly any people or cars."

"Did you go outside or make any phone calls?"

"I had to call the office and tell them I wouldn't be in."

"With your personal phone?"

"Yes."

Jo swore again. "They're somehow tracking your phone."

"I'm sorry."

"Too late for that."

He sucked in a breath. "Will they come for me?"

"If they wanted you, you'd be dead or taken by now."

"Right." The one word held a mixture of relief and fear for his daughter.

"Have your burner phone available in a few minutes, okay?"

"I will. What should I do?"

"Stay there. If the feds come for you, don't tell them anything just yet." Jo didn't trust the feds, and in her mind, there was always one more thing she could do. She wouldn't give up. There had to be something she could do to get Brooke back.

"Okay," he said.

Jo ended the call and texted Irena, telling the woman she didn't know where Fran was.

While she waited for a reply, she got out of the car. Now that Brooke had been taken, Jo didn't have time to delay. She had to get Fran to understand what was going on. She glanced around, then hurried across the street and up the motel steps. It was quiet as she hurried down the walkway and paused in front of Fran's door. She knocked and thought she heard movement inside. Fran was probably close to the door.

"Fran, my name is Jo Gunning. I'm helping your husband, Connor." She needed to be detailed, so that Fran would know she wasn't lying. "I know all about the feds, Irena Garin, and Yuri Orlov. Connor told me about Easton, and how you bought that painting in your living room, that you met the artist. I'm going to put a prepaid phone on the ground. Call the last number. It's another prepaid phone I gave to Connor. Irena has Brooke, but I'll help you get her back."

Jo backed down the walkway. The woman wouldn't have much of a choice. On the one hand, it would be a risk getting the phone. On the other hand, she would need to know what was happening with Brooke.

Jo waited, and the door finally opened. She caught a glimpse of a frightened face. Then a hand came out and snatched the phone before the door quickly closed. She continued to wait. A few minutes later, the door opened again. Fran beckoned her, and Jo hurried down the hall and into the room. The woman shut and locked the door, then handed the phone back to her.

"I just talked to Connor," Fran said. Her voice was low and edgy, her eyes wet from crying. She was about five-six, with shoulder-length highlighted blond hair. No makeup, wrinkles at the corners of her eyes. Her jeans hung a little loosely on her thin frame, and her shirt was creased. "He told me about Brooke." Her voice broke. She trembled as she drew in a few breaths. "Connor told me what was going on, and that I should listen to you."

Before Jo could respond, she received another text from Irena.

"Find the woman."

Jo held up a hand as she dialed.

"You'll come to me," Jo said, her voice low and menacing. "If you hurt Brooke, I will end you."

"We want Fran," said Irena.

"I'll find her and be in touch."

Jo ended the call without giving her time to respond.

She wanted to dictate the terms to the Russians, and she knew she could because Irena was clear that she wanted Fran, not Brooke. If Irena hurt the girl, she'd have no bargaining power.

"What?" Fran asked.

"Hold on."

Jo called Connor next.

"I talked to Fran," he said when he answered. "She doesn't want to involve any of our agencies, and she won't turn herself in. I tried to convince her that was best, but she won't listen. I told her she can trust you."

"I know. Have you seen anyone there?" Jo asked.

"No. What's going on?"

Jo quickly filled him in. "Stay put. Fran and I will get Brooke back."

"Okay." The one word held a lot of emotion: confusion, anger, resignation. "What if they hurt Brooke?"

Jo glanced around the tiny room. The walls with their faded wallpaper seemed to close in as she spoke.

"They want Fran, not Brooke. Stay out of sight, and I'll call you when I can." Jo ended the call and turned to Fran. "Have you seen anybody suspicious around here?"

She shook her head. "No. I told the hotel staff I was running away from my abusive husband, and I paid them to bring me food. I also asked them to let me know if they see anyone suspicious." She pointed to the door. "The girl today said someone had asked about me, but that they'd left. That was you?"

Jo nodded. "I knew you were here when she delivered the food."

Fran grimaced. "I wanted to find some way to get some fake IDs, then get Connor, Brooke, and myself out of the country."

Jo frowned. Wishful thinking. "It's too late for that now," she said. "We have to get Brooke back."

Fran sank onto a queen bed. "How're we going to do that?"

Jo had been thinking it over. "They want an exchange. Brooke for you." Fran's eyes widened in fright, and Jo held up her hand. "Don't worry, we're not actually going to do the exchange. I need to get Irena and her people out here, isolated from everything around them, from what they know. Then we'll get Brooke away from them."

"How?"

"I'll text Irena and tell her I found you, and that she needs to meet us at a place we designate. She won't know the area, so she won't be able to prepare." Jo tipped her head with a grim expression. "She's going to come with other people, so we need to get them in a remote place."

She checked Google Maps for the lay of the land, and then something occurred to her. "That picture of the abandoned barn in your living room."

"What about it?"

"How familiar are you with the area around it?"

Fran shrugged. "It's out in the middle of nowhere. Isolated." Then her eyes lit up.

CHAPTER FORTY-EIGHT

This could be it.

"Tell me about the barn," Jo said.

"I don't remember who owns it, but the artist we talked to said no one's ever there. It's too far off the beaten track. No houses around. There's a long dirt road off Ocean Gateway that you take to get to the barn."

"Is the area wooded?"

Fran nodded. "Yes."

Jo googled the area and had Fran point out the exact location of the barn.

"If it were me," Jo said as she pointed at the map, studying the layout, "I'd drop people off to the north, let them approach the farm from that direction." She pointed to a different area. "You'll stay to the south. Here." She pointed once more. "We'll find someplace off the dirt road to hide the car."

Fran looked over her shoulder. "I guess that would work."

"You've got a gun, right?"

The woman nodded. "Yes, and I've taken classes. I'm a

decent shot. But . . ." she gulped. "I've never shot at anyone."

"I'm not asking you to. But you need it, just in case." Jo sat back. "Get your things while I contact Irena."

Fran moved around the room, and Jo called Irena back. The Russian woman answered brusquely.

"I don't like to be kept waiting."

"I needed to find Fran."

"That was fast."

Her words sounded sarcastic—likely, she knew Jo had already found Fran when they'd spoken before.

"I have a place for the exchange," Jo said. "You need to come alone, just you and the girl."

"Of course," Irena said.

"If you harm Brooke in any way, the deal's off. You won't be able to talk to Fran to find out what she knows."

"I understand. Where are we meeting?"

"There's an old barn off Highway 50, also called Ocean Gateway." Jo gave more specific directions. "You can find it with GPS, can't miss it. Bring Brooke into the barn at ten o'clock tonight. I need to see her first before Fran shows."

"That's a long drive." Irena must've been looking at the map.

"You can handle it," Jo said. "Remember, nothing happens to the girl."

"Of course not." Irena ended the call without another word.

Jo looked at Fran. Her face was pale, her eyes wide as she sank back onto the bed.

"They won't hurt Brooke, will they?"

Jo shook her head. "No. They want what you have, or what they think you have."

Fran glanced around the tiny room. "I'll die if they do

anything to Brooke. I never meant to get her or Connor involved in anything."

Jo nodded tersely and signaled for Fran to follow her.

They went over a couple more details, and then Fran gathered her belongings and they left the motel. Once Fran's things were in the back seat of Jo's SUV, they drove out of Oxford. Dark clouds hung low to the north, and Jo worried that a storm would roll in. Fran seemed nervous too, though for different reasons. She began talking.

"Connor said that Brooke ran away and you tried to help her."

"Yes," Jo said. "Who knew it would lead me to Russian spies?"

Fran let out a humorless laugh. "You met Kent Jacobs?"

Jo glanced at her. "Yuri?"

The woman frowned. "I still have a hard time thinking of him as Yuri. When I met him, he was Kent." She cleared her throat. "Man alive, he was so good looking, and I was so needy. We just started talking, and . . . we hit it off." She was quiet for a moment. "He had me completely fooled. I couldn't believe he would want me, and I did things I don't normally do. I craved the attention, and when he started asking about my work, I was careful at first. But then he seemed to withdraw, and I was scared of losing him, so I talked, tried to keep him interested in me. And before I knew it, I was in over my head."

"Did the Russians pay you?"

"No." She was adamant. "I did what I did for love, not money."

Jo gave her a thoughtful nod. An age-old story. As she drove, the terrain changed from flat and grassy to more wooded. Buildings grew scarcer.

"We'll get all of this resolved," she said.

Fran bit her lip. "I didn't want Brooke to know about this, but now she does." She stared out the window. "I can't stand the thought of her seeing me in prison."

"Depending on how you cooperate, you could get a good deal," Jo said.

She laughed derisively. "What would I tell the feds? That I was a sucker for a Russian spy, and then when I realized that, I tried to fool him by giving him false information? Like they'll believe me." She shook her head. "If the feds take me in, I'll go to prison for a long time." Jo kept her eyes on the road as she listened. "I don't want Brooke to see me behind bars." Then Fran gasped. "If the Russians get me, they'll torture me, and then kill me. It'd be better not to be taken alive."

"The Russians won't get you, I promise."

Fran was quiet for a moment. "I really made a mess of things, didn't I?"

Jo didn't reply. The other woman continued to look out the windshield. The sun was setting as they came upon the dirt road that led to the abandoned barn. Jo turned off of Highway 50, and the surroundings grew more wooded, bathed in shadows. When they were about a mile from the barn, she slowed the SUV and looked for a place to hide the vehicle. She finally found a grove of tall trees, and she hit the brakes and pulled in. Cutting the engine, she looked at Fran.

"You need to stay here. I'll go to the barn and wait for whoever arrives."

Fran looked panicked. "They'll have Brooke, right?"

Jo winced. "I highly doubt it. Irena agreed to my stipulations too fast. She'll want to know if it's just you and me, or if the CIA or someone else is involved, and then she'll plan her next moves. I'll handle whoever shows at the barn, and you stay here. If you see anybody other than me, get out of here and call the police."

Fran didn't say anything. She knew what that meant. If Jo didn't come back, the jig was up, and Brooke would probably die.

"You have your gun?" Jo asked her.

The woman reached into her bag in the back seat and retrieved a Novak Browning hi-power 9-millimeter handgun. Jo resisted a smile. In her experience, the semi-automatic, although a good weapon and functional, was a bit of a status symbol. More expensive than a Glock, the Browning showed pride of ownership.

"I'm ready," Fran announced.

Jo took her free hand. "It'll be okay. I asked Brooke to trust me earlier, and I need you to trust me now. I know what I'm doing."

Fran locked eyes with her and nodded. They got out of the vehicle, and Fran came around and got in the driver's seat. Jo shut the door, silenced her phone, and gave her an encouraging nod. Then she struck out through the trees, keeping the dirt road in sight.

She figured she had about a ten-minute walk to the barn if she moved quickly. The air was thick around her, and lightning flashed in the distance. Hopefully it wouldn't rain before she could finish at the barn.

The last bit of light was fading fast as Jo hurried on, careful on the uneven terrain. It was hot still, and she felt herself sweating. As she neared the barn, she could smell rain in the air. It was almost completely dark when she finally saw a silhouette of a building in the distance. The barn sat in a small clearing, and she crouched near some trees and studied it for a minute. She saw no movement, so she stealthily crept through the darkness up to the barn, then around a corner.

Finding a door, she quietly opened it. Hinges creaked, and Jo instinctively braced herself. But no one was there. She had calculated how long it would take someone to drive from the DC area to the barn. Irena, or whoever she was sending to this remote area, were at least an hour away.

Jo stepped in and closed the door. A fraction of gray light seeped through a small, broken window high up near the peak of the roof. She looked around.

The barn was large, with several empty stalls, some still containing hay. A few containers sat in a loft. Good. She could attack from higher ground, a standard tactical move. She went to a ladder and tested it. It seemed solid. Jo wasted no time climbing up to the loft, where she positioned herself behind one of the boxes, keeping a good view of the barn door.

She hunkered down to wait.

CHAPTER FORTY-NINE

Jo marked the minutes. Whoever was coming would be getting close. She drew in a deep breath and let it out slowly. A sliver of moonlight shone through the high barn window. The hay smelled sour and moldy, like wet dirt, and she wrinkled her nose.

It was hot and muggy in the loft, and she wiped her hands on her jeans. She didn't know what kind of weapons Irena's people would have, probably some kind of short-barreled entry guns. She could take them out with the Sig P220, but her shots had to be quick and precise. Stretching, she listened. Doubts crept in. She hoped she had guessed right with her plan.

If not . . . She shuddered to think of the consequences.

More minutes ticked by. Then she heard it. A small squeaking of the hinges on the barn door. Jo tensed and peered into the darkness. Nothing happened for a moment, and then she saw a figure step into the barn. A man. He wore a black shirt and black cargo pants, and she was unsurprised to see the profile of a Colt M4 Commando rifle in his hands. The weapon had a flash suppressor clamped to it.

She was thoroughly familiar with the M4 Commando. It had a short 11.5-inch barrel, with a lower muzzle velocity than a longer M16 rifle, but it was still a good weapon, used by Army Special Operations Command Groups. The man scanned the barn, and as his head tipped upward, Jo ducked behind the box. She waited a second and then peeked around.

Another man had stepped into the room, same dress, same weapon in his hands. Jo heard them underneath the loft, checking the stalls. She held her breath and didn't move. Then they stole back into the center of the barn, their guns lowered.

She waited. If they had Brooke, Jo would hear something from Irena. But her phone remained silent. One of the men spoke into a mic on his shirt, his voice quiet. She wasn't sure what he was saying, but she heard Fran's name, and "Nyet." He nodded again and signaled to the other man.

No Brooke.

One of them moved toward the ladder, and Jo shifted and aimed down on them.

"You were supposed to bring her," she said.

Both swung their guns upward.

The first one saw her, but he didn't have time to react before she shot him twice. His head jerked back as the bullets slammed into his body, and he fell in a heap.

Jo moved to her right, pulling the trigger again. The other man's gun was up, and he fired a round toward where she had just been. He missed, but she didn't. He dropped to the barn floor, the M4 Commando falling next to him.

She waited and listened, thinking she heard something outside the barn. When no one else entered, she hurried down the ladder and put an insurance round in each man's head to make sure they were dead. Then she checked their pockets.

Nothing.

Jo put the Sig in her waistband, took one of the M4 Commando's, and moved silently to the barn door.

CHAPTER FIFTY

The two men had left the barn door open. That was good for Jo—no squeaky hinges to deal with. She glanced outside. Her vision was limited, but everything looked clear, so she crouched down and slipped through the doorway. She pressed herself against the wall and scanned all around.

The moon had disappeared behind clouds, and scattered raindrops fell around her. She listened, but the storm wasn't helping. Lightning streaked across the distant sky, the flash just enough to momentarily illuminate the area as bright as day. And that was all she needed to see movement at the edge of the trees to the south of the barn.

Another man, darting quickly in the trees near the road. Toward the SUV and Fran.

He was taking chances that he probably shouldn't be, moving fast with little attempt to disguise his whereabouts. His image in that flash of light was seared into Jo's brain. The broad shoulders. The short hair.

Yuri. He had to get to Fran, had to clean up his mess.

But she wasn't going to let him.

Jo ran across the clearing and toward the road. No shots, so she figured it was just the two of them. The rain fell harder as she darted into the trees. She hurried, and like Yuri, she was making more noise than she wanted to. He was far ahead, and faster than she was.

Then he spun around. He'd heard her. He held a M4 Commando as well, and he wore PVS-15 night vision goggles, making it easy to spot her. Something whizzed by, and then she heard the air disruption of a bullet. A near miss. Jo dropped to the ground. Yuri dashed into the trees again. She pressed herself down. The ground was wet, and she wiped moisture off her face. The storm would mask both of their movements, but it didn't help her with visibility.

She waited a moment, then got into a crouch and moved forward, her rifle aimed in front of her. She'd lost the Sig, but she couldn't afford to find it. Yuri was out there somewhere. A jagged bolt of lightning streaked across the sky like a brilliant white river. She dropped to the ground again as she saw Yuri up ahead. He still wore the night vision goggles, but he would've been temporarily blinded by the light. He stood still for a moment, and she fired once at him. The rain obscured any ability to know if she'd hit him.

Then the darkness enveloped her again. Thunder rumbled loudly around her, shaking the earth. Jo used the noise to disguise her movements as she eased forward, shielded by the trees. The rain came down harder, and lightning flashed again. Looking left, she didn't see anything, but to the right, there was movement.

She tried to think as Yuri would. He had to get to Fran as fast as he could, but he would know he needed to get rid of Jo first. He had a few options. He could run away from her, but that would get him nothing, put him in a defensive position. Or he could move toward her, put her at a disadvantage as she was forced to guess where he was. Or, if he was really good, he'd stay where he was. It would still keep her guessing.

Jo chose option three for herself, stealing just a few feet to her left and waiting. A moment later, she heard the whiz of a bullet passing, close to where she'd just been. She squatted down and didn't move.

Another lightning strike hit, and she looked all around. Yuri had moved closer, now to her left. He ducked down, temporarily blinded again, and waited. Jo took a hasty shot, but it was lost in the storm and the noise.

She went right and waited again.

The next lightning strike, Yuri was in a different place. He was trying to bluff her, movements in one direction, then backtracking in another direction, then moving toward her again.

During the next flash, she didn't see him.

Where was he? Jo raised the rifle.

Had he given up, and he was headed after Fran? Or was he thinking of her movements as well, figuring she'd stayed in place? If so, that gave him an advantage. He could get to Fran. Jo knew she couldn't take the risk of Fran being left alone, so she moved out into the darkness again. The rain continued to fall, and then a sudden flash of lightning split across the sky again. She aimed, looking left, forward, then right.

Nothing.

The darkness returned, along with the thunder. She crept forward again, but she couldn't hear Yuri. For a second, she wondered if he'd fooled her, outflanked her and gone around behind. She glanced over her shoulder, but with the rain and darkness, she had no idea if he was there.

A bullet could come from that direction and hit her, and she would never know it.

Jo crept forward, and when the next flash of lightning came, she held the M4 in front of her. Then her eyes widened.

Yuri was fifteen feet away, his gun pointed right at her. But he couldn't see.

She fired off two quick rounds, and the man dropped to the ground. Jo waited for return fire, but none came. Just the thunder. She darted to the right, then crawled toward the body, even though she couldn't see it. She held her breath. With the next flash of lightning, she ran. Still no movement as she approached and looked down. He remained still, so she kicked off the night-vision goggles. She could just make out Yuri's dead eyes staring up into the sky.

Jo put an insurance round into his head, then glanced around. His gun lay nearby. She kicked it away, bent down, and emptied his pockets. Nothing but a phone, which she pocketed. She took his gun and started down the road. No need to worry about noise now. If Yuri'd had help, they would've appeared already. Once she'd put distance between herself and the barn, she pulled out her phone and dialed a number.

"Well?" Irena said.

"Where's Brooke?" Jo asked.

A pause, and then Irena laughed quietly. "Where's Yuri?"

"He won't be coming back. You want Fran, produce Brooke."

Irena had planned for every option. She knew there was a chance Yuri might not make it back.

"Meet me at Great Falls Park, in Virginia," Irena said. "You should be able to make it there by 2 a.m. Leave your car at the Visitors Center and hike north to the falls. Then wait there. And make sure you have Fran."

"Make sure you have Brooke."

The call went dead.

Jo shoved the phone in her pocket and hurried back to the SUV. It took her over five minutes, and was still raining hard when she approached. She didn't see Fran in the driver's seat. Raising her gun, she looked all around.

"Fran?" she called out.

A light appeared from inside the SUV, and Fran opened the back door.

"I was scared," she said, "so I hid in the back seat."

"Let's go."

Jo yanked open the car door and slid behind the wheel. She was soaked, but there was nothing she could do about that. Fran shut the back door and slid into the front passenger seat.

"What happened?"

"They didn't bring Brooke," Jo said.

Fran swore softly. "Is she okay?"

Jo nodded. "She's back in Virginia. We have to go there now."

"Do you need a new shirt?" the woman asked, looking her over.

Jo nodded. Fran reached back into her bag and pulled out a T-shirt. Jo peeled off her soaked shirt and donned the fresh one. It was a little small, but it would do. Fran had the car key, and she handed it to Jo.

"Let's get my daughter."

CHAPTER FIFTY-ONE

As Jo drove down the dirt road toward Highway 50, she pulled out her phone.

"Call Connor and tell him what happened, and tell him to stay put for now."

Fran's hand shook as she dialed. "He's not answering. What's going on?"

"Irena knows where Connor is."

"Oh no! What do we do?"

"I'll get him somewhere safe."

Jo had been resisting Dack's help, but she called him now. "I need you to get Connor Whigby," she said when he answered. She wasn't on video call, so she couldn't see his face. She waited for him to type his reply.

"Where is he?"

Dack wasn't wasting any time.

Jo told him where the motel was.

"I'll head there now."

Now that she knew he was on his way, she briefed him on the situation. "I don't know if Connor's still there, but let's hope."

"I'll find him and let you know," Dack replied.

"Take him somewhere safe and stay with him."

"I will."

He ended the call, and Jo handed the phone to Fran.

"Keep trying Connor."

Fran did, and Jo stared into the darkness as she drove. Rain battered the windshield and pounded the roof of the car. She put the wipers on high. As they swiped back and forth, she thought through the logistics of their upcoming situation.

"He's not answering," Fran said. "What do we do?"

"I'm not sure," Jo said. "I don't know how many people Irena will have to help her. I took out three of them, but who knows what resources she has at her disposal?" She glanced at Fran as she cranked the air conditioner to try to help dry her clothes, running a hand through her wet hair. "This time, we need to show your face. We won't be able to bluff anymore."

Fran was silent for a moment. Then she said, "You need help."

Jo nodded and went over options. "I've been to Great Falls. The trail where we have to meet Irena is rugged, and part of it meanders close to the falls. Irena wants us isolated, making it harder for us to have backup."

Fran's tongue ran over her lips, and then she pointed to Jo's phone.

"Call the CIA, or whoever else is involved in this. They can help get Brooke back safely."

Jo stared straight ahead for a moment. "Are you sure? You said you didn't trust anyone in our government."

"I can't let Irena do anything to Brooke. I'll deal with whatever else later." Her voice shook.

Jo agreed, and had Fran dial Borland's number. The

woman handed the phone to her, then looked away. The phone rang a couple of times, and Borland answered, barking his name, a hint of weariness in his voice.

"It's Jo Gunning. I need your help."

"What's going on?" He was suddenly alert.

She interrupted. "We can talk about that later. I have Fran Whigby, and Irena Garin has her daughter, Brooke. Irena wants an exchange. I can't risk Brooke or Fran's lives, so I can't do this alone."

Borland didn't take time to argue. "Where's the exchange?"

"Great Falls." She relayed Irena's instructions. "We have to be there at two. That's not much time."

"I'll have things in place," he said. "Where exactly are you meeting Garin?"

"She didn't say. Fran and I are supposed to walk that trail. Irena's going to get us isolated, and then she'll show. I have to get the girl back."

"Of course. Nothing will happen to her."

"I have your word?"

Borland grunted. "I promise, okay? Follow Irena's directions, and don't do anything stupid."

"Right."

Jo ended the call and sped up.

"They'll help?" Fran said.

Jo nodded. "They don't have a lot of time, but their teams are good." She thought for a minute. "Take your gun with you. We'll hike the trail exactly as Irena said. But be ready for anything. I don't think she'll ambush us—she knows I've already taken down three of her men."

"Okay," Fran said, her voice barely more than a breath. "And then what?"

"We see what happens," Jo said.

They drove north on Highway 50 in silence, through Easton. The rain eased up, and Jo turned the wipers down. Their slow back and forth was hypnotizing. Fran was tense, her jaw working. The highway swung west, and they soon passed through Kent Narrows and Stevensville, then started across the Chesapeake Bay Bridge. Few cars were about, and the rain finally stopped, leaving glistening blacktop.

Dack called back.

"I've got Connor. He got scared and left the motel room, but I found him at an all-night diner down the street. I'll stay with him."

At least that was one worry she didn't have to deal with. She told him about Borland.

"Good," he said, sounding relieved that she would have backup.

"I'll keep you posted."

She ended the call. Fran glanced at her and drew in a deep breath. She was too nervous to say anything.

Once they reached the other side of the bay, Jo stayed on Highway 50 to the I-495, finally crossing the Potomac River into Virginia. Fran tensed as they merged onto the Georgetown Pike and headed to Great Falls Park, driving into the Visitors Center just after 1:50.

The park sat on eight hundred acres in Virginia, situated along the banks of the Potomac River. A series of cascades poured over steep, jagged rocks as the water flowed through the narrow Mather Gorge. It was a popular destination, especially on weekends, but at this time of night, the parking lot at the visitor center was empty. Jo pulled into a spot with the headlights of the car on the trail entrance. It didn't look like anyone was around.

"Do you think our backup will show?" Fran asked.

"Don't worry. They'll be smart about this." Jo turned Fran. "Are you ready?"

Fran held up the Browning and nodded.

"Let's get Brooke back."

They got out of the SUV. Jo's pants were still damp, but she ignored that. She held her rifle at the ready as they started toward the trailhead. It had rained here as well, and the parking lot and surrounding foliage were wet. They started forward, guided by the moonlight. The trail was rocky and muddy in spots, and they walked carefully. Jo was alert for everything. The air was crisp. In the distance, they could hear rushing water, but close by, there was only the sound of their breathing as they exerted themselves.

Where's Borland? Jo thought.

They hurried on. The trail curved, and a louder noise filled the air. They were getting closer to the falls. A few feet off the trail, the terrain dropped sharply. Hopefully Borland had had enough time to get a team out here. Just as the noise from the falls was growing deafening, she heard a voice.

"Stop."

Jo and Fran halted.

"Put your guns down." Irena's voice came through the darkness.

Jo hesitated, then whispered, "Do as she says."

They bent down and carefully put their guns on the ground. Then they straightened, hands visible and open.

"Where's the girl?" Jo called out.

Farther down the trail, Irena stepped from behind a tree. She had Brooke in front of her, tape covering her mouth, her hands behind her back

"Have Fran come forward," Irena said. "Don't do anything funny, or the girl dies."

Even at this distance, Jo could tell Brooke was terrified. *Where was Borland?*

"Don't do anything to my baby," Fran said. She stepped out in front of Jo.

"Let the girl go," Jo said. "No funny business on either side."

Irena smirked. "You cost me three men."

Jo shrugged. "I knew I couldn't trust you."

"And I can't trust you."

Two men dressed in black stepped out of the trees between Jo and Irena. Both held guns trained on Fran.

"Come forward," Irena commanded. Fran stayed rooted in place. Then Irena barked, "Move!"

Fran took a halting step.

Suddenly, three other men stepped out of the shadows, guns pointed at Irena and the first two.

"Don't move! Hands up and turn around." one of them said. "You're surrounded!"

Jo recognized the gear and the way they carried themselves. It was an HRT team—extremely well trained, Delta Forces types.

At that moment, all hell broke loose.

Irena's men crouched and turned, guns up, and Borland's men opened fire on them. Brooke screamed through the duct tape. A voice called out.

"Move away from the girl! You're in our sniper's crosshairs."

"Don't do anything to Brooke," Fran yelled.

Irena spun Brooke around to the voice, using her as a shield. At the same time, Jo dove for the weapons on the ground, tossing the Browning at Fran. Rolling to her knees, Jo aimed the rifle toward Irena. At the same time, Fran ran into the fray and shrieked.

"Leave my daughter alone!"

She was blocking Jo's line of sight. Irena's men turned to Fran, and shots rang out. One of the Russians went down. The other fired at Borland's men. Irena pushed Brooke forward, then darted off the trail. Brooke tumbled to the ground.

Jo turned and saw movement. Irena crouched, aiming at Fran.

"Brooke!" Fran yelled.

"Get down!" Jo hollered back.

Irena fired, a few quick rounds. Fran jerked suddenly and fell to the ground. The agents exchanged more gunfire with the Russians, but one man broke off and ran toward Fran, his gun raised. Irena's weapon swung toward Jo, and she saw a look in the woman's eyes, one she'd seen before. The will to never give up, to fight to the end. Irena would take Jo out rather than lose to her.

Jo ducked down and looked toward Brooke. One of Borland's men was shielding her. A bullet sped past Jo. She stared off the trail—Irena was firing at her. Jo scrambled into the rocks and ran after the woman. She was far up ahead, but she slipped and her gun went flying. She started to search for it, then glanced back and saw Jo making up ground, so she kept running down to the rugged terrain by the waterfall.

Jo continued to race after her. The falls pounded loudly to her right. She clambered over larger rocks on a barely defined trail. More than once, she stumbled, but righted herself. The path turned, and she moved forward more carefully, sweeping left and right with her gun. The falls were loud, but she soon heard another sound nearby.

CHAPTER FIFTY-TWO

Jo saw the figure a moment too late. Irena hurtled out of the darkness, her motion muted by the falls. She slammed into Jo, knocking her down. Jo's M4 Commando scattered onto the rocks near them. Irena's momentum carried her past, and she rolled into a crouch, scrambling to her feet at the same time Jo did.

Irena glared at her, arms raised, ready to punch. Jo feinted left, and Irena went right, then punched. Stepping aside, Jo deflected the blow, her momentum carrying her forward. She hit Irena with a left. It connected, but the woman was tough, not fazed at all.

They both spun around.

Irena swore in Russian, her eyes crazed. Everything had fallen apart, and she had to know Borland's men would be coming for her. No way she was going with them. She launched forward and punched. Jo jerked backward as the blow connected with her cheek. Irena was stronger than she looked. Jo's head buzzed. She turned and feinted again. Both women raised their fists and stared at each other.

Irena dodged, and Jo deflected. They were breathing

hard. Each got in a couple of blows, then Irena swung with her leg. Jo grabbed it with both hands, one on her shoe, the other under the ankle, and shoved her back. The Russian woman fell to the ground. Jo scrambled for the rifle, but was tackled from behind before she could reach it. They twisted on the ground for a moment.

Irena pressed her forearm down on Jo's neck, but Jo struggled and broke the grip, then exerted herself and threw the woman backward. Jo turned and felt on the ground for the rifle. At the same time, out of the corner of her eye, she saw Irena grab a large rock. She rolled over as Irena snarled and raised her arm. Jo's hand closed on the butt of the rifle, and she aimed and fired.

The bullet hit Irena square in the chest. She jerked and dropped the rock. Jo scrambled away as the woman fell to the ground and didn't move. Jo's chest heaved as she gasped for breath. Crawling over to the body, she felt for a pulse.

Nothing.

Jo's body shook with adrenaline as she stood up. The waterfall rumbled nearby, but over that, she heard voices. She stepped past the body and threw the rifle as far out into the river as she could. Then she put her hands in the water and let the current wash away any gunshot residue. She didn't want to get involved in what would be an ongoing investigation. If Borland knew she'd shot Irena, she'd be tied up in red tape for weeks or months. Moving back from the roiling water, she turned around. She was staring at Irena's body when Borland and three other agents arrived, guns raised.

"Don't move!" Borland yelled at her.

Jo raised her hands. "About time you got here."

One of his men dropped to a knee and felt Irena's neck. Then he turned and shook his head.

"You shot her?" Borland asked Jo.

"I don't have a gun." She jerked her head. "There was a guy. He ran off."

Borland signaled with a thumb, and two of his men ran farther down the river. The third agent stood back. He stared at Jo, and she realized he was the rookie agent she'd subdued at the building where she'd been questioned. His eyebrows formed a thin, angry line.

"No hard feelings," she said.

He didn't reply.

Borland looked at Jo. "Are you going to stick with that story?"

"How are Brooke and Fran?" she countered.

"Fran's dead."

Jo swore under her breath. Borland holstered his gun and put his hands on his hips.

"Brooke will be okay," he said. "She's pretty shaken up. You know where her dad is?"

Jo nodded. "Safe at a restaurant."

"She'll want to see her dad. We have a lot of questions for both of them, though."

She breathed a sigh of relief. It didn't sound as if Irena had hurt the girl, not physically, anyway. She pointed toward Irena's body.

"How many people did she bring with her?"

"Besides the ones you saw, we took down three others."

"Good."

"Where's your gun?" Borland asked.

Jo shrugged. "I never had one."

He contemplated her, but before he could say more, someone spoke in his earpiece. Borland put a hand to his ear and listened, staring at Jo the whole time. Then his hand dropped to his side.

"So far, my guys aren't finding anybody out there."

Jo shrugged. "I don't know what to tell you."

Borland contemplated her for a minute. "I'm taking you in for questioning." He surveyed the ground. "You have a lot of explaining to do."

"I told you everything."

He bent down and looked at the body, then straightened and gestured toward the other man.

"Take her in, Engel. I'll get to her when I can."

Engel holstered his weapon and approached Jo.

"You gonna give me any problems?" he asked her.

Before she could answer, Borland spoke. "She's smart enough not to do that. She's already in enough trouble."

Engel searched her and took her phone, the fake ID and credit cards, and her money. Over the sound of the falls, more noise came as men approached. Borland barked instructions to them, then signaled Engel.

"Come on," the man said to Jo.

He zip-tied her hands while Borland watched, then guided her by the elbow along the rocks on the trail. It grew quieter, just the distant water crashing over the falls.

CHAPTER FIFTY-THREE

Engel took Jo back into DC, to an unassuming building that she didn't recognize. He drove the car into an underground garage, where two other agents met them and escorted her inside the building. There was nothing on the walls to indicate where they were. They rode up an elevator and soon were in a typical interrogation room. Engel cut the zip tie and had her sit down, and then the agents left the room.

Jo waited a long time. The room smelled unpleasantly antiseptic, like it was covering something bad. All adrenaline had left her on the drive, and she was tired. She fought sleep as she went over the events at Great Falls Park and wondered what she could have done differently.

Fran had wanted Borland's people involved. She knew they'd needed the help, but how quickly she'd suggested calling the agents told Jo that Fran expected she wouldn't come out of the confrontation alive. She'd said multiple times that she didn't like her choices, whether it was the US government or the Russians who took her. That had to be

why she'd pulled her gun and run into the fray. She'd
known someone would see her as a threat, that they would
take her down. It was why she'd yelled to distract attention
from Brooke. Fran had sacrificed herself for her daughter in
the end. No one could've stopped her.

After a while, Jo yawned and stretched, then got up and
walked around the room. She knew she was being watched,
but she didn't care. It had to be daytime. Ignoring the
hunger pangs she was now feeling, she sat at the table again
and closed her eyes. She dozed, but kept herself from falling
into a deep sleep.

The door finally opened, and Borland stepped into the
room, followed by three men, including Engel. They spread
out, and Borland sat down across from her. He set a file
folder on the table.

"We meet again," he said, sounding trite.

"How's Brooke?"

"We talked to her."

Jo arched an eyebrow. "Tell me what happened to her
since she was taken at the motel." He hesitated, and she
smiled at him. "It's not going to hurt anything."

After considering for a moment, he said, "She told us all
about being locked in the safe room, why her dad did that,
and how you helped her, how you got her and her dad to a
motel room. She thought it wouldn't be any big deal to get a
soda, but when she went down to the vending machine,
someone snatched her. They used a chloroform-soaked rag
to knock her out. She woke up in a small room, but she
doesn't know where it was. They kept her tied up, but they
left her alone." He ran a finger along the table. "They didn't
want her, they wanted Fran."

"So I assumed," Jo said. "And Connor Whigby?"

"We let him know what happened at the park, and we questioned him as well."

"And?"

His eyes narrowed. "He says he didn't know what Fran was up to until recently, and that she was feeding the Russians lies. She wanted to make things right." He didn't say anything about the Whigbys' plan to go somewhere safe, to assume new identities. "Connor said it was all Fran, that he didn't know about Yuri Orlov or Irena Garin until he went to the Clarion Hotel."

Borland's lips were a thin line. She didn't think he fully believed Connor.

"And you interrogated him for how long?" she asked.

His lips twitched into a little smile. "That's confidential."

"Sure," Jo said.

"You knocked out one of my men." He glanced at Engel, who turned red. "And you ran a car into a ditch."

"You were holding me against my will."

Borland held her gaze long and hard, then consulted his file.

"What did Fran tell you?"

Jo shrugged.

"She said about the same thing as her husband." She felt protective of Fran now, even in death.

"Did Fran tell you she was a spy?"

Jo shook her head. "She worked for the Department of Defense."

"Did she tell you she was getting money from Yuri?"

"No."

"Was Fran working for anybody?"

"Not that I know of."

"How did you find her?"

She glanced at the others, the audience for this game between her and Borland.

"Lucky guess," she said.

Borland eyed her, not amused.

"Who hired you?"

"Nobody," Jo said. "I was trying to help Brooke."

"Was it your idea to meet at Great Falls Park?"

"Those were Irena's instructions, like I told you."

"Did you go there with plans to kill Irena?"

"No."

"When you saw Irena push Brooke away, why didn't you stay where you were?"

"I didn't want Irena to come back for Fran, so I went after her."

"And you shot her."

Jo shook her head. "No."

Borland tapped the file for a moment, impatient.

"Who shot Irena?" he asked.

"A man."

"What did he look like?"

Jo thought for a moment. "Average build, dark clothes, dark hair."

Borland's eyes were cold. "That's not much of a description."

"It was dark."

He sat back and crossed his arms. "I know you're lying. You shot her."

Jo stared at him. "If so, where's my gun?"

"My guess is you tossed it in the river. We can get divers to look for it."

She smiled. "In those falls? That'd be difficult to do."

He held her gaze, but it was clear he knew she was right.

"Did you find Irena's gun?" she asked.

His expression was almost a sneer. "I'm sure you knew where it was."

"Where's my car?"

"We have it."

"So you searched it."

Borland didn't answer that. "Why not tell us what really happened? It's not a big deal."

She looked at him, amused. "If I did shoot Irena—and I'm not saying I did—I'd be tied up in DC for a long time." Weariness washed over her, sudden and strong, like a violent waterfall. "I want to be done with all of this. I want to know Brooke is okay, and then I don't want to see you or anybody in any agency like yours again."

He uncrossed his arms and leaned forward. "I don't want to see you, either. Assuming you left the military for a reason, you need to stay gone."

They locked eyes for a long time. The room was quiet. Then Borland drew in a breath.

"One last chance to tell me what really happened."

She held his gaze and didn't say anything.

"I'll keep you here," he said.

Now she leaned forward. "No, you won't. You have a mess to clean up." She ticked things off on her fingers. "A US citizen with access to information that the Russians want. Spies operating freely in the DC area. And dead bodies. You have plenty to handle without dealing with me. You can't keep me here forever, and I've got nothing to lose by exposing it all, either. If you give me a reason to, I will."

His jaw worked as he thought through her response. Then he grabbed the file and stood up.

"I don't want to see you again," he said.

"You won't."

He glanced at his men. "Get her out of here."

They all stepped into the hallway. The trio walked her to the elevator while Borland went the other direction.

CHAPTER FIFTY-FOUR

Engel and the two men rode with Jo down to the basement. When the doors slid open, they walked through the garage to her SUV.

"How thoroughly did you search the car?" she asked.

One of the agents unlocked a nearby Suburban and held the back door open for her. Jo got in, followed by the other. The first shut the door and went around to the driver's side and started the car. She looked out the window. Engel got in her rented SUV. The driver headed out of the garage, followed by Engel.

The sun was bright as the Suburban emerged from the parking garage. The driver turned onto the road. Jo squinted, but the two agents just looked out the windshield, sunglasses on. Neither said a word.

They drove a few blocks before the driver parked at the curb. They got out and opened the door for Jo. The SUV pulled up behind them, and Engel got out and handed her the car key.

"Thanks," Jo said, her voice wry.

Engel handed her a small plastic bag. "We're keeping the fake IDs and credit cards, but we're returning your original ID and credit card," he said. The bag also had her phone and money.

The man who'd driven the Suburban just looked at her. All she saw was her reflection in his sunglasses. She watched them get back in, and the vehicle pulled into traffic. She waited until it turned the corner before she slid behind the wheel of the SUV and checked the console. Her binoculars were still there. The car manuals were in the glove compartment, and the wet shirt she'd taken off near the barn was on the passenger seat. She touched it—dry and wrinkled now. She ran a hand over the T-shirt Fran had given her, and sadness swept through her. The woman had made so many bad choices. But in the end, she'd made the choice that had really counted.

Jo sighed as she took the phone out of the plastic bag and video-called Dack. His face was close to the screen as he studied her.

"Well?" he asked.

"It's over, and Brooke's okay."

He tipped his head with a small smile. "When Borland's men came for Connor, I disappeared."

"Good."

Jo told him everything. Traffic zoomed by— she was sure she was being watched, but she didn't care.

"Everything I have has been compromised again," she said. "They'll be tracking me, so I can't use my own ID and credit card. I don't want them following me. I just want to get some rest."

"Return your car to the rental place, then ask to use the phone there and call me back."

She nodded, smiled, and ended the call. Googling Hertz

car rentals, she selected one nearby. As she pulled into traffic, she checked the rearview mirror. A dark sedan tailed her. Jo was too tired to care. Fifteen minutes later, she was turning in her car, and she asked the clerk to use their phone.

The man smiled and handed it to her. She called Dack's untraceable number. She couldn't see him, but he used a voice translator and gave her an address.

"Go there. It's a hotel in Arlington. It's safe. Tell them you're Heidi Furlong. They'll give you a key."

"Thanks."

"Call me when you're in your room."

"Will do."

Jo thanked him again and hung up. She walked out of the car rental office and headed toward a Metro station. On the way, she lost the surveillance man who was following. Then she took a train to the hotel in Arlington.

She went inside, and it was exactly as Dack had said. The receptionist had a key and a package for Jo, and no one questioned her lack of luggage. A bellboy escorted her to a suite on the seventh floor. Once he left, she opened the package. Dack had provided a new burner phone, along with a new ID, a credit card, and cash.

She sat down on the couch and video-called him.

"You made it," he said with a smile.

"Thanks for all of this."

"Sure thing. Stay as long as you want, and charge anything you need to the room. Get some rest, and then you can figure out your next move."

Jo glanced down at herself. If she'd seen someone else in this condition, she'd have wondered if they were homeless. "I need clothes first thing."

"You look great."

She laughed. "Thanks."

He studied her. "You okay?"

Jo was slow to respond. "I will be."

"You can't feel guilty about Fran. You did all you could for her, and for Brooke."

"I guess so."

Dack knew better than to push anything now. "Call me later."

"I will."

After looking around for a minute, Jo ordered room service. While she waited for the food, she took a long hot shower, then donned a hotel robe. She called to get her clothes cleaned, and then she turned on the TV and flipped channels, but didn't see any references to the events at Great Falls.

A while later, a knock came at the door. She went over, listened, and peeked out. A young-looking waiter with a long ponytail stood in the hall with a tray. She opened the door.

"Here's your lunch, ma'am."

She stepped aside, and he came into the room, put the tray down on a table, and handed her a bill. She signed it with a big tip, and he thanked her. After he left, she locked the door, put a chair under the handle, and wrapped a towel around the door stopper.

Finally, she sat down to eat. She'd ordered a steak, a baked potato, and steamed vegetables, along with apple pie. Her appetite was voracious, and when she finished, the hotel staff already had her clothes cleaned. Jo put them in the bedroom closet, then slipped out of her robe and slid under the covers. Soon she was fast asleep.

It was light when she awoke, so she knew she'd slept for a long time. She checked the time. Nine o'clock—she'd been out for over sixteen hours. Again, she ordered room service, this time a big breakfast of eggs, sausage, toast, juice, and coffee. She took another shower, and when the food arrived, she ate it with gusto. The eggs were perfect, not runny, the sausage spicy, the toast with just the right amount of brown. After days of running and rushing, the meal was wonderful.

She dressed, then texted Brooke, but the teenager didn't respond. Jo pocketed the fake ID, credit card, cash, and phone, then left the suite. She took an Uber to a Target for clothes, a duffel bag, and toiletries. As she paid, she smiled to herself. Maybe this set of things would last a little longer.

Jo spent the next several days at the hotel, working out in the gym, running, and even lounging by the pool. At first, she felt guilty, but Dack told her not to be. With everything that had happened, he assured her that she deserved it. He knew she would move on when she was ready to, even if that meant back to a motel kitchenette of her choosing. In her mind, Jo knew she wasn't going to do that, but she still needed to take care of some last details.

Finally, she texted Connor Whigby, identified herself, and asked to meet him. He agreed, and they arranged a time at a coffee shop near his house.

When he entered, she was already sitting at a table. He walked over and sat down.

"May I buy you a cup of coffee?" she offered.

Connor shook his head. "I should be buying you a drink. Dinner, even."

She let out a small huff of laughter and studied him. Some of the tightness that he'd been carrying around had vanished, replaced by a film of sadness in his eyes. He ran a hand through his hair.

"I just . . . I don't even know what to say."

Jo didn't reply. The sounds of other conversations hung in the air, but he seemed oblivious to them.

"How's Brooke?" she asked.

He sighed. "It's been tough. She's got a rough road ahead, but she's a strong girl, and she'll make it. She's already seen a therapist, and I'm sure she will for a while. She's not happy that I locked her in the safe room, but she gets it. She wants to see you."

"I'll meet her."

"She'd like that." He hesitated. "I'd like that. It'll make her happy."

"And you?"

He frowned. "We got through the funeral. I had to tell everyone Fran died in a car accident. National security and all." A grimace. "It's for the best. I don't want people to know what Fran did, and she wouldn't, either."

"How's the senator?"

He laughed, bitter and short. "She's acting as if things are okay, but they're not. They're keeping an eye on me, asking a lot of questions. It's just a matter of time before I lose my job."

"And then what?"

His face grew distant for a minute. "I don't know. I have some money in the bank, and I'll figure out something. Once Brooke graduates from high school, maybe I'll move away." He looked out the window. "I'm kind of tired of DC."

She nodded. "Yeah, so am I."

His laugh held a little humor this time, but then he grew serious again. "I can't believe Fran's gone, that it all went down the way it did. But you brought Brooke back to me."

Jo sipped her coffee. Connor didn't say anything more. After a while, he made eye contact.

"Call Brooke, okay? She wants to talk to you."

"I will," Jo said.

Connor looked at her, his brown eyes crinkled, his lips in a slight sad frown, and then he got up and left the coffee shop.

True to her word, Jo called Brooke and met her the following day at a Five Guy's. Jo ordered hamburgers, fries, and Cokes, and they sat at a booth in the corner. Brooke picked at her food, mostly just staring at Jo.

"My dad isn't telling me everything, but I know my mom messed up."

Jo considered her answer carefully. "It's true she made some mistakes, but in the end, she was there for you."

Brooke's face twisted up. She ate a few fries, then sat back. "I'm going to miss her."

"As you should. Just remember the good times with your mom, the fun things you did." Jo spoke from experience.

Tears welled up in Brooke's eyes. "I will."

They ate for a minute in silence. Then Brooke reached a hesitant hand across the table, resting it on Jo's for a moment.

"What're you going to do?"

"When I got out of the military, I wanted to lead a quiet life."

Brooke laughed. "Guess I kind of messed that up."

Jo winked at her. "It's okay. The quiet life starts now."

"Where will you go?"

It took a second for the words to come out. "I'm going to head west. But I'm going to take my time getting there."

"Why?"

Jo let out a deep breath. She didn't want to explain the tension she felt with her father and sister, that she wasn't ready to face them just yet. She knew she'd have to, but not now. There'd be time.

"It's complicated," she said. "I think I'll head south first. With winter coming, it'll be warmer."

Brooke smiled. "Will you stay in touch?"

"Sure."

Jo gave her the number from a new phone that she'd purchased. Brooke texted her, and the phone rang.

"Now you have my number," Brooke said

"Thanks." Jo added it into her contacts.

They finished their meal and left the restaurant. Jo watched the girl get into an older Subaru and drive away. Then she took the Metro back to the hotel in Arlington, where she was spending one final night.

The next morning, she called Dack.

"It's time for me to move on," she said to him. "Thanks for everything you did."

He smiled. "Anytime. Where're you going?"

"I'm going to head south, then make my way west."

"You'll end up in Colorado?"

She swallowed hard. She was leaving a familiar place, going toward one that was strange, and far away, both physically and emotionally. Jo wasn't sure when she would get there, or what awaited her. "Eventually."

"At some point, you'll need to face your father."

"I need a little more time."

He nodded thoughtfully. "Keep in touch."

"You know I will."

Dack raised a hand as if to touch the screen. She did the same thing, and he told her goodbye.

Jo ended the call, put her things in her duffel bag, and left the hotel for the last time. She took an Uber to a Greyhound bus station, got out, and walked inside. She didn't know where she was going just yet, but it was away from here.

It was time to move on.

Are you ready for a new Jo adventure? Preorder book two in the series: Gunning for Truth.

Turn the page to read the first two chapters right now!

GUNNING FOR TRUTH

CHAPTER ONE

The thump awoke Jo Gunning from a fitful sleep.

She lay on the bed and listened. It was dark in the small motel room, just a hint of moonlight trickling its way in through a crack in the heavy curtains that covered the lone window. Jo listened and assessed, a habit as natural as breathing.

No one was in her room. They couldn't be—she'd wrapped a hand towel around the door stopper and placed a chair under the handle. Also habits.

She was always careful, had been since she was in Civil Affairs, the Army branch where she'd worked alongside Special Operation Forces in some of the most dangerous areas around the world.

Another thump.

Jo sat up and swung her legs over the side of the bed. She stared at the far wall, past the armoire and television. The noise had come from the next room, and raised voices now broke through the silence. She glanced at the clock.

Just after two in the morning.

She sighed. All she wanted was a decent night's sleep before she traveled on. The motel was near Marion, Alabama, a rural community in the middle of nowhere. It wasn't much, but it was cheap and halfway clean. Perfect for anonymity.

The voices grew louder, the decibel about to hit shouting level. Then a popping sound, a bit tinny, slightly muffled. She knew exactly what it was. Quieter than the thumps on the wall, but far more dangerous. Not uncorking a champagne bottle either. That was a gun shot.

Jo jumped up, slipped on jeans and a T-shirt, and strode to the door. After removing the towel from the door stopper and pulling the chair away, she put her hand on the doorknob. The voices had grown louder.

"... gonna let me..."

That was a man, loud and furious.

Then something from a woman that Jo couldn't understand.

She opened the door and peeked out.

The parking lot was washed in a hazy yellow glow from the lights hanging along the side of the building. The lone, flickering streetlight at the far end was useless. A dark Dodge Ram pickup truck, parked a few spaces down from Jo's door, was the only vehicle. No other guests at a small motel in a lazy town with hardly any people.

The shouting continued, and Jo stepped out to the sidewalk, then strode next door. The window was partially open, the voices clearer.

"What the hell were you thinking?"

The man's voice was low now, with a thick Southern drawl that couldn't mask the lethal mix of anger and threat.

"I said I was sorry." The woman sounded shaky.

"Sorry don't cut it."

A crack, like skin on skin. A palm on someone's face.

"I oughta kill—" the man started to say.

Jo knocked on the door before hearing anymore, almost out of reflex. So much for anonymity.

"Now you've done it," his voice came from inside.

Footsteps, and the door opened to reveal a man in black boxers. He stood a couple of inches taller than Jo's five foot nine, with big arms and legs, a bit of a paunch, and thinning, reddish-blond hair.

"What?" he snapped, the smell of alcohol heavy on his breath. He stared at her with bloodshot brown eyes.

Jo glanced past him. Light from a nightstand lamp shone on a woman perched on the edge of a queen-size bed. She looked to be about forty, with streaks of gray weaving through her long brown hair. All she had on was underwear and a plain bra. Even though the light was dim, Jo could see red on her cheek.

"Grady . . ." she said as she put a hand to her face.

"Are you okay?" Jo asked.

"She's fine," Grady said.

Jo glanced back and forth between them, taking the whole scene in. "Is there a problem here?"

He swore. "Mind your own business."

Jo tilted her head, considering him. Grady seemed like the kind of man who expected to be listened to, for people to jump when he said jump. She'd run into his type before. They didn't bother her. She smiled at him, friendly.

"I'm in the room next door, and you're arguing woke me up, so this"—she gestured toward their room—"is my business."

Grady's eyes narrowed, and he jabbed a finger toward her room. "You better get back there right now if you know what's good for you."

Jo stared past him to the woman. "Do you need help?"

Before she could answer, Grady took a step to the left. Jo followed his glance to a half-empty bottle of whiskey, which sat next to a Glock 43 pistol on a round table underneath the window. Grady looked back at Jo.

"Don't go for it," she said.

His spine stiffened. "What're you going to do?"

Jo sighed. "I don't want any problems, okay? Why don't you get your stuff and go." She pointed to the woman. Just leave her alone."

The man puffed out his bare chest and took a step toward her. "I said, what are you gonna do about it?"

He was bigger than Jo, but his muscles looked flabby, out of use. And he was drunk. As he raised a fist, she stepped toward him, grabbed his wrist, and pulled him in front of her. The move was rapid and unexpected, and it took him off-guard. Just as quickly, she spun him around. He swore and tried to twist out of her grasp, but unlike him she kept herself fit, and she had the element of surprise.

Jo shoved him against the door jamb. His head bounced off the wood, and blood spurted from his nose, a cartoon-bright red spattering the wall. Grady grunted in shock and pain. He tried to resist, but she held him firmly in place.

"I'm going to mess you up good," he snarled, his face against the wood.

Jo yanked his arm up until he winced again and even let out a small mewl of pain. She looked at the woman.

"Get his clothes."

The woman blinked at Jo, then went to the end of the bed and picked up Grady's jeans, shirt, socks, and boots.

"Darlene, you better—" he said.

Jo twisted his arm to shut him up. Darlene stood rooted in place.

"Is that his truck?" she asked Darlene.

The woman nodded.

"Put his clothes in it," Jo said.

Darlene took a couple of hesitant steps, then dashed past Jo and into the parking lot. She hurried to the truck, opened the door, and tossed in Grady's clothes.

When she turned back, Jo nodded toward the room. "Now get me the gun."

Darlene hurried back inside, ignoring Grady's threats. The man continued to struggle, but between the booze and being out of shape, he was no match for Jo. He cursed even more as Darlene grabbed the Glock and handed it to Jo. She took the weapon, then stepped back and aimed it at Grady. He turned around carefully, his hands up, hatred in his eyes.

"What, are you gonna shoot me?" He sneered. Blood dribbled over his lips, and he snorted and spit onto the sidewalk. The space was probably becoming a biohazard.

Jo shook her head. "That would be a waste of a bullet." He glared at her, and she gestured with the Glock. "Get into your truck."

"Can't I at least get dressed?" he asked.

Jo let out a snort of laughter. "Get in now or I'll make you strip down and walk away naked."

His foul language filled the air as he walked barefoot to the truck and got in. Jo removed the Glock's magazine and locked the slide to the rear to eject the live ammo from the chamber. Pocketing both, she walked to the truck. Grady rolled down the window but didn't say anything, just continued that hateful glare. She handed him the gun.

"Go home, wherever that is," Jo said. "Try to mess with Darlene again, you'll have to deal with me."

His eyes burned like they wanted to consume her, but he seemed to believe her threat, and he rooted around in his jeans for his keys. He didn't say a word as he started the truck and jammed it into reverse.

"You better move on if you got any sense," he said, though his threat didn't sound nearly as serious as hers, choked by the blood in his nose and throat. "I don't want to see you anywhere around here again."

Tires squealed as he backed up and peeled out of the parking lot. She waited until the taillights disappeared down the road and then turned back to Darlene.

"What a pleasant guy."

Darlene laughed nervously.

"Will you be okay?" Jo asked.

Darlene nodded and waved toward the road.

"You really pissed him off."

Jo shrugged. "I've dealt with worse."

"What do I do if he comes back?"

Jo started toward her room. "He's not going bother you," she called back.

Darlene crossed her arms over her chest. "I don't have a car."

At that, Jo looked around the empty parking lot. "Grady brought you here?"

She nodded. "I guess I could call somebody in the morning to give me a ride back to Greensville."

"Why not now?"

Darlene sighed and shook her head, looking down. "I don't want to bother anyone at this time of night."

"How far is Greensville from here?"

The woman scrunched up her face. "About ten miles

southwest."

Glancing up at the stars, Jo took in a deep breath of the night air. "It's quiet around here."

Arlene looked past her at the empty two-lane highway. "What if he comes back?" she repeated.

This time, Jo gave her a reassuring smile. "I'll deal with him. Put a hand towel around the door stopper and jam a chair under the doorknob." She pointed at Darlene's room window. "And I'd close that, too."

"Okay. But it's hot out, and I gotta sleep."

"Use the air conditioner."

"It don't work so well," Darlene muttered.

Jo tried not to let her exasperation show on her face. It was almost as if the woman was hoping Grady would return. She didn't want to get beat up by him, of course, but she couldn't resist him, either.

As Jo opened her door, she said, "I'll keep an eye on things. You get some rest. We'll deal with everything else in the morning."

"Why do you wanna help me?" Darlene asked.

Jo didn't hesitate. "You sounded like you were in trouble. I couldn't let it go."

"Let's hope trouble hasn't found you," said the woman.

With a grim nod, Jo opened her door and went back into her room.

CHAPTER TWO

She awoke early the next morning. The motel room smelled musty, but it was quiet, peaceful. She listened for a moment, hearing no noise from the other room. It was 6 a.m., just after sunrise. If Darlene had been drinking like Grady appeared to have been, she was probably hung over and still sleeping.

Jo got up and did a series of exercises, then threw on shorts and a T-shirt, slipped on running shoes, and went outside. Jogging away from the parking lot, she soon passed a couple of abandoned buildings near the motel. Even though it was early, the July heat beat down on her, the air heavy with humidity. The road was quiet, with empty fields on both sides as far as she could see. The occasional vehicle passed by, mostly giving her a wide berth. Farther down the highway, she passed a gas station, but it didn't look like anyone was there this early.

She ran for half an hour, then turned and headed back to the motel. After finishing her run, she showered and dressed in jeans and an Oxford shirt, then headed over to the motel lobby. An older man, who was sitting behind a short counter, looked up when she walked in.

"I need to stay until four," she told him.

"You'll have to pay another day."

It wasn't like he had a line of people waiting to rent rooms, but he clearly could use the money, so she acquiesced and paid him.

"Alright, you're all set. Leave the key on the table in your room when you leave," he said.

"Any place to get breakfast?" she asked.

He shook his head. "There's a restaurant at that gas station down the road. There ain't never been much in this town." Then he frowned, his eyes distant even though they were looking right at her. "Don't know how much longer I'll be able to keep this place going."

She thanked him and started back down the road to the gas station, at a brisk walk this time. A couple of pickup trucks were gassing up by now, and a few cars had parked outside the small convenience store and attached diner.

The moment she stepped inside, the two men sitting at the short counter gave her an inspection. A waitress told Jo to sit wherever, and she took a booth by a window where she could look out to the parking lot. The pair at the counter talked in low tones, their eyes now conspicuously avoiding her. She ignored them, and when the waitress walked over, she ordered coffee and a big breakfast of eggs, bacon, and pancakes.

She had just finished eating when she saw Darlene appear out of the haze of the road, heading toward the restaurant. Jo signaled her when she walked in, and the woman sauntered over.

"How're you doing this morning?" Jo asked as Darlene slid into the booth across from her.

"I've got a hangover," she pronounced, her cheeks red.

Jo nodded. "I'm not surprised."

The waitress came over, and she ordered coffee. The server eyed Darlene as if she knew her, but Darlene gave a little head shake, and she moved away.

Jo studied the woman over her coffee cup. Darlene had tried to pretty herself up with some makeup, but she couldn't hide the bruise on her left cheek, nor could she do anything about the crow's feet flaring from the corners of her eyes, or the worry lines across her forehead. Life had been hard on her, and not just last night.

"Come around here often?" Jo asked.

Darlene shrugged. "Once in a while."

"Are you from around this area?"

Darlene nodded out the window. "Down in Greensville. It's about twenty miles."

"Are you still planning to get a ride back there?"

"Not until this afternoon. My friend works at the grocery store, and she doesn't get off until four." She surveyed Jo. "Where're you from?"

Jo thought about that. "I'm just passing through."

Darlene laughed, a low, guttural sound. "No one passes through this area. Nothing's out here."

Jo smiled. "I spent some time outside of Montgomery as a kid. I passed through there on my way west. I just wanted something out of the way, off the beaten path."

Darlene snickered. "You certainly found that here."

After taking a sip of coffee, already lukewarm, Jo said, "If you're from Greensville, why were you with Grady at that motel?"

The stare she got in return was hard as rock. "You know the reason why. Grady and me needed an out-of-the-way place."

"It seems to me you could do better than that guy," Jo said.

Darlene opened her mouth, but then she hesitated. "Probably." Her back went rigid. "He wasn't happy about what you did to him, and he won't forget it."

"I'll keep that in mind. Like I said, I'm just passing through, so hopefully he and I won't run into each other again."

"You don't have a car?"

Jo shook her head. "The bus didn't come this way. I got off in Birmingham, and I thumbed my way south, and walked."

"You hitched a ride? Hard to do these days."

"Every once in a while someone will still stop."

Darlene gulped some of her own coffee. "If you want to wait until four, my friend Mona could give you a ride to Greensville."

"That'd be great." Jo looked out the window to the fields, to all the nothingness around them. "What are you going to do until then?"

"Probably go back to my room, throw up this coffee, and sleep it off."

Jo couldn't help but laugh. "Honestly, that sounds like a good plan."

"Nothing else to do on a Sunday." Darlene cocked an eyebrow. "And you?"

"I'm going to see the sights."

Darlene laughed as well, then winced and put a hand to her temples. "Oh man, do I have a headache."

"Time for you to get some rest."

The woman nodded, and Jo paid the bill, including Darlene's coffee. Darlene thanked her, and they left the restaurant together, remaining quiet as they walked back down the road to the motel. Jo felt beads of sweat trickle down her spine. She didn't want to have to change a second time after already changing out of her running clothes. When they got back to the motel, Darlene took her hand and looked her in the eye.

"Thanks for what you did last night. Grady can be . . . a handful."

"You should watch yourself," was all Jo said.

Darlene shrugged, opened her door, and disappeared inside.

Jo went into her own room and turned on the TV. She

flipped channels for a while until a special ringtone on her phone interrupted her. Dack Pendleton, her friend and former colleague from the Special Forces, was video-calling. She answered, and his tanned face appeared on the screen. He was good-looking, with closely cropped brown hair, an angular jaw, and a wide smile. Dack looked at her with soft blue eyes, then glanced down, and she knew he was typing.

"Hey, lady. How's life?"

Jo enabled the live-caption feature and waited. A moment later, Dack's typed message came through. It was transferred into an altered electronic voice, somewhat tinny and impersonal, but she imagined hearing his tenor voice. She smiled.

"It's not bad."

He made a point of looking past her. "I see you're in another charming luxury abode."

Jo laughed. "Yeah, this place is a real joy." She took a moment to tell him exactly where she was, and about the incident with Grady the previous night. When she finished and looked back at the screen, Dack was studying her.

"What?" she said.

"Don't get yourself into any trouble. Any more trouble, I mean."

She held up her hands. "In this place? What trouble can I get into?"

He shook his head slowly. "You already did. You always think you need to help people."

Rolling her eyes, she shrugged. "There's nothing going on here."

"I think it's best to give that guy Grady a wide berth."

"I plan to," she said. "I'm getting a ride to Greensville later today, and I'll probably spend the night there, then keep heading west."

"If you're looking for something to do, I could always use the help."

Dack had his own contract security firm that offered incident response, security consulting, and training services. It was a perfect fit for him, given his past in the Army. Like Jo, he was an expert marksman, was skilled at hand-to-hand combat, and knew how to gather intelligence. Starting his own company hadn't been in his plans, but when the operation they'd been on together in Syria went badly, that had changed everything for him.

He stared at her, then typed, "You've got that brooding look."

"It's nothing," she said.

"I know what you're thinking. If you came to work for me and something went wrong . . ."

She sighed. "I can't help it."

Dack moved closer to the screen, and his eyes danced.

"How long are you going to blame yourself for something that wasn't your fault?"

She held up her hand. "We've been over this before. It *was* my fault."

He shook his head vehemently and opened his mouth, showing a stub where his tongue should've been. Jo forced herself to look at it, to at least do him the favor of not looking away. Then he clamped his jaw shut and typed. She imagined anger in his voice.

"My tongue was cut out by an enemy insurgent. You didn't do that."

She stared at him. "I was the one who said we could trust the woman. It was my intelligence that said where to execute the raid to get the HVT." And the raid for the high-value target, who was supposed to give them information on a terrorist cell, had gone terribly wrong. "I should've realized I wasn't getting good information, and we shouldn't have gone to meet him."

Dack swore at her. "Your intelligence was good. You vetted that woman, and you had no way to know that she was setting us up. You were cleared of any wrongdoing. We've been over this a hundred times and it doesn't change."

"I *should've* known," she repeated, as she always did.

He jabbed a finger at the screen. "It wasn't your fault, and you need to remember that you're the one that made sure I was rescued. You know a rescue normally doesn't happen. Most people who are caught in our positions are tortured and killed, their bodies drug through the streets, or worse. That didn't happen to me because you were there to get people going, to get a team back in. It was your intelligence that knew where the terrorists had taken me." He swore again, then looked at her intently. "You know that's true. I owe my life to you."

Jo glanced away.

"Jo. Let go of yourself for a second and listen. You know I'm right," he said.

She finally nodded. "It's hard to hear that. I doubt myself all the time."

His expression softened. "I know you do, but you don't need to. You were a great soldier, the best I've ever seen. You have to stop blaming yourself, and you have to stop trying to right a wrong that never was—and that couldn't be changed even if it had been."

She looked at his eyes for a long time before she answered. "All right."

Dack exhaled and smiled. "Good. Now that we're done with that, you know you have to go see your family at some point."

She let out a little laugh. "You're not going let me off the hook today, are you?"

"Nope."

Jo drew in a breath. "Dad's still mad at me because I put the Army before my family. He didn't understand that I couldn't get home when Mom was sick."

"Sounds like you two have to work out some things."

She knew she did, and he knew she was avoiding going back to Colorado, where her father lived, where she'd purchased a small mountain cabin in Salida as well several years ago. She'd hardly been there since, too busy with CA to visit, but she'd wanted a quiet place to go to when she retired, a place where she could be anonymous. Somewhere that no one would bother her. But that also meant her father and sister would be nearby, and every painful piece of the past would be dragged up to address. Her father still hadn't forgiven her for not returning home when her mother had gotten sick. And it didn't help that Jo had chosen to go into the Army in the first place. Her father had pictured some other career for her. All that had created a rift that still needed to be addressed, but Jo wasn't ready for that just yet. She wasn't sure she ever fully would be.

Dack glanced at his watch. "I hate to do this, but I need to go. You're okay?"

"Never better." She smiled at him.

"If you need anything, don't hesitate to ask. And let me know where you end up next."

Jo nodded, and he put his hand to the screen. She did the same, and then he ended the call.

Sitting back for a moment against the thin, stiff pillows of the motel bed, she thought about her father. Dack was right. She did need to talk to him, and at some point, she would. But not today.

Jo put the phone down next to her, then lay back on the bed and waited for Darlene's ride to arrive.

Preorder Gunning for Truth on Amazon!

FROM THE AUTHOR

Dear Reader,

If you enjoyed *Gunning for Trouble*, would you please write an honest review?

You have no idea how much it warms my heart to get a new review.

And this isn't just for me.

Think of all the people out there who need reviews to make decisions, and you would be helping them.

You are awesome for doing so, and I am grateful to you!

ACKNOWLEDGMENTS

The author gratefully acknowledges all those who helped in the writing of this book, especially: Beth Higgins, Marie Lynch, Becky Neilsen, Tracy Gestewitz, and Randy Powers.

A special note to Don Calvano, former U.S. Army Cav Scout/SWAT Operator/Detective. He answered a lot of my questions, and any mistakes regarding the military and weapons are mine alone.

If I've forgotten anyone, please accept my apologies.

To all my beta readers: I am in your debt!
Dianne Biscoe, Sheree Ito, Louise Ohman, Albert Stevens, Marlene Van Matre

ABOUT THE AUTHOR

Renée's early career as a counselor gives her a unique ability to write characters with depth and personality, and she now works as a business analyst. She lives in the mountains west of Denver, Colorado and enjoys hiking, cycling, and reading when she's not busy writing her next novel.

Renée loves to travel and has visited numerous countries around the world. She has also spent many summer days at her parents' cabin in the hills outside of Boulder, Colorado, which was the inspiration for the setting of Taylor Crossing in her novel *Nephilim*.

She is the author of the Reed Ferguson mysteries, the Jo Gunning Thriller series, the Sarah Spillman police procedurals, and the Dewey Webb historical mysteries. She also wrote the standalone suspense novels *The Girl in the Window* and *What's Yours is Mine, Nephilim: Genesis of Evil*, a supernatural thriller, along with children's novels and other short stories.

Visit Renée at www.reneepawlish.com.

RENÉE'S BOOKSHELF

Jo Gunning Thrillers:

Gunning for Trouble

Gunning for Truth

The Sarah Spillman Mysteries:

Deadly Connections

Deadly Invasion

Deadly Guild

Deadly Revenge

Deadly Judgment

Deadly Target

Deadly Past

Deadly Premonition

Deadly Price

Deadly Christmas

The Sarah Spillman Mysteries Boxsets:

Sarah Spillman Mysteries Books 1-3

Sarah Spillman Mysteries Books 4-6

Standalone Psychological Suspense:

The Girl in the Window

What's Yours Is Mine

A Gun For Hire

Cool Alibi

The Big Steal

The Wrong Woman

Reed Ferguson Mysteries Boxsets:

The Reed Ferguson Series: Box Set 1-3

The Reed Ferguson Series: Books 4-6

The Reed Ferguson Series: Books 7-9

The Reed Ferguson Series: Books 10-12

The Reed Ferguson Series: Books 13-15

The Reed Ferguson Series: Books 16-18

Reed Ferguson Stories: Five Mystery Short Tales

The Reed Ferguson Series Boxset Collection

Dewey Webb Historical Mystery Series:

Web of Deceit

Murder In Fashion

Secrets and Lies

Honor Among Thieves

Trouble Finds Her

Mob Rule

Murder At Eight

Second Chance

Double Cross

Dewey Webb Historical Mystery Series Boxsets:

The Dewey Webb Series: Box Set 1-3

The Dewey Webb Series: Box Set 4-6

The Noah Winter Adventure

(A Young Adult Mystery Series)

The Emerald Quest

Dive into Danger

Terror On Lake Huron

Take Five Collection (Mystery Anthology)

Nephilim Genesis of Evil (Supernatural Mystery)

Codename Richard: A Ghost Story

The Taste of Blood: A Vampire Story

This War We're In (Middle-grade Historical Fiction)

Nonfiction:

The Sallie House: Exposing the Beast Within

Printed in the USA
CPSIA information can be obtained
at www.ICGtesting.com
LVHW040620250923
759196LV00003B/296